◇◇◇◇◇◇◇◇◇◇◇◇◇◇◇◇◇◇

A Man For Susan

By

Charlotte Kent

The Second Novel in the Series

Captain's Point Stories

◇◇◇◇◇◇◇◇◇◇◇◇◇◇◇◇◇◇◇◇◇◇◇◇

For Steve and Jean,
who have provided so much inspiration and
encouragement to me
Annie Acorn

To my husband, John, the love of my life
Juliette Hill

Charlotte Kent is the pseudonym used by
Annie Acorn and Juliette Hill
when writing their collaborative contemporary
women's fiction/family saga series
Captain's Point Stories

You may contact and/or follow the authors at:
charlottekentromances@gmail.com
@CharlotteKent20

This is Max's third starring role in a work of fiction.

The true story of his actual rescue can be found in
Annie Acorn's *Chocolate Can Kill*

The novel, *A Man for Susan*, is a work of fiction. Any resemblance to real people or events is completely accidental. A few literary liberties may have been taken when it comes to geographic locations, medical treatments, sailing terms, tidal charts, and helicopter rescue protocols in the interest of creating great literature.

CHAPTER I

Shots rang out as Anderson flung open the door, and Marsha felt her heart stop as she crouched behind the bureau only a few feet away. But then a thud sounded from the unseen room, and she could see the detective still standing tall in the doorway.

Slowly releasing her breath, she remained where she was as he had commanded, fighting the urge to run to him as the antique clock ticked the seconds away in a rhythm that matched her heart's renewed beat. Finally, he moved forward into the room, only to return a few moments later to the foyer that his long strides crossed to join her.

"You're safe now." He held out his hand, and she allowed him to draw her up and to him.

For what seemed like a lifetime, he held her gaze as he crushed her in his strong grasp, and then he lowered his lips onto hers.

The End

"Anders, turn off that computer and come help me," Elizabeth Chesterton called to her husband as she checked in the foyer mirror to see if strands of her auburn streaked-with-gray hair were already sliding from the loose coil she had twisted onto the back of her head. Satisfied, she crossed to the bottom of the broad staircase. "Susan has already texted to see if we're running late."

"Susan?" To her relief, her Nordic god look-a-like husband appeared at the top of the stairs - carefully smoothing back his blond hair with one hand, his blue eyes focused on her. "Not Adrianna?"

"Adrianna is too much in love with Chase Sheffield to think of anything else on their wedding day," his wife said, "and

Chase hasn't noticed anyone but her since she arrived here in Captain's Point."

"Well, she's done him a world of good." Her husband straightened his wine-colored cummerbund.

"Yes, she has," Elizabeth agreed as he joined her. "You know, Anders, I never knew before those two were engaged that a man in his early thirties could actually bloom."

"Now that's not true, dear." Her husband slid a strong arm around her and planted a kiss on her lips, dislodging at least two wisps of her hair. "I sprouted all over when I caught you."

"Liar." His wife caught a stocky, blond four-year-old by the arm as he attempted to run by her. "Hold still, Daniel, and let me fix your hair." She pulled a comb from her purse. "Ring bearers should always act like they've been taught at least a modicum of good manners."

"Like in one of Grandpa's plays?" Her grandson's eyes widened.

"Exactly." Elizabeth smiled down at him. "Now let me look at the two of you." She eyed them both up and down. "Yes, I think that we'll do."

A mere four blocks away in the living room of the caretaker's cottage on the grounds of Montgomery House, Susan Chesterton adjusted Adrianna Montgomery's veil and, unbeknownst to them both, almost mimicked her mother's words.

"I think that will do." She smiled over her friend's shoulder at their reflections in the cheval mirror that was providing a much needed service on a temporary basis, but then a worried expression filled her face. "I hope Mom and Dad get here soon. At least, Courtney texted that she's on her way with Lizzie." She referred to her older sister and the niece who would walk down the rose-carpeted aisle beside Daniel.

"Don't fret," Adrianna said, checking to make sure that her pearl earrings were firmly in place. "This wedding won't start one second before we're ready for it. You know, I'm beginning to think that I made a mistake when I asked you to stand up beside me. You may outshine the bride."

"There's no danger of that," Susan stated with all sincerity. "You look lovely."

Side by side in the cheval mirror they formed a picture of contrasts. Susan stood slightly taller, blonde and blue-eyed. Adrianna shone forth, slim with dark waves and dark eyes that were capable of flashing with anger, but much more often twinkled with pleasure.

Always a bridesmaid never a bride – the familiar phrase tripped its way through Susan's mind, although strictly speaking that wasn't true. She had been a bride, almost six years ago, but her prince on a white horse had turned out to be a jerk on a mule. At least, she now had her Daniel, the frown which had darkened her countenance smoothed into a smile.

Still, there was part of her that wished it were she who would be walking down the aisle this day, although not to marry Chase Sheffield. Adrianna and he were made for each other. Surely, somewhere, there was a good, kind man for her, too.

"Penny for your thoughts." Adrianna smiled at her, but received no answer as the cottage's front door opened at this moment and allowed the much awaited ring bearer and flower girl to enter along with their entourages.

"Just in time." Susan sent her mother a look of relief. "Now, Dad and you go and prepare to be seated right before Penny Plunk in lieu of Chase's parents. Then Penny will be seated, I'll follow, and then Edmund will change the tune and Otis will escort Adrianna and give her away before joining Penny in the front row of the bride's side in lieu of her parents."

"That was a mouthful," Anders stated and turned to his wife. "Did you get it all?"

"You stick with me." She slipped her hand through the crook of his arm. "You and the pavilion look lovely, dear." She blew a kiss towards Adrianna. "I don't know how Otis and you managed to get it constructed in time, but the setting overlooking Captain's Point and the ocean is beautiful."

"The plans were already in place, so it wasn't too hard," Adrianna responded. "I'm just glad we're having nice weather."

"Time," Susan said as she glanced at the mantel clock and then addressed Adrianna. "Chase isn't going to know what's hit him when he sees you."

"Thank you again for your help." Adrianna encompassed everyone in the room with her glance. "All of you mean so much to Chase and me."

Susan shooed everyone except for Otis through the doorway, leaving him to fulfill the role of father of the bride.

"Your mom and dad would've been proud and happy for you today." Careful to avoid Adrianna's pearl drop train, her property manager stepped forward and brushed her cheek with his lips. "And so would've been your Great-aunt Martha."

"Thank you, Otis." Adrianna blinked back tears that had sprung unexpectedly to her eyes. "If you'll hand me my mother's Bible and my flowers, we'll be ready."

At the back of the rose-colored carpet, Susan firmly wrapped the hunter green leash of a tuxedo-clad Chihuahua-Beagle mix named Max twice around the left hand of the ring bearer and sent them and the flower girl along the aisle, following closely behind. Taking her place opposite the groom and her cousin Larry Chesterton, the best man, she smiled and gave the briefest of nods to the pianist.

Once he had received his cue, Edmund Robinson swung into the familiar notes of *Here Comes the Bride*, and Penny Plunk, having risen from her seat as a sign to the other guests, watched with pride as her husband escorted their young employer forward.

The groom took one look at his intended and knew he would never see anything else as beautiful or love anyone more, even if he were to live three full lifetimes. The bride kept her eyes on her groom, glad for his calm strength that she would always rely on, secure in the knowledge that she was marrying her soul mate. A few minutes later, Chase Augustus Sheffield placed the ring on Adrianna Maria Montgomery's finger that ended their search for each other and marked the beginning of their new life together and, once she had placed a ring from her on his own finger, shortly thereafter kissed his bride.

Edmund progressed into the more flamboyant strains that proclaimed the ceremony to be over as the sunset sent streaks of rose and pink across the sky, gulls flying overhead added their sharp cries and Max barked his approval.

The reception afterwards at the soon to open Sheffield Place Inn was presided over by Edmund, the new manager, and his wife Marissa. The food was proclaimed to be marvelous, the music was phenomenal, the bride was radiant and the groom couldn't take his eyes off his new wife. Once the champagne had been drunk, the sun had set and the cake had been cut, fireworks delighted the guests and most of the population of Captain's Point, who sat on the cliffs overlooking the sea and enjoyed them in response to a notice in the local newspaper.

At the end of the display, Adrianna tossed her bouquet of roses cut from the Montgomery House garden into the air, aiming for Susan who caught it. Then a white limousine drove the happy couple away, presumably on their honeymoon.

A few minutes later, the bride and groom disembarked at the caretaker's cottage, where Penny awaited them in order to help Adrianna change from her wedding dress into something more comfortable. This done, the young couple walked the short distance to the front of Montgomery House, the bride's ancestral home that was comprised of granite and graced by an octagonal tower, where the groom opened the door to reveal Max who greeted them eagerly with a wag of his tail.

Then Chase turned his wife so that she faced him. "Remember when I explained that you were Captain's Point's princess, and you took exception saying that, if it were so, then I was its prince?"

"Yes."

"Well, I'm putting the whole notion to rest." He lifted her into his arms. "You are now entering our new home together with me as my queen." And with that he carried his now giggling bride over the threshold, closed the door and turned the bolt with her still in his arms, and then carried her up the broad staircase and through the doorway of the tower suite bedroom where he paused just inside.

"Guard!" he commanded Max, who immediately dropped to the floor in a ball, ears alert, eyes directed at the stairway. "Now, stay!"

Then his new master pushed the door closed with his foot and returned his wife to an upright position.

"I can't believe you taught him to do that," Adrianna attempted in vain to control her giggles.

"It was worth every minute of time spent on it for the privacy it will afford me with you," Chase assured her. "Now, my beloved, may I ask if it is your intention to giggle your way through our wedding night?"

"Quite possibly." She fought to control herself. "I'm afraid it's all of the happiness welling up inside of me."

"Then we'll have to see what can be done about it." Her groom gathered her to him and, for a moment, gazed down at her adored face with a soft look in his own eyes before he resolutely lowered his lips onto hers.

As soon as the bride and groom left the reception, seeing how tired her little boy was, Susan took him to Chesterton Cove where they lived, just two blocks away, so she could put him to bed.

"I married Adrianna today, didn't I, Mama?" Daniel asked, his eyelids drooping.

"No, Pumpkin, you helped Adrianna marry Chase," his mother explained. "There's a difference."

"One I should remember?"

"It would probably be best if you did." She tucked him in, smoothed a lock of blond hair from his forehead and then brushed it with her lips, thinking as she did so how lucky she was to have him, but knowing in her heart of hearts that she would still like a full-blown man of her own.

A few hours later, Adrianna lay with her head on her new husband's shoulder, his left arm wrapped around her holding her close, and wondered how any one body could hold as much joy as hers was at that moment. Typical of her interest in the welfare of those around her, she then considered how she could best put to use this wonderful feeling.

Susan…

As she treasured the sound of Chase's steady breathing beside her, her thoughts rapidly centered on her best friend in Captain's Point. There had been a moment at the reception when she had glimpsed her wedding attendant standing by a chatting group of guests, a wistful look on her face. Susan would be the focus of her new campaign. She would find someone as wonderful as Chase for his law partner.

Well… Maybe not quite as nice as her Chase, she snuggled closer to his warm body as his right hand came around and found the spot on the small of her back that made her shiver. After all, there was only one of him, she thought, as she molded her body to his.

CHAPTER II

You are invited at eleven o'clock to a post-wedding day brunch at Montgomery House, the select, gilt-edged invitations had read. *Please come in jeans and be ready to assist us if you are willing to help with a small task after the meal.* All ten invitees had accepted.

"The hollandaise sauce is ready." Chase looked up from the stove in his new home's large, square kitchen where he was preparing the final ingredient for his fast becoming famous Eggs Chesapeake – a morphed Eggs Benedict for which he substituted lump crabmeat for the more traditional ham.

"The fruit salad is on the table, as are the baskets of scones and muffins." Adrianna didn't even look up from drizzling thin white icing on the warm homemade apple strudel she had removed from the oven a short time before no longer surprised that, since he had lived alone and appreciated good food, her new husband had long ago trained himself as a gourmet chef with the help of the new owner of Montgomery's restaurant, John Thornburg.

"That smells wonderful!" Otis nodded appreciatively from the island where he was mixing a Mimosa for Edwina Foster, the elderly widow who now lived in Montgomery House's recently renovated dependency.

Next to him, his wife and the newlyweds' housekeeper, Penny, plopped a celery stick into a Bloody Mary and handed it to Larry Chesterton.

Noticing that the only one of the party who seemed at all bleary-eyed was Max, Jim Laidlaw – the groom's track buddy from high school and now Max's vet – picked up the dog to check for infection, soon satisfied that the animal only needed some sleep.

"Arthur," Adrianna greeted the tall, white-haired gentleman who had let himself in and found his way to the kitchen per a note taped to the front door. "Have you met Edwina? Edwina, Arthur is the one I mentioned who was lucky enough to meet Luciano Oliveira in his youth," she completed the necessary introduction, referring to the world famous artist whose paintings Chase had inherited upon his aunt's recent death.

"Okay, everybody, soup's on," their host announced. "Grab a plate from the dining room table if you want to risk the Eggs Chesapeake."

"Penny, can you let Susan, Edmund and Marissa know that we're ready?" Adrianna asked. "I think they're checking out the changes in the front parlor."

"Am I on time?" Paul Lynch entered through the doorway to the mudroom - his normal mode of entrance since he had rented the caretaker's cottage from Montgomery Properties.

"Just in time," Otis assured him. "What will it be – a Mimosa, a Bloody Mary, or there's coffee and tea."

"I'll risk a Bloody Mary," the newly installed associate minister of the bride and groom's church named his poison, leaning his lanky frame against the island. "After all, I gave a great sermon at the early service this morning."

"So where are you going for your honeymoon, and when are you leaving?" Larry addressed their host and hostess once everyone was settled around the dining room table, surprised when both of the newlyweds burst out laughing.

"We're not." Chase regained control of himself first.

"You're not going on a honeymoon?" Penny's face reflected her astonishment.

"That's nuts!" Jim proclaimed in his usual forthright manner.

"Or crazy," Susan maintained.

"Well, they are crazy in love," Otis reminded his fellow guests.

"Even so." Susan waved the comment away and directed a stern gaze at her law partner. "You've taken a month off from the firm and left me holding the bag."

"Says the woman who just hired two new associates," her host reminded her.

"Don't get us wrong," Adrianna attempted to draw attention away from her spouse. "We plan to make good use of the time. It's just that we've been having so much fun setting up Sheffield Place Inn, rearranging things here, and sorting out boxes from Chase's aunt's house. Neither of us could name either a place that we would rather be or anything we would rather be doing than to remain here together right now."

"Although we're going to visit the cabin in Maine before the month ends," Chase continued their sad tale. "Adrianna's never seen it."

"And we want to take a grand tour of all the places in Europe that I've been to and want to revisit with Chase," his wife added. "We're planning to wait until spring, and we're hoping that Otis and Penny will come along."

"You want to take us with you on your delayed honeymoon?" Penny asked aghast as first surprise, then pleasure and then dismay crossed her face.

"My bride believes it's the least we can do, given that next year is your fortieth wedding anniversary." Chase came to his bride's defense.

"Well, I never," Otis beamed at his employer. "I may just have to talk Pen into taking you up on that one."

"I still say you're both nuts." Jim helped himself to a slice of strudel. "Now what exactly is the small task you need help with once we've all eaten too much of this rich food to want to move?"

"Actually, there are a few things, and given we'd like to keep a low profile for these next few days, we thought we would call on you for assistance." Chase's voice took on a business-like tone. "There are a couple of pieces of furniture we could use some help moving, I want to discuss care and treatment of Oliveira's paintings more in detail with Arthur, we both want to discuss a humidifier for the piano with Edmund, and my wife wants the ladies' opinions on placement of some of the smaller objects we've brought here from my aunt's house."

"That doesn't sound too bad." Larry accepted a carafe of coffee from Penny. "Count me in."

As the others nodded their agreement, Adrianna sat quietly enjoying the sensation of having been referred to as Chase's wife, wondering how she could pass the pleasure on to Susan. Knowing that Susan and Jim occasionally met for lunch or dinner, she pondered their relationship, but then decided they were too much like brother and sister to make a match of it. Paul Lynch, of course, was another viable candidate, and no one could say the new minister wasn't good looking in a boyish kind of way with that lock of sandy brown hair that kept falling onto his forehead.

"As long as everyone's in a helping mood…" Jim's voice broke through her thoughts. "I'd appreciate it if you would mark the Animal Shelter's box luncheon on your calendars – honeymooning couples excused. It's scheduled for two weeks from yesterday at eleven o'clock, and they're holding it on the grounds of the shelter. Single women are required to bring a box lunch. Single men are required to bid on the lunches and the pleasure of the cook's company for one hour while the lunch is consumed."

"How fun!" Edwina exclaimed. "I haven't been to a box luncheon since I was a girl growing up on the farm."

"Sounds like you've invited an experienced professional," Arthur said in his quiet voice. "I, for one, will be there to bid. Tell me, Edwina, do you generally include a slice of cake or pie in your boxes?"

"We always considered chocolate cake as the standard." A pink flush now graced the elderly woman's cheeks. "But with all the allergies…"

"Chocolate cake sounds fine to me." Arthur glanced around the table. "What do you younger fellows think?"

As this brought on a heated discussion of the merits of one type of dessert over another, Adrianna once again found herself in a position to observe Susan and was concerned to find her friend systematically crumbling a bite of scone onto her plate.

"What will you put in your box, Susan?" Adrianna brought the matter to a head.

"I don't know." Her friend looked up surprised. "I may not be free."

"Your calendar isn't that full, Cuz," Larry teased her. "We'll go together, and I'll bid on your box if no one else does."

"I might even throw in a dollar myself," Jim said, following suit.

"Does anyone want more coffee?" Adrianna drew their attention to herself, wishing she hadn't broached the question, for the first time recognizing the size of the task she had set for herself. Finding a man for Susan, she now realized, might not be as easy as she had first thought.

CHAPTER III

At nine o'clock the next morning, Chase's cell phone rang, as he was lounging on the morning room couch, Adrianna curled up beside him, each enjoying a second cup of coffee.

"Susan…" He sat up a little straighter and set his mug on the side table. "I'd better take it."

"Of course," Adrianna agreed. "Let's see what she needs."

"I'm sorry to be the bearer of bad news," his law partner opened their conversation, "but Captain Reb is demanding to see you, and he won't take 'No' for an answer. Apparently, he saw you two walking along the cliff this morning, while looking through his binoculars from his boat."

What she refrained from telling her partner was that the captain's exact words had been, "Don't try and fob me off by telling me that those two lovebirds are on their honeymoon, because I saw them smooching with each other right there at the end of Captain's Point with my very own eyes. Now, I want you to get on the phone and tell them I'm on my way over there to Montgomery House, so they'll let me in."

"Did he say what it's about?" Chase rolled his eyes at his bride.

"No, he says it's important, but personal, and he insists he has to speak with either Adrianna or you directly," Susan filled him in. "Right now, I have him waiting in the reception room."

"Let me see what my bride has to say." Chase turned to his new wife. "Apparently, we have been spotted by paparazzi from the ocean off Captain's Point, and Captain Reb is now demanding an audience with either you, my queen, or me about some highly important, but strictly personal matter. What sayeth you? Should we see him, or should we tell them off with his head?"

"Don't be silly." Adrianna tried hard to maintain a straight face, intrigued as she was by the captain's request. "Would he come now?"

"That appears to have been his plan, but Susan and Bridgette currently have him on ice."

"Well, tell them to thaw him out and send him right over," Adrianna said. "We can talk about what we want to do with Montgomery House afterwards."

"Send him on," Chase advised his partner, "but be advised that we consider your actions in this instance to be treasonable. You are currently but one step away from being locked up in the tower."

"Have you two been drinking Bloody Marys again?" Susan asked. "Or are you both suffering major cases of the sillies?"

"Must be the latter," Chase told her. "I promise you we've consumed nothing liquid but our coffee."

A scant ten minutes later, Penny ushered the beer-bellied captain and Tiny Slocum – the tall, big-boned, middle-aged woman who had saved Chase from serious injury during a sailing accident earlier in the summer – into the library, interrupting the young couple who had been peering over several large pieces of paper spread across the big oak table.

"Captain…" Chase stood and extended his hand.

"Tiny! How nice to see you!" Adrianna beamed a welcome as she, too, rose and left her husband's side to give the older woman a quick hug. "How's your ankle?"

"Fancy your remembering about that on your honeymoon," Tiny responded, a pleased look on her face. "It's fine, except when a storm's brewing, and then sometimes I get a twinge."

"As good as my barometer," the captain confirmed.

"So what can we do for you two this morning?" Chase remained standing, not wanting to prolong the session.

"Well, the fact is," Captain Reb began in his gruff manner, "I've asked this here little sailor to be my wife." At which point, he clasped his intended, who was half a head taller, to his left side, and the newlywed couple shared the unusual experience of watching a middle-aged woman morph into a blushing, young schoolgirl.

"Why that's wonderful news!" Full to the brim with romance herself, Adrianna felt an immediate kinship with the other woman, no matter how unfortunate her pick of a husband might be. "Chase, I believe this announcement calls for champagne." She turned to her spouse, who promptly resigned himself to his fate.

Glasses having been raised to the happy couple, the captain cleared his throat. "The thing is," he began, "I've come here this morning to turn in my resignation."

Having discussed at some length only a few days before the fact that neither of them believed the captain was giving his position as General Manager of Montgomery Marina the attention it needed, both Chase and Adrianna worked hard to hide their pleasure at this bit of news.

"Are you planning to retire?" Adrianna asked, the first to recover.

"Not exactly retire," Tiny spoke up. "It's the bait shop you see. With my dad gone, there's too much important work for just me. I can't trust the responsibility to the kids we've always hired to help out, but someone like my Reb here... Well, he can handle anything."

In the same way as couples who have been married for much longer often do, the newlyweds at this point exchanged a quick glance in which each one clearly communicated to the other that they doubted it.

"I'll continue to hire out my boat for deep sea fishing," the captain filled them in, "so I'll still rent the boat slip, but I'll vacate the marina office in two weeks, giving you enough time to find a replacement."

Chase's immediate reaction to this disclosure was to glance sharply at his wife, but if she was appalled at the prospect of locating a replacement having become part of their honeymoon period, her face showed no signs of it.

"Well, I'm sure we'll both dance at your wedding." Adrianna took two steps towards the foyer and paused, putting an end to the discussion. "You will send us an invitation, won't you?"

Tiny assured the newlyweds that theirs would be the first names on the list of perspective wedding guests, and Chase firmly closed the front door behind the engaged couple less than two minutes later, catching his wife's hand as she turned away from him and pulling her to him.

"Are you okay?" He read her face. "You're not regretting that we didn't go somewhere like most people do on their honeymoon, are you? Because if you are, I'll make reservations right now, and we can fly anywhere you want by tomorrow. All we'll need to pack is our overnight bags, and we'll buy new luggage and clothes when we get there."

"Now you listen to me loud and clear, Mr. Chase Sheffield." She slid her arms around his neck. "There's nowhere in the world that I would rather be than right here in our own home with you."

"You're sure?"

"Positive." She smiled up at him. "After all, I went into this marriage forewarned. You asked me to share with you the wild and crazy ride that was destined to be our lives when you proposed, remember?"

"Yes, but I never envisioned this."

"Look at the bright side," she told him. "I married you and not Captain Reb."

And with that he threw back his head and laughed, before he planted a sound kiss on his wife's lips, glad that Fate had wedded him to the woman in his arms and not Tiny Slocum.

CHAPTER IV

Edwina Foster marveled at her reflection in the cheval mirror that her late husband, Hamilton, had given her on their fifth wedding anniversary. Her baby blue cotton blouse accentuated her snow-white hair and crystal blue eyes. A pair of white slacks and stylish high-heeled summer sandals completed her outfit. While her husband would've been pleased by her appearance, she wondered what he would think of her mission.

How her life had changed in a few short months, ever since Adrianna had shown her that moving to Captain's Point was an appropriate next chapter in her life! Whether or not he would've approved of her move, Ham certainly couldn't have found fault with her current home - the newly restored dependency on the grounds of Montgomery House, far from the Indiana cornfields of her youth.

Determined on her course, Edwina straightened her diminutive shoulders, recognizing that while she was grateful for her grandson Jason, his wife Ginny and Lucy, her new great-granddaughter, living close by so she could experience the precious milestones of their lives, she still must venture out on her own.

A ding from the kitchen timer indicated that her freshly baked, oatmeal raisin cookies were cool, and Edwina moved to her breakfast bar area in response, where she arranged the cookies on a delicate china plate edged with tiny blue flowers. Covering the plate with a sheet of plastic wrap, she secured it with a thin navy blue ribbon, again pleased with the results of her efforts.

But then, doubt assailed her. Things were so different these days, and she barely knew Mr. Stern – Arthur – having only met him the one time at the newlyweds' brunch. What would the soft-spoken man think of her, popping up from nowhere with a plate of food in her hands?

"A man would be crazy not to love these," Ham had said the first time she had made the cookies as a young bride.

Her mind settled, she slipped into a white cotton sweater that Ginny had knitted for her and picked up what she now viewed to be the perfect welcoming gift for the first tenant to have rented one of the new retail spaces in what had once been Montgomery House's carriage house.

Leaving the security of the dependency, she made her way along the garden walkway to welcome Arthur Stern, artist, to the home of his new combination teaching studio and gallery, Artful Soul.

Nip, the mainly black outdoor cat, appeared out of nowhere meandering along the stone path just ahead as if acting as a tour guide, meowing here and there as he led Edwina closer to her destination. Approaching the shop, she paused as a sudden bout of nerves overwhelmed her, persuaded by Nip's rousing encouragement to continue.

Finding Arthur's back turned to the shop's doorway that was propped open, Edwina tapped softly three times on the doorframe.

"I hope I'm not interrupting," she found her voice belying the schoolgirl shyness welling within her. "Adrianna told me you were setting up here today, and I wanted to welcome you with a small shop-warming gift." She handed him the wrapped plate. "They're oatmeal raisin."

"Now isn't that sweet!" Flashing a wide smile, Arthur rested the painting he held on a folded drop cloth before taking the gift from her. "What a nice surprise! How did you know oatmeal raisin cookies are my favorite?"

"It was a lucky guess." Edwina wished she could have thought of something witty to say.

"Please forgive my manners." The artist pulled up a velvet-covered, high back chair for her. "Won't you sit down for a few minutes?"

Not having intended to stay, she could think of no reason for leaving and obliged as her host placed the plate of cookies on an intricately carved oak desk.

"These are too pretty to eat, but I'm afraid I'll still over indulge after lunch." He secured a metal folding chair for himself. "Actually, I'm glad you've popped in. I could use your advice, if you have a few minutes."

"My advice?" Edwina suddenly felt woefully out of her depth.

"Yes, you're obviously a woman of refinement, and I noticed you at the opening of the Williams's gallery back in July," Arthur explained. "I've never had a retail space before, but my son insisted that I shouldn't let this opportunity pass me by. Still, I'm having trouble deciding where to hang what and which paintings could either be housed in accessible folders or stored until needed."

His faded brown eyes were filled with such hope that Edwina straightened her shoulders and prepared to give this new challenge her best shot.

"My late husband, Hamilton - I always called him Ham for short – dabbled in both watercolor and oils. He was quite talented, but his father discouraged him from making art his career, so he became a corporate attorney."

"I became a math professor here at the college," Arthur shared, "but I interrupted." He gestured for her to go on.

"What a coincidence!" Edwina sent him a shy smile. "Back before time, I was a high school history teacher."

"Small world."

"Yes, it is." Edwina was pleased by how easily their conversation flowed.

"I'm sorry about your husband."

"Thank you, I lost him years ago, but I sense that he's still watching over me."

"I feel the same way about my late wife." A wave of loneliness passed over the artist's face. "It was three years in May since she passed away."

"I'm sure she would be happy to know that you're opening your new shop."

"Indeed, she would." Arthur's expression smoothed. "How understanding you are, but tell me more about your husband. Did he continue to paint?"

"Ham maintained a large studio at our main house and a smaller one at our summer place on Burns Lake in Minnesota," Edwina continued. "He welcomed the occasional retail traffic that came our way thanks to the rental cabins and other homes planted here and there around the lake." Her face brightened as she remembered romantic carefree days at the lake with her husband before Ham, Jr.'s, birth – immersed in art by day and swept away by passion at night.

"Do you mind?" Her host reached over and retrieved the china plate. "I really can't wait until after my lunch." Untying the ribbon, he lifted one section of the wrap and offered the plate to her, taking a cookie for himself once she had selected one.

"These are delicious," he declared having taken a bite. "Just what the doctor ordered. So what would Ham advise me to do if he were here?"

Not wishing to say the wrong thing, Edwina took time to examine the various works that were propped up along the walls of the large room, taking in as well that the room was wider than it was long when viewed from the front door.

"It strikes me that your beautiful paintings fall into three categories – seascapes, large and small, those that reflect inland scenes, and ones whose subjects are people," she began.

"That's a good point. Which ones do you prefer?"

"Honestly, I would be hard pressed to say." She met his gaze. "I could pick ones that I'm personally drawn to from each group, and all of them call to me in one way or another. I love the power represented in some of your seascapes, but then I appreciate your treatment of the sunlight as it finds its way among the trees in some of the woodland scenes. And, of course, who wouldn't be delighted by the faces of those children playing ball in a meadow filled with wildflowers?" She pointed towards a small painting outshined by larger works leaning against the far wall.

"Imagine your having picked that one out from among the rest!" Arthur's face filled with pleasure. "It's always been a particular favorite of mine, although I felt others might find it too romantic."

"Not at all," Edwina assured him before continuing. "Ham always said you should hit your customers with your strongest work first. Given that, I would suggest that you hang your larger seascapes along the back wall, where you have more space to devote to them and those entering the front door will see them right away. The inland scenes and those containing human subjects could then be grouped on the two side walls, each category being given the opportunity to show off to advantage."

"Amazing!" Her host beamed at her. "You have just distilled into a nutshell what I've struggled to figure out all morning. Would you have time to give me your opinion as to individual placement?"

"Sure, if you think it would be helpful," she agreed, welcoming the feeling of being needed.

Two hours later found most of the major works having been hung and decisions having been made as to how best to display the smaller paintings.

"If you don't have any plans, I would love to continue our conversation over lunch." Arthur placed his hammer on a box of printer paper. "There's a tea room I frequent in town."

Flattered by the unexpected invitation, Edwina felt herself blush. "That sounds lovely, but I must take a rain check. I promised Ginny, my granddaughter-in-law, that I would babysit Lucy this afternoon while she runs some errands." She glanced at her watch. "Goodness, I've been having such fun that I had no idea of the time. She'll be here to pick me up in ten minutes."

"Some other time then." Arthur escorted her to the main entrance of his new space, where he ran a long, thin finger along a delicate cable as it carried down the upper arm of her sweater. "What precise knitting. You rarely see fine handiwork these days. My wife was hardly ever without her needles."

"Ginny recently completed the sweater and presented it to me for good luck," Edwina filled him in, glad to give credit where credit was due. "She's quite talented. Once the baby gets a little older, I'm hoping to convince her to open a shop. You never know, do you?"

"Well said!" Her host gestured her to step into the sunshine first. "Thank you again for your help and the cookies. I'll be calling you about taking tea with me soon."

"I'll look forward to it," Edwina assured him as she turned to leave, wishing with all of her heart that she could've stayed.

CHAPTER V

Susan Chesterton sat on a bench in front of Chester's Crab Shack, fighting an uncharacteristic urge to cry as she waited for her cousin Larry who had asked her to join him at his restaurant for lunch. First Adrianna and now Tiny Slocum, where was the fairness in that? Soon she would be the only woman in the world or at least in Captain's Point who wasn't married.

Rummaging in her quilted-cloth purse, she pulled out a small car, a ball and a set of jacks in a zipper bag and laid them on the seat beside her, confident that somewhere beneath them was a packet of tissues hidden away in case of emergencies. But then, she remembered the peanut butter and jelly incident the previous Friday and knew she wouldn't find them, determining it would be better if she just didn't cry.

"You've never given yourself a chance to grieve for the death of your marriage," her psychologist friend from college had pointed out to her, when she had shared in an email that she verged on crying all the time. "Take the whole experience out, review it and then find a place for it."

Probably good advice, Susan had felt, but between Daniel and work, she was still having trouble finding the time in which to do so. The toys once again stored safely away, she stood and slung the bag over her shoulder, preferring a stroll along the boardwalk to remaining on the hard seat.

"Susan!" Bitsy Wilder, the owner of Long and Short, billed as the best hair emporium in Captain's Point, hailed her. "Where've you been?" Expert fingers examined her hair's ends. "You need a trim. You'll never get another man if you let yourself go like this. Stop by on your way to your car, and I'll work you in."

"Thanks." Susan forced a smile, thinking it might be time to look for a new stylist – an unmarried one. "I'm not sure that I'll have the time, I have an appointment with a new client at three."

"It never hurts to keep a man waiting." Bitsy sent her a knowing look before hurrying on her way.

How could you keep a man waiting when you didn't have one? Susan wondered as she stood next to the wooden railing and watched the sailboats on the water. Not that she had time for one anyway or even a place to put one for that matter, living as Daniel and she were at the big, old Chesterton Cove house with her parents. Recently, Chase had been gone from the office more than he had been there, and although he had told her to bring in three more associates, so far she had only been able to find two who were eligible.

Not wanting to miss her cousin when he arrived, she shifted her position, resting her left forearm on the top plank and giving herself a full view of the western end of the boardwalk. Everywhere she looked there were couples – gray-headed ones, big-bellied ones, and a large group of teenaged ones, who seemed bent on eating the candy store's entire stock of gelato.

No, wait, she told herself, one solitary person was reading a newspaper and appeared to be male from his shoes. Perhaps, he was the man of her dreams. She turned her face away as he looked up from his paper, one glance having set her straight.

Deeply tanned, a paint streak running along the leg of his jeans, his dark hair worn slightly long – she rejected his being the true love for her, despite his looking about her age.

But then the simple, innocent world she had always known changed in a flash. One minute she was standing where she had stood hundreds of times before - in full view of her friends and neighbors, perfectly at ease. The next minute she felt a sharp tug as her purse was jerked from her shoulder by a long-haired teenager who rapidly lengthened the distance between them as he made a run for it.

Catching a glimpse of her cousin rounding the corner several shop fronts away, she started to call for him to grab her purse and return it, but the words never left her. With one fluid motion, the man she had dismissed so casually only a moment before rose from the bench upon which he had been sitting and grabbed the fleeing teen's wrist, bringing the young criminal's hand and arm around and up the boy's back parallel with his spine.

"I believe this is yours, ma'am." The stranger held out her purse as Susan hurried over, dimples forming on both sides of his mouth as he sent her a slow smile.

His hair that had appeared brown in the shade of the building now revealed itself to be shiny black in the sun. Springing from a widow's peak on his forehead, it swept away from his face on either side of high cheekbones, but it was the broad shoulders and chest set atop his slim waist and hips that set her spine tingling.

"Thank you." Susan accepted her property as Larry rushed to her side. "That was amazing!"

"Are you okay?" Her cousin threw an arm around her shoulder and then looked over at the culprit, who had long since given up trying to squirm loose from the man's iron grip. "Billy Spooner! I might have known. It's a good thing your victim here isn't a prosecutor. How many times have you been in trouble now, Son? Six or seven?"

"The gentleman asked you a question." The stranger addressed the sullen teen. "Not that it matters. Whatever the number was before, it's now that number plus one."

"What's going on here?" The marina's young security guard, whose main duty was to empty the trash receptacles, sauntered up having finally noticed the crowd that had formed.

"Billy, here, snatched my cousin's purse from her shoulder," Larry filled him in. "I trust you'll hand him over to Sheriff Ward, now that this gentleman was kind enough to waylay him for you." He turned to the man who had come to his cousin's aid. "I'm Larry Chesterton. My cousin Susan and I are in your debt. Won't you join us for lunch?" He nodded towards Chester's.

"That's a nice offer, but I've already eaten." The man withdrew a card from the wallet he had pulled from his pocket, Billy now in the care of the law's representative, and handed it to the security guard. "Here's my name and temporary contact information should the sheriff need me to make a witness statement. In the meantime, I'm almost late for an appointment so you will have to excuse me."

And with that he left the scene of the crime, looking neither right nor left as he walked towards the small crowd of onlookers who parted and let him through without a sound as Susan watched, spellbound.

Not since she had witnessed a herd of gazelles part in a similar fashion for a male lion at a wildlife park had she witnessed such power and control emanating from one so obviously the ultimate male of his species. And his eyes – those dark hooded eyes – that had met her gaze and read her soul as he had nonchalantly returned her purse, still controlling the struggling thief with one hand. So much power, so much quiet strength – it had sent a wave of electricity through her body and taken her breath away.

"Come on, you." The security guard puffed out his sunken chest and steered the now wrist-shackled Billy towards the marina's office, hoping that he still had the handcuffs' key.

"Wish your fellow had taken us up on my offer," Larry took Susan's arm and headed her towards Chester's. "He seemed like a nice guy. Did you get his name?"

At which point, his sophisticated, every-hair-in-place cousin gave him a shock as she burst into tears.

CHAPTER VI

"Did you see him?" Bridgette popped her head into her one available senior partner's office two hours later.

"Did I see whom?" Susan looked up from the document she was checking for errors.

"That man! That gorgeous hunk of a man!"

"Here?" Susan put her pen down for a moment, taking in the fact that, if her secretary had been a dog, she would've been panting. "In Captain's Point?"

"In our office." Bridgette moved forward and shut the door. "He needed some deeds shifted or something."

"Who did he see?"

"That new guy, Gary." Her secretary's face filled with dismay. "What a waste! Marsha should've given him to you or, at the very least, to Barbara."

"Because he's a man?" Susan asked.

"No, because he's a gorgeous hunk of a man," Bridgette insisted. "I'll bet you a fiver right now that the Chamber of Commerce will be after him to replace Chase in next year's *Most Eligible Bachelors Calendar*."

"What exactly did this paragon look like?"

At which, to Susan's amazement, her secretary described point by point the stranger who had reacted so quickly on the boardwalk, grabbing hold of Billy Spooner and returning her purse.

"Oh, him," she replied, doing her best to sound nonchalant. "Larry and I met him earlier today. I'm sure Gary handled everything well, but just in case, would you bring his file to me when Gary's done with it?" Then she picked up her pen and returned to her document, signaling their conversation was over.

An hour later, Bridgette was back.

"Yes." Susan looked up from a *Law Review* volume.

"I have that file you requested." Her secretary laid the folder on her desk.

"Which file?" Susan glanced casually at the name on the tab.

"The one Gary was working on."

"Right." With the tip of her finger, the senior partner pushed the folder aside as she returned to her research. "Thanks."

Disappointed, Bridgette left her boss to her work, thinking as she walked to her own desk that it was no wonder such a beautiful woman was going to waste, unaware that as soon as she had left the firm's first female senior partner behind, Susan had pulled the file towards her and read the name *John Jefferson*.

Anderson looked up from his three-day-old newspaper as sounds of a sexy female voice addressing Bernice in the waiting room reached his ears. A quick check of his desk revealed it to be fair to middlin', although he did sweep the remains of yesterday's lunch into the metal trashcan in preparation for receiving what he hoped would be a new client.

A few seconds later, she entered his room – slightly over medium height, large blue eyes, natural blonde, with legs that could fell a strong man at five hundred paces.

"Mr. Brooks?" she asked in a voice that, up close and personal, made him wish he could hear it spoken again and again. "I'm Susan Carlisle, and I need your help."

And at that moment, Anderson knew he would move Heaven and Earth to do whatever he could for this woman.

Larry Chesterton turned from his computer and gazed out of his office window, his mind lost in thought. What in the world was wrong with Susan? Sure, Billy Spooner had stolen her purse right from her shoulder with a suddenness that had probably shocked her. But still…

It wasn't as if Billy would've harmed her, and she should've known that. Even her purse had been returned by the quick-thinking guy who had come to her aid. So why had she burst into tears after the incident was over? He had only said that he wished he had gotten the fellow's name.

Maybe she was overworked with Chase out of the office. Hadn't she mentioned something like that at the brunch?

Well, there were two things he could do. He could either take Susan for dinner at Montgomery's, giving her a nice evening out, or put his Aunt Elizabeth on the case. For a moment, he considered before picking up his phone and punching the number he wanted that was on speed dial.

"Bridgette? Larry Chesterton here. Could you put me through to Susan? … Thanks."

As he waited for his cousin to take his call, his brow cleared. Maybe if he plied her with a really good chardonnay, she would tell him what was bothering her.

Pleased with her cousin's invitation, Susan hurried along the produce aisle of Captain's Point's local organic market after work, planning to pick up some tomatoes her mother had requested she bring home and drop them off at The Cove on her way to meet Larry. As she reached for a perfect specimen, though, her hand halted in mid-air at the sound of a smooth voice beside her.

"We're going to have to stop meeting like this." John Jefferson's dark eyes twinkled at her as she glanced up, even as she felt his animal magnetism once again sucking her breath away.

"I'm…" She found her mind couldn't remember the words as her eyes fell to the watch on her wrist. "I'm late." She clutched at the handle of her shopping cart. "If you'll excuse me…"

And with that she abandoned the tomatoes and hurried to the front of the store, confused and embarrassed, unable to explain even to herself what had come over her, while left behind the man she had disappointed watched her escape through narrowed eyes.

Still wanting to take her mother what she expected to receive, Susan now found herself having to resort to the franchise grocery further along the main street where she managed to purchase the required vegetables. Having delivered them to The Cove, she then headed for Chester's where Larry had said he would wait for her after leaving his brokerage firm, preliminary to their walking to Montgomery's for dinner.

Arriving later than she had planned, she found her cousin deep in a discussion with his own restaurant's manager and promised to wait outside, preferring the pleasant evening air to the bedlam of the crab shack's interior.

As she approached the boardwalk's railing, though, she was surprised to hear Jules Massenet's *Meditation* from his opera *Thais* as played by a solo violinist. One of her favorite pieces, she felt herself drawn to its source, her footsteps taking her away from the strip of stores and restaurants to the string of boathouses projecting off the western end of the marina.

As the sky filled with the rose, pink and mauve of the spreading sunset above, Susan spotted him - standing with his back to her on the end of the final pier, his violin's case abandoned on the boards at his feet. With a tenderness and skill she hadn't heard in person before, John Jefferson played to the gentle waves lapping against the pilings beneath him, even as she heard the song of her mate in the haunting strains, calling her to him and beyond in a way she now knew she could never resist.

CHAPTER VII

Anderson sat at the table for one in the upscale restaurant, keeping his new client in view as she enjoyed a meal at another table with a blond Adonis who looked to be either her brother or a cousin.

Why was it that every blonde-haired, blue-eyed woman named Susan he had ever known had turned out to be an ice maiden? Was it something in their genes or the way they were raised, knowing from birth that blondes always have more fun? Either way, in his far flung experience, there were no exceptions.

Still the stack of C-notes she had left on his desk had stood tall next to the pile of his unpaid bills, and all she had asked for was reasonable surveillance. Even the barely dead steak on his plate was being paid for. It was a tough life, but someone had to live it, he guessed.

Jim Laidlaw turned off his laptop and leaned back in his seen-better-days lounge chair as the familiar living room of his childhood home dimmed around him. Sometimes life was tough, sometimes it was great, and sometimes it was downright disappointing. Not that he wasn't glad for Chase Sheffield, he was. Anyone could see that Adrianna and he were made for each other, but still…

Why now? Why this sudden urge to get married? Was it because of his birthday that loomed at the end of the month?

Susan… Now there was a pretty filly, and no one could say that Susan Chesterton wasn't fun. He had enjoyed escorting her on their occasional lunch or dinner dates, but who was he kidding? She wasn't in love with him, and he wasn't in love with her, not that he wouldn't have liked to have been.

And then the face that he normally pushed from his mind rose in front of him. One mistake, his inexperienced foot pushing a little too hard on the accelerator of his dad's '89 Oldsmobile, and in a matter of seconds, he had lost a chance with the love of his life – too young, too stupid, too embarrassed to turn things around. And with a sigh, he turned off the reading lamp by his side and made his way through the darkened house he shared with an aged gray cat and his childhood memories.

The storm broke at two o'clock in the morning, as a bright light flashed its presence into the tower suite bedroom around the edges of the drapes followed by a sharp crack of thunder. In an instant, Max, who had been allowed in to take his place in his bed on the hearth, had sprung onto the half-tester where he balanced precariously on the edge as he frantically attempted to burrow beneath the covers and down to Adrianna's feet.

"Bless your heart!" His mistress rolled from her husband's arms and gathered the dog to her. "It's only a storm."

"We really must consult Jim about what, if anything, can be done for him." On the other side of the mattress, Chase stretched his long frame. "Do you need any help?"

"No, he just wants to be held." She rose from the bed, Max still in her arms and slid open one side of the drapes that concealed her favorite window seat. "Go back to sleep."

Relaxing against the pillows, she held the still shivering dog close with her left arm as she absentmindedly stroked his back with her right hand, until he gradually calmed down.

In her large bedroom at The Cove, Susan threw back her own covers, slid her arms into a silken robe and slipped quietly through a connecting bathroom into her son's room. Here she found him still asleep - a stuffed monkey held in his arms, a large golden retriever curled in a ball atop the bed at Daniel's feet.

"I see you have everything under control, Casey," she whispered to the dog, who had opened one eye and lifted his tail in a brief half wag of acknowledgement at her approach.

Satisfied, she made her way back to her own room where she returned to bed, soon drifting back to a sleep in which she danced in the arms of a strong, unidentified man to the haunting strains of a violin.

In the master bedroom of the Montgomery House's dependency, Edwina sat bolt upright in her bed as the shriek of what sounded like a woman's scream merged with a roll of thunder and rain lashed against her windows as if bent on making its way in.

"A banshee!" her maternal grandmother's voice seemed to call in her ear.

Shaken, she flipped on the bedside lamp and rose from her bed, before heading to the kitchen where she turned on the heat beneath the kettle kept on the stove and prepared to brew a cup of vanilla chamomile tea that she hoped would help her get back to sleep. Waiting for the water to come to a boil, she turned on the gas logs in the living room's restored fireplace with the remote, glad for the warm glow that it cast over the room, thinking it sufficient to fill her needs.

A few minutes later, as she sat in her favorite chintz armchair sipping on the warm, sweet, milk-laced tea – the storm now having abated outside – she knew she had been silly. There had been no real scream, merely a blending of a nightmare she must have been having with the storm's outside wrath.

How comfortable her new home had become in such a short time! How lucky she was to have it!

Her tea now consumed, she turned off the logs, rinsed the cup in the sink of her neat, well-equipped kitchen and slipped back into bed, secure once again in the knowledge that she had made the right decision when she had moved to Captain's Point.

Drawn to the window of what had formerly been Chase Sheffield's childhood bedroom in the newly restored Sheffield Place Inn, John Jefferson remained standing there as the wind moved the storm northward along the coast. Gradually, the trees peppering the lawn here and there beneath him stilled as the clouds thinned, allowing a full moon to peek through, disappear and then reveal itself completely.

Then, his mind moved from the scene outside now to the pair of beautiful blue eyes that had looked up at him so full of gratitude on the boardwalk, but later had filled at the grocery with…what?

Fear? A bit. Confusion? Certainly, but there had been something else. Slowly, he sifted through twenty years of adult memories until he landed on the precise one.

He had been twenty-two at the time and working on a dude ranch in Wyoming – green to the point of being dangerous. The ranch's foolish owner had caught and placed in a corral a wild stallion that had managed to break loose during the night, pausing on his way to freedom beyond the compound to break into a neighboring enclosure, releasing three mares.

The next day had been a circus as the owner had insisted that the mares and stallion must be retrieved. It had taken their small, mainly unschooled group the better part of the day to locate and corner the tiny herd in the narrow end of what was thought to be a dead end canyon.

Following his boss's instructions he had ridden his horse along a small passage between the rock outcroppings that should have brought him out on the back right side of the herd. Instead, he had discovered one of the mares at a true dead end, where she had looked at him with eyes filled with the same fear, confusion and longing all rolled into one.

Dismounting, he had remained where he was as he had spoken soft words of encouragement. Gradually, she had calmed to the point where he had felt comfortable removing a coil of rope from behind his saddle and fashioning it into a small lasso, the loop of which he had held loosely in his hand.

For about ten minutes, he had waited meeting her gaze, before he had turned slowly and faced the side of his own horse, pleased when the loose mare had taken a step towards him, then another, until finally she had allowed him to slip the rope over her head.

Leading her back to the group, he had been greeted with anger instead of the gratitude he had expected, the stallion having outwitted the ranch owner by leading the other two mares through a cave and onto open plains that stretched beyond. Two weeks later, he had left the dude ranch behind and taken the memory of the mare's haunted eyes with him.

Satisfied, he pulled the drapes back across the window and returned to the desk where he had been working, turning off the mica-shaded lamp and preparing for bed.

Back in the tower bedroom, Adrianna rose from the window seat where she had been dozing with Max held in her arms, closed the drapes and returned the sleepy dog to his bed on the hearth before slipping once again beneath the covers on the half-tester, trying not to disturb Chase.

"It's about time you returned." He surprised her by rolling over and drawing her to him, so that they lay together like two spoons. "I was beginning to think I had lost you to another."

"Never," she whispered as her head found its accustomed place on his shoulder and she snuggled contentedly against the warm body of her new husband, glad to have his strong arms around her once more.

CHAPTER VIII

"Oh, no!" Adrianna exclaimed the next morning as she was sorting through a large stack of mail - a business letter from their accountant in her hand. "Charles Stoddard is retiring."

"Can't say I'm surprised," Chase said. "Charlie must be seventy if he's a day. Is he leaving Captain's Point?"

"The letter doesn't say." She glanced through the missive again. "The office will continue to process work as needed for six months to allow time for his clients to make the necessary adjustments. Do you have any suggestions for a replacement?" Her fingers searched 'Captain's Point, Maryland, accountants' on her laptop.

"Not really." Chase leaned back in his chair at the other end of the long library table that now served as their joint home office desk and stretched out his legs.

"There aren't very many choices," his wife told him as she scrolled down the listings that had appeared. "Wait a minute – Stephen McKinney. Isn't that Belinda McKinney's son from church?"

"Now that you mention it, I think he is an accountant." A clear picture of a tall, slim man of about his wife's age coaching the church's teenaged boys' basketball team took shape in his mind.

"Do you know him?" Adrianna asked.

"Well enough to like him," Chase answered. "According to Paul, he's generous with his time when it comes to the church. Why don't we send him an invitation to Robin's event at Sheffield Place Inn and give you a chance to meet him in an informal setting. If you like him, too, then we can make an appointment with him at his office."

"I appreciate the compliment of your respecting my opinion," his bride stated, "but if you like him, I know I will. Why don't I send him the invitation like you suggested and make an appointment to meet with him at his office next week? It strikes me that he may not have much staff as recently as he's gone into business, and our joint holdings would dramatically change the complexion of his firm. We would be doing him a disservice if we didn't give him as much time as possible to work through the transition with Charles."

"Come here." Her groom held out his arms, and hopefully, she rounded the big table and plopped onto his lap. "Do you have any idea how delightful you are – beauty, brains and perception all rolled into one? Not to mention the fact that you're an amazingly sexy little vixen." He bent his head and kissed a spot on her neck that sent shivers up her spine.

"Chase…" Her voice held a firm tone belied by the laughter in her eyes. "You simply cannot allow every single thing that I do to turn you on."

At which her groom slid his lips along the opening of her V-necked top until she let out a small gasp of pleasure. "Why not?" he asked as he stood with his giggling bride still in his arms and headed up the tower stairs to their bedroom.

Work abandoned for the rest of the morning, the honeymooning couple had enjoyed a picnic lunch at the table in the kitchen garden with Otis, Penny and Jeff Stuart, their college-aged, part-time grounds man, before adjourning to what had once been a formal parlor and now served as their music room.

Engrossed in frolicking through a fast-paced, ragtime duet at the baby grand, neither of them heard the front door open or the footsteps crossing the foyer that heralded Larry Chesterton's arrival.

For a moment, he stood in the room's arched doorway and watched them unawares, not wishing to intrude and unable to pull himself away, so happy and in love did they look. But then, the piece came to an end as Chase ran his right hand upwards along the keys to the highest C and pinged it with a flourish as he reached over and kissed his bride's cheek.

"Bravo!" Their broker announced his presence. "Glad to see you two are allowing yourself at least some down time."

Remembering their mid-morning activities, both newlyweds immediately burst out laughing as Adrianna blushed and Chase pulled her to him on the piano bench. "You see, my love," he said, working hard to keep a straight face, "even our broker thinks we should spend more of our time down than we do upright on our honeymoon."

"You two will be the death of me one of these days." Larry rolled his eyes before moving further into the room and checking the clock on the mantle. "Aunt Elizabeth should be here in a few minutes."

"What are you boys up to now?" Adrianna's expression immediately sobered, even though the corners of her mouth twitched, as she looked from one of the miscreants to the other, completely unaware of whatever plans had been set in motion.

"I thought you might enjoy a little field trip," her new husband explained, "so I've organized a small party. We're going to explore the tunnels under the house on the off chance that your great-grandfather left behind some of his Prohibition contraband."

"Oh, Chase…" His bride's eyes widened as memories of her near drowning in a room at the seaward end of the tunnel flooded her mind. "I'm not…"

"Never fear, my queen," he assured her, his eyes filling with understanding. "All has been made safe. Otis oversaw that for me on the day Elizabeth, Susan, Penny and you went to Baltimore to shop for your wedding gown."

"Do you really think we may find some cases of Franklin Montgomery's liquor still stored in one of the rooms or an offshoot tunnel?" Adrianna asked as she gathered her courage, determined not to spoil her husband's fun.

"Who knows?" He released her and stood as sounds of other arrivals reached them from the foyer. "But we might as well see."

"Here they are," Elizabeth Chesterton announced from the arched doorway where she stood with two college-aged girls – one tall and willowy, her thick, dark hair falling to her shoulders and the other diminutive in stature, her tight, dark curls cut close to her head above the mocha contours of her face. "This is Becca Tate, she gestured to the taller girl, and this is Sandra

Williams. They're the interns I'm working with this quarter. I hope you don't mind that I brought them along."

"Not at all!" Adrianna sent both young women a welcoming smile, unsure as to why they would've wanted to come.

"We really appreciate this opportunity," Sandra said in a soft voice. "It's not often you're given the chance to prove a theory concerning events that may or may not have occurred a century and a half before."

"I've known for some time that there was a central drop off and exit point somewhere along the coast near Captain's Point," Elizabeth shared, "but I've never been able to pinpoint it. When Larry mentioned the tunnels and rooms under Montgomery House the other evening, I jumped on it as a possibility."

"You're talking about the Underground Railroad," Adrianna said as she remembered that Elizabeth Chesterton was considered to be the expert on the subject as it pertained to Maryland. "How exciting!"

Chase relaxed by her side, relieved that she now seemed to be looking forward to revisiting the catacombs beneath the house where he had barely saved her from drowning only a few weeks before.

"John's arrived," Otis announced from the doorway. "Do you want us in here, or will all of you be joining us in the kitchen?"

"The kitchen, I think." Chase took his wife's hand. "If you will all follow me, we'll pass out flashlights and supplies. My hope is that we can fashion some sort of map of the tunnels and rooms as well as discover what, if anything, has been stored there."

"That would certainly help us," Becca spoke up from the rear of the small procession as they made their way to the back of the house where they discovered John Thornburg, the owner of Montgomery's restaurant and a trained sommelier, along with Penny and Jeff.

Adrianna was reassured by a box of flashlights and a supply of batteries that awaited them on the granite-topped island.

"My wife hasn't seen it yet, but I've recently had rough lighting installed along the main tunnel," Chase told them, giving Adrianna's hand a gentle squeeze as Otis dealt out the flashlights, legal pads and pens.

"Wrought iron safety gates have also been added at the bottom of the first stairway and at the far end of the main tunnel above the high-water line, where it opens onto a boat dock," Chase continued his description of their destination. "There is one dead end room beyond the tunnel at that end that I will allow you to take a quick glimpse of if the tide is low enough. Both times I've been in that room it was completely empty, but it would have provided a temporary waiting room at certain times of the day, if one were anticipating the arrival of a boat."

"I would like to see it," Elizabeth said. "Sometimes travelers left their marks along the way."

"We should head straight there then," Chase said, "before the tide starts coming back in."

"Are you planning on our sticking together, or should we fan out?" Larry asked.

"Let's stick together at first," their host said. "The tunnel, the walkway and rooms I've seen have all been carved out of rock, and I can't imagine that they extend very far. If we find something completely unexpected, then we can change gears. If we come upon another point that accesses the ocean, Otis and I will need to check it out first. Is everyone ready?"

A murmur of agreement passed around the room.

"Otis, why don't you lead the way to the Captain's study then," Chase suggested, allowing the others to clear the room.

"It's like falling off a horse." He gazed down at Adrianna's wide eyes once they were alone. "I don't want you to know fear ever again in this house."

"I'm never afraid with you beside me," she assured him as she felt his strong arms go around her and draw her to him, trying hard to release her concerns about the tunnels and rooms beneath them once and for all as he kissed her.

CHAPTER IX

Adrianna and Chase joined the rest of the group in the Captain's study as the room was still called in honor of the home's builder, Captain Jebediah Montgomery, whose portrait as an older man hung over the room's fireplace.

"Why don't you explain how you discovered the tunnel?" Chase suggested, turning to his wife.

"When I first returned to Captain's Point, my great-aunt Martha had left me a clue that was designed to help me meet some of the conditions of inheritance under her will," Adrianna explained. "The clue read simply '*The answer is in the garden...*' A photo of my great-aunt reading to me while I played in my sandbox as a child in the kitchen garden was also included in the envelope."

"What a strange thing for Martha to have done!" Elizabeth exclaimed.

"Actually, I had already satisfied the requirements by the time I discovered the meaning of the clue," Adrianna continued, "but until that point, I had been systematically searching for it both within the house and on the grounds, uncovering several things along the way that meant a great deal to me."

"Amazing!" Larry interjected. "I had no idea you had been doing all of that."

"Chase and Susan both knew." Adrianna smiled up at her husband. "In fact, Chase was quite perturbed with me when he learned that I had looked over the parapet on the roof as part of my endeavors."

"I should think he was!" Larry's eyes widened as he stood up for their host.

"On the Saturday evening after you two returned from his aunt's home in Boston," Adrianna addressed their broker, "I was sitting at the desk here in this room and realized that the frieze above the wainscoting was comprised of a carved garden."

"Then, being the inquisitive creature that she is," her husband picked up the story, "my wife proceeded to test each flower and leaf until she discovered this." He reached over and twisted a large peony at which a panel in the five-foot high wainscoting slid open revealing a stairway carved out of the cliff's rock that led down to a locked wrought iron gate, beyond which a tunnel could be seen.

"How ingenious," Elizabeth whispered under her breath.

"If you'll let me go first, I'll lead the way to the boat dock as we discussed in the kitchen." Chase bent his head and proceeded down the stairs, pausing to unlock the gate where he flipped a switch that illuminated the tunnel.

Otis gestured for Larry and John to go next, followed by Elizabeth, the two interns, Jeff and his own wife, Penny.

"Chase asked me to keep an eye on you when he was busy." Their property manager smiled at Adrianna, holding her elbow until she had passed through the sliding doorway, then leaving a brick to hold the doorway open before following along behind.

"You two did a good job with the gates and the lighting," she said as she moved forward through the tunnel, which had been plunged into darkness the first time she had entered it, leaving her to find her way by sliding her hand along the rough-hewn stone walls to the sea entrance, where she had made a false move and almost met her death.

"Your husband drew up the specs the day after you two got engaged," Otis said, "but he swore me to secrecy – not that he had to twist my arm to get me to agree."

"No, I imagine you were right there with him on the need to get this done." Adrianna chuckled, glad for her fatherly friend's company. "Two of you against one."

"Might as well make that three," Otis filled her in. "Penny was thrilled when I told her afterwards how I'd spent my day while you ladies were away."

"Look at all the rooms!" Elizabeth's excited voice carried back to them, followed by a quieter reply from one of the interns that Adrianna couldn't make out.

"Every time I come down here, I'm surprised by the length of this tunnel and how many rooms extend off of it," Otis stated as the scent of salt air became stronger and a dim light shone up ahead.

"Here we are." Chase's strong voice reached the two stragglers, followed by the squeak of another wrought iron gate being opened. "As you can see, we're at low tide, but at high tide the water comes over this walkway and into the room beyond to the level of several feet. It might not have come quite so high when the whole shebang was completed, but you would have to verify this through some research."

"Make a note, girls!" Elizabeth's excitement was palpable.

Adrianna noticed that a kayak and oars had been hung at her eye level across the tunnel from the first iron boat ring, which had been placed just beyond what was now the high water mark.

"In case the panel slides shut on someone again," Otis explained as Adrianna turned to him.

"You two thought of everything, didn't you?" she whispered, her eyes filling with tears.

"No, your husband did." Otis hugged her to him. "You'll never be in the same position again."

"He tied the rope he brought with him to this ring and then wrapped it several times around his wrist before wrapping more of it around his waist," she explained. "Then in the room he put a beach towel around my waist, wrapped more of the rope around me and tied me to him. If he hadn't done that we would have been carried out to sea by the rip tide. As it was, he swung me between him and the wall as we were coming back across the walkway around the corner here and took the full brunt of the huge wave that hit us, shielding me from it. How he held onto those rings in the wall, I'll never know."

"Sheer determination, I imagine," Otis said. "That was quick thinking on his part to grab the beach towel and the rope. He never told me how he had used them, but, of course, he'd been here before so he knew what he was getting into."

"I was bruised the next day, but I didn't have the chafing you saw on his wrist because of the towel." Realizing that everyone else was now entering the room where she had been trapped,

Adrianna dabbed her eyes on the sleeve of her shirt and then followed along behind, determined to get the worst over.

Entering the room, she was surprised once again to find that the grate in the ceiling ten feet above them had been cleared of vegetation, sunlight now streaming through the aperture.

"Where does it come out?" She turned back to Otis.

"Right at the edge of the woods. Chase had a wrought iron fence installed around it, so no one would accidentally send their foot between the bars."

Like one of our future children, Adrianna thought as she turned back around, met her husband's eyes filled with concern for her and sent him a smile.

"Look!" Elizabeth pointed the beam of her flashlight sideways across the rock forming the far corner of the room, revealing indentations in the rough surface.

"Here." Chase retrieved a canvas gym bag from Otis. "We brought some bottled water, if you think it would be appropriate for us to wash the wall clean. We can always replenish with sea water if more is needed."

"Let's see what it shows us," Elizabeth agreed, taking a roll of paper towel that he offered her.

A few minutes later, the wall had revealed a series of carved marks – some as high as six feet above the floor, others almost at floor level as if the carver had been sitting as he or she had worked.

"I recognize several of these." Elizabeth stepped back so the others could see better. "This one – the cross in a circle – was made by James White, a slave who had run away from a plantation in Mississippi, and the pine tree is documented as having been the mark used by Lazarus Russell, who became a very successful merchant and landowner some years later in the Midwest."

"I count twenty-seven marks," Sandra said.

"No, I think there may be even more over here," Jeff pointed out from where he had been working quietly closer to the room's entrance, a shy smile taking up residence in his face as Becca beamed at him.

Standing quietly near the doorway, Adrianna watched as her strong husband helped first this person and then that one, perfectly at ease despite their horrific previous experience. As her heart filled with pride, she sent Otis a calm smile – now firm in her belief that all of Chase's efforts on behalf of her and their future children had indeed made their home safe and secure, above ground and below, and recognizing she had no further need for her fear.

CHAPTER X

Managing to break away from the office a few hours earlier than usual, Susan arrived home at The Cove only to find it devoid of inhabitants except for Casey and her mom's mixed breed terrier, who was known to the household as Terror. Assuming that Daniel was running errands with her mother, she quickly changed into a pair of jeans, a blue Chester's T-shirt that set off her eyes and her trainers. Then she gathered her thick blonde hair into a ponytail and headed out the home's back door for a rare solitary walk.

Once outside, her footsteps took her along the cliffs, past the new Sheffield Place Inn, Montgomery House and its neighboring farm, and onto her own family's farm where she had been raised and her sister's family now lived. For a moment, she paused and enjoyed the breeze off the ocean as she pondered whether or not to drop in for a visit with Courtney.

But then, she continued along the cliff. Having cleared the short distance that comprised the farm's narrow access to the sea, she turned right onto the familiar path that would lead her through the pine woods to a large rambling Victorian. Formerly the home of the deceased Ivan Lancaster, gentleman farmer, it now stood empty awaiting the appearance of his heirs - its wide porches providing a broad view of the ocean spread beyond the long slope down to the cliff and a comfortable place for a solitary think.

Cool and quiet, the woods soon worked their magic as she felt her worldly cares melting away. To her left two squirrels chased one another up a tree, while deeper within the close-packed trees on her right a mockingbird sang a lone tune.

"Listen," Ivan had once told her as evening had begun to spread its shadows around them. "Listen and the trees will whisper to you."

What would they tell her about the stranger who had so touched her, she wondered?

The trees, though, were not whispering - quite the contrary. Today, they were filled with the sound of an axe falling, and the noise was coming from the direction of the house that was under her firm's care, her uncle having been named administrator of Ivan's will before his own death.

Making her way silently towards the edge of the woods, she had just pushed aside the overgrown branches of a large rhododendron bush, when John Jefferson lifted an armful of fresh cut pine logs and turned around.

"Checking up on your firm's new client already?" He sent her a warm smile that immediately precluded any intention she might have had to turn away. "That's what I call customer service!"

Suddenly, the dots connected in Susan's head. "You're Ivan's heir."

"Guilty as charged." He added the logs to what appeared to be a growing pile. "I'm ready to take a break. Why don't you join me for a glass of lemonade on the porch?"

Not wanting to appear churlish, she nodded her agreement.

"If you go around to the side facing the sea, you'll find some fine old Brumby rockers and a very nice view," he told her. "I'll be with you in a minute."

Making her way to the ocean side of the house as directed, Susan wondered how long she should stay before she could gracefully make an exit, all thoughts of a quiet think now completely out of the question. Expecting her host to reappear through the door beside her, she was surprised when he rounded the corner of the house carrying a tray that held two glasses, a pitcher of lemonade and a plate of what appeared to be homemade iced sugar cookies.

"Here we are!" He placed the refreshments on a sturdy, hand-hewn pine table that Susan knew had not been on the porch before and then served the lemonade. "Help yourself to some cookies. I'm staying at the new Sheffield Place Inn, and Marissa baked them."

"But the inn isn't open yet." Susan chose one of the cookies that did indeed look delicious. "They're holding the big pre-opening PR event this weekend."

"It's open if you know how to get around Edmund." Her host sent her a grin, revealing his dimples, as he took a seat in the rocker on the other side of the table and stretched out his long legs. "I told him that since I was going to be knee deep in renovations here, staying amongst them there wouldn't be any bother at all and at least the plumbing would work at his place."

"How much work are you planning to do before you sell this property?" Susan asked, wishing that she had viewed the contents of his file back at her office instead of merely glancing at the name on the tab.

"I'm doing serious renovations, although I've kept it in pretty good shape for Uncle Ivan over the past several years when I've visited." He took a drink from his own glass and set it on the table. "I have no intentions of selling, because I'm making Captain's Point my permanent home. Now, what was it that you wanted to see me about?"

"Actually, I was inadvertently trespassing," Susan admitted. "I didn't realize you were in residence, and I've been in the habit of coming here when I wanted to be alone and think ever since I returned to Captain's Point back in April. I spent hours on this porch with Ivan as a child, and I knew he wouldn't mind."

Once again, her host surprised her when he responded by laughing. "You're Uncle Ivan's 'my sweet little Susie.' Although he was holding out on me, when he described you as being the cutest thing in pigtails he'd ever seen."

"And you're his 'that rascally nephew of mine,'" she replied as understanding dawned within her.

"Is that what he called me behind my back?" Jefferson's dark eyes twinkled. "He meant it as a compliment, you know."

"I'm sure he did," Susan assured him. "He was obviously quite fond of you."

"Well, he would've been, wouldn't he?" Her host sent her a twisted smile. "After all, we were the black sheep in our family, so we had to stick together."

"The black sheep?" She wasn't sure that she understood, surprised by the pain that had filled John Jefferson's eyes.

"We were the throwbacks, or didn't you know that?"

"I have no idea what you're talking about," she admitted, not sure that she really needed to know more.

"Describe my uncle."

"Tall, broad shouldered, with dark hair and eyes like yours, although his hair had turned silvery white in recent years," Susan obliged.

"Exactly. Both Uncle Ivan and I took after my maternal great-grandmother, a full-blooded Cherokee," her host explained. "The dark looks had skipped a generation, but then the two of us came along one generation after another, much to the shame of our blond-haired, blue-eyed, Virginia's-finest relations. They weren't outwardly hostile to either of us, you understand, but they made us both aware in subtle ways that we weren't really wanted, even my mother. In my uncle's case, he left them all behind and settled here, while I've spent most of my adult life traveling the world."

"But, surely, your dark hair and eyes couldn't have made that much difference to your family." Susan immediately wished she could take back her words and rushed on. "You know we're probably related somewhere back along the ancestral line."

"You have Lancaster or Jefferson relations?"

"No, through our Cherokee heritage." It was her turn to surprise him.

"Not with that blonde hair and those blue eyes," he stated.

"Now who's judging someone on their appearance?" she asked. "True, I take after my father's Norwegian side of the family, but when you meet my mother, you'll see that her hair is auburn. Her many times great-grandmother was a member of the Blue clan who married a red-haired, Scottish trapper after he was found dying of what was probably pneumonia and was adopted by the Long Hair clan, who nursed him back to health. My great-grandmother, who was, of course, still a member of the Blue clan due to the matriarchal laws of the Nation, moved to Maryland with her husband, the son of a farmer from somewhere near Asheville, North Carolina."

"You do know your Cherokee," he admitted.

"My mother's an historian," Susan filled him in. "Her work primarily centers on the Underground Railroad, but Cherokee history is close to her heart. When you meet her, don't get her started on the subject if you have any plans for the next hour or two of your life. What are your clans?"

"Wolf and Paint – Paint being my great-grandmother's." Savoring the phrase 'when you meet her' in his mind, her host offered Susan the plate of cookies, which she found unable to resist and took yet another one. "Small world, isn't it?" he asked.

"Yes," she agreed as she gazed at the calm ocean spread before them, slowly rocking in her chair. "I can't tell you how many happy hours I've spent here with your uncle. As you probably know, he didn't suffer fools gladly, but for some reason he took a shine to me when I wasn't much more than a toddler and he found me wandering in his woods."

Jefferson wondered if the original attraction for his uncle had been that she reminded him of a younger sister who had died of leukemia, but he kept that to himself as he asked, "So what were you coming here to think about, or is that too personal?"

"I have a son named Daniel." Susan kept her eyes focused on a yacht that was making its way up the coast. "He's been very hurt by his father and our divorce. I brought him back here to Captain's Point when a partnership at my uncle's law firm opened up to me thanks to Chase Sheffield, who owns the inn where you're staying. Daniel and I now live with my folks at Chesterton Cove, known by the locals as The Cove, on the other side of the inn."

"Probably a good move on your part," her host stated, "although the man was a fool to let you and his son go."

"You can't possibly know that." She turned sharply in his direction.

"Yes, I can." He met her gaze, and once again, she knew without a doubt that he had indeed read her clear down to her soul. "Was he dumb enough to have an affair?"

"Worse than that." Susan looked down at her hands where they were folded in her lap. "He said he had grown tired of having a wife and child always hanging around his neck, and it wasn't as if I wasn't pulling my weight. I worked full-time at a law practice in the D.C. area, and once I realized how cold he was towards Daniel, I took full responsibility for everything that pertained to him. Basically, he threw us away with the trash."

"Look at me!" Her host's angry tone forced her to meet his gaze. "You are not trash, and neither is your son." Then his voice softened. "How old is your child?"

"Daniel's four."

"Four years old – what could he possibly have done that would bring on that kind of contempt from his own father?" Her host asked.

"Nothing," Susan admitted, embarrassed as she felt the prick of tears in her eyes.

"Here." He handed her a couple of napkins from the tray. "Have a good cry. It'll do you a world of good, and I've seen plenty of women cry in my time – not that any of them ever cried because of something I'd said or done to them I hope."

"Thank you." Susan dabbed at her eyes, fighting to gain control of herself. "I'm not normally this emotional. My friend says I haven't processed the divorce in my head yet, and I've been carrying a fair-sized load at work due to unforeseen circumstances."

"Sounds like you've had a lot on you."

For a few moments, they sat in silence as they both gazed at the ocean before them lost in their own thoughts, Susan gently rocking in her chair once again.

"Would you believe that as much time as I've spent on this porch, I've never been in the house," she broke their silence. "The most I've ever seen of the inside is a partial view of the kitchen beyond the mudroom as glimpsed from the back door."

"I'd invite you in and show you around," her host said, "but I've just stained the downstairs floors except for the one in the kitchen, which I did when I laid a new tile floor in the mudroom. That's why I came around the house with the tray."

"You have been busy," Susan said.

"Why don't you join me for dinner on the pier at the marina tomorrow," he suggested. "We can come by here on our way to the restaurant, and I can show you what I've been up to besides replacing all the windows, refinishing the floors, making this table and doing some clearing around the grounds. In exchange, you can educate me on all the ins and outs of Captain's Point."

"I'd enjoy that." She sent him a shy smile, but then turned her gaze back to the ocean, part of her pleased this man would ask her out knowing that she had a small child, even as she remembered that their date would cut into her time with Daniel. "It's always so peaceful here," she added as they again shared a few minutes of comfortable silence before she rose and explained that it was time she returned home.

"Will six o'clock be okay?" he asked as he escorted her back to the woods.

"Yes." She paused for a moment before stepping onto the path, pleased with how much more relaxed she felt than when she had started out. "Thank you for being so understanding back there. Ivan was wrong to call you a rascal. You've been very kind to me this afternoon."

"I've treated you with the respect you deserve." Once more, he held her gaze with his dark eyes, before she turned quickly away and headed into the woods, overwhelmed by a desire within her for him to have drawn her to him, held her close and asked her to stay.

CHAPTER XI

At the same time that Susan was making her way back to The Cove along the cliffs, Arthur locked up his new gallery and headed along the walkway that connected Montgomery House's former carriage house with the dependency, Edwina's china plate in his hand. Having reached his destination, he stepped onto the covered porch and rang the doorbell that gave off a pleasant chime within, pleased when his new friend opened her door.

"I've come to thank you again and return your plate," he said, holding it out to her. "I'm afraid I made short work of your delicious cookies."

"I'll take that as a compliment." She sent him a smile as she took the plate. "Won't you come in?"

"For a few minutes," Arthur accepted her invitation, curious as to how she had decorated her new home.

As an artist, the paintings hung here and there on the walls were the first things to which his eyes gravitated, including a work from the Hudson River School that had been given pride of place over the fireplace. But then, he spotted a smaller piece done in the Impressionist style leaned against the back of the second shelf in a tall bookcase and strode to it.

"One of my husband's," Edwina told him with pride. "I always recall the smell of paint when I think of our marriage."

"He certainly knew what he was doing." Arthur reached out his hand to remove it from the shelf for a closer look. "May I?"

"Certainly."

"I love the way he's captured the light," the artist said. "Where was it painted?"

"Along the shores of Burns Lake," she told him.

"So the woman and child are you and your son?" he asked, pointing to the image of a young woman in a floral print dress, bending over a brown-haired boy who was intently digging with a brightly colored shovel and pail.

She smiled wistfully at the painting. "The hardest thing about downsizing from our house was closing up Ham's studio. I had insisted in all of our houses that he allow a couch in his special room, so that I could comfortably spend time with him while he painted. I can't tell you how many sketches he did of me in various poses on one or another of those couches. I have one completed as a full blown painting in the other room, if you'd like to see it."

"Of course." He replaced the small canvas on the shelf and followed her along the short hall where she pointed to a mid-sized frame that had been hung over a small writing desk.

In this work, the artist had turned to Realism. Supported by pillows, a young Edwina reclined at the end of a green couch, the folds of a loose-fitting, white cotton dress falling from a gathered bodice, her sun-browned arms and legs bare. Her right arm and hand lay along the base of her rounded belly as if supporting the child that she carried, her face lit from within as she gazed with love at the painter.

"Stunning." Arthur forced himself to speak, the single word unable to articulate how struck he was by both the subject and the painting.

"Ham should've pursued his art more aggressively," Edwina said, her voice taking on a slight edge, "but his father insisted that he pursue a 'real' career. He always said that Ham, Jr., would be allowed to choose for himself, but our son preferred a similar kind of professional course as his father's."

"I can sympathize with that story, although in my case my father may have been right," Arthur admitted. "I never have had the talent of say an Oliveira or your husband."

"But I love your paintings!" Edwina exclaimed. "They're filled with so much emotion, and you play with the light in such marvelous ways."

"Thank you," he accepted her compliment in his simple, quiet way. "Hearing that from someone as knowledgeable as you are means a great deal to me."

Suddenly realizing that they were standing alone in her bedroom, embarrassment washed over Edwina. "Would you like a cup of tea or, perhaps, coffee?" she asked as she led the way back to her living room where they were soon settled in for a quiet chat.

CHAPTER XII

"Obviously, you're going to want to spend more time in this room, perhaps taking pictures or making tracings," Chase addressed Elizabeth and the two interns, once they had viewed Jeff's find in the rock-walled room off the tunnel. "At this point, though, I would suggest we move to some of the other rooms we passed on the way here in case they reveal other interesting details." He stepped back and allowed the others to leave the room first.

As they returned along the tunnel, the group entered and passed their flashlight beams over the walls of six empty rock-walled rooms, each measuring approximately ten feet by ten feet, three on each side of the tunnel. Disappointed murmurs could be heard as they headed to the next opening, this one on their left just before the bend to the right that would put them in view of the steps leading back to the Captain's study in the main house.

Entering this room first, one thing immediately stood out to Otis. "None of the other rooms had shelves in them," he pointed out, nodding towards what appeared to be a simple bookcase made of bare wood that centered on the wall opposite the room's doorway.

John Thornburg moved forward and held aloft a battery operated storm lantern he had thought to bring along, running his hand along the top shelf until he felt what seemed to be a knot hole on the back left corner next to the rock. "Hold on a minute," he said, excitement underlining his tone as those closest to him heard a sharp click and the right side of the unit moved an inch towards them.

The others formed a semi-circle, clearing the space directly in front of the bookcase as Chase took hold of the side of the shelves and pulled them easily into the room, revealing a void beyond.

"It's another room!" Elizabeth's eyes shone, but it was John Thornburg who was destined to be delighted this time as the room was found to contain what had been used in years past as a wine cellar and still held a number of what proved to be choice vintages whose labels proclaimed their having been bottled in the late '30s and '40s.

"Will any of them still be drinkable?" Jeff asked.

"Quite possibly," John assured them as he carefully removed and dusted off the label on yet another bottle. "And they will certainly fall within the collectible category."

"They were probably purchased by your grandfather before he served under General MacArthur," Otis addressed Adrianna. "If I remember correctly, he died of a heart attack in the Philippines sometime after the treaty of surrender was signed."

"That's right," Adrianna confirmed absentmindedly, as the beam of her flashlight ran along the top of the shelves that in this room had been constructed in a way that reflected the care given to the woodwork found within the main house. "Chase, are you seeing what I'm seeing?"

Her husband turned around from where he had been speaking quietly with the sommelier in the far corner. "No, what have you found?"

"There's a carved frieze running along these wine shelves." His wife pointed to where her flashlight beam was now focused onto a large peony carved into the top right corner of the most prominent set of shelves that resided opposite the room's entrance.

"Now that would be too good to be true." Chase hurried forward, twisting the ball-like flower first one way and then another, his efforts being rewarded by this unit swinging forward as well.

"A third room!" Larry exclaimed.

"How far back do these rooms go?" Penny wondered aloud as Chase slowly pulled the shelves into the room where they stood, not wanting to disturb the wines stored on them any more than necessary as he revealed a much smaller space behind.

"John, perhaps you should go first," their host suggested, the beam of his flashlight having shown him that the room was filled with wooden crates stacked along the walls – two deep and five crates high – some carrying labels, others branded with burnt symbols and two carrying wax seals.

Stepping into the small space, John let out a whistle and gestured for Chase to join him. "We've hit the mother lode," the sommelier's strong voice carried back to those eagerly awaiting his verdict. "These crates are from the '20s and '30s. Does the name Lafite-Rothschild mean anything to you?"

"You're kidding!" His host took his wife's hand and drew her forward with him into the room.

"This crate here and here and those two over there that I can see." John moved his lantern overhead as he pointed to various parts of the room. "If I'm correct, some of these bottles may be worth upwards of $5,000 dollars each, and we're looking at cases of them."

"Good old Great-grandfather Franklin, the old scoundrel!" Chase hugged his bride to him as he grinned down at her.

"We may have to raise a glass in his memory." Adrianna beamed back at him.

"I would suggest that we lock this all back up until we can make an accurate inventory another time," John stated. "These rock walls have done a great job of keeping the temperature in line with proper storage requirements, so there's a good chance that at least some of it can still be enjoyed, sold or kept as a resource for future generations to draw upon."

Everyone in agreement with John's suggestion, the group moved on to the final room on the other side of the tunnel. This room revealed itself to contain a mid-sized hutch that resided in the center of the opposite wall.

Hurrying forward, Elizabeth and Penny opened the cabinet's doors and drawers, but they were all found to be empty.

"Looks like we've found all that there is." The housekeeper stepped back, almost tripping over her husband who was bent over behind her rummaging through the canvas bag he had been carrying.

"Let me check something out." He drew forth a metal tape measure and proceeded to measure the depths of the cabinets and shelves as well as the length of the cabinet as it stood out from the wall. "Now that is strange," he stepped back.

"What is?" Elizabeth asked, her eyes shining in anticipation.

"The shelves are eight inches deep and extend nine inches out from the wall, just like you would expect," Otis explained, "but the cabinet is twelve inches deep, but extends eighteen inches from the wall."

"Are you saying that there's a false back?" Larry asked, taking a step forward.

"There may be." Otis opened the cabinet's doors again and sat on the floor in front of it, then worked at the shelf that divided it horizontally, lifting it off the four wooden support pegs – two on each side – that had held it in place, revealing what appeared to be a fifth, but metal peg at the back that was shaped like a clock key.

"Will it turn?" Sandra asked.

"Let's see," Otis said as everyone else in the room held their breaths, but the key didn't turn. Instead it allowed Otis to pull the false cabinet back forward, revealing a dark void behind it.

Stretching out on his stomach, the property manager worked his upper torso into the cabinet. As he felt around the aperture, his fingers soon discovering a simple wooden latch that he was able to push up easily, loosening the hutch and allowing it to be pulled towards the room in which the group stood.

Elizabeth and her interns made no attempt to hide their glee as the group walked through a series of three long rooms beyond, each separated from the next by an open archway until they reached a dead end.

The first room was lined with wooden bunks that contained some evidence of straw mattresses that were now covered with rotted bits of sheeting. A quick pass over the walls of this room with their flashlight beams was enough to verify that many more marks had been carved into the rock walls here.

The next room held a rough table made of long planks laid over three basic sawhorses, while the third room still held a variety of upright chairs and stools, one or two with cane seats, but most simply fashioned of rough wood.

"It's marvelous!" Elizabeth exclaimed. "Way more than we had dared to hope."

"You must come and do whatever you need to document everything," Adrianna said. "You know you're always welcome."

"Thank you, dear!" Elizabeth gave her an excited hug. "I can't tell you what this means to me."

"What is it, Pen?" Otis asked his wife, who was working at a small chest trying to pull it away from the wall that marked the dead end.

"I think there's another door and latch behind this like the one you found that let us in," his wife answered.

"Show me," her husband hurried forward along with Chase.

"See?" the housekeeper pointed.

"I think she's right," Otis said.

"You see what's on the other side," Chase told him. "I have an idea I want to investigate." He headed back through the three rooms.

"Are you going to the main house?" John followed his host. "I need to get back to the restaurant, if you don't mind letting me out."

The chest having been pulled from the wall by Otis and Jeff, a latch similar to the one at the other end of the series of rooms was indeed found. Once lifted, it released what appeared to be the back of yet another cabinet on the other side of the wall, which when pushed aside revealed a short tunnel – a small grate in its high ceiling allowing some light to filter in - that led to a flight of stairs rising to a plain door.

"The odd wiring," Otis muttered under his breath, and Adrianna looked over sharply even as she worked to figure out what her husband was up to.

Meanwhile, above ground, Chase had reached the dependency where he knocked on the front door at the same time that a series of sharp knocks emanated from the guest bedroom.

"What is that?" Edwina asked, rising quickly from her chair.

"I think the front door first." Arthur strode forward and opened the door a crack, before throwing it wide open.

"Have they reached here yet?" Chase asked as he entered the room, immediately taking in Edwina's worried gaze. "There's nothing wrong," he assured them, taking note of the sounds coming from the back of the house. "We've just made the most startling discovery. If you'll allow me?" He indicated the hallway to the bedrooms with a nod.

"Certainly!" The older woman's face cleared. "This is all so exciting!"

The knocking clearly coming from a built-in wardrobe in the second bedroom, Chase knocked back to let the group know that their efforts were being acknowledged. "Give me a moment!" he shouted through the wooden back, then turned to Edwina. "Would you mind if we put these clothes on the bed?"

"Not at all!" Her eyes beamed back at him.

Arthur assisting, the work took but a matter of seconds, including the removal of two small boxes from the wardrobe's shelf. Then Chase lifted the shelf to reveal that it, too, rested on this time two metal pegs that looked like oversized clock keys. Between them, the two men were soon able to swing the wardrobe inward with the help of Otis and Jeff pushing from the other side, and the excited group beyond quickly made their way into the dependency.

"That grate in the ceiling explains your banshee scream during the storm last evening," Arthur said in an aside to Edwina, referring to her having shared her uncomfortable experience with him earlier.

"And why we found no wiring in this wall when we were doing the renovations," Otis stated, looking across the room to Adrianna, who nodded her head in agreement.

Larry's phone chose this moment to ring. "Susan," he said to the room in general, before stepping into the hallway to answer.

"Tell her to come to the house, and we'll show her what we've found," Adrianna followed him.

"I must say this field trip has turned out even better than I expected," Chase addressed the group.

"It's certainly been a thrill for us," Elizabeth said, "but we had better head to The Cove now. Anders should be getting home with Daniel any minute."

"And I've got a class," Jeff excused himself, "but it's been a fun afternoon."

"Why don't you two join us for supper," Adrianna suggested to the older couple once Elizabeth, the interns and Jeff had left. "We can fill you in on everything that we've found. Susan and you, too, Larry." She turned to Penny. "We'll order in pizza, salad and cheesecake from Armando's, and I hope Otis and you will stay as well."

Suddenly realizing that she hadn't asked her husband if he was willing to share an evening of their honeymoon with half of the county, she turned so she could see him behind her, pleased when he sent her a brief nod and a slow smile, a twinkle in his eyes. Reaching out, she slipped her hand into his before turning back to their guests.

"I'm in," Arthur accepted her invitation. "What about you, Edwina?"

"Wild horses couldn't keep me away," the older woman stated firmly. "More and more, I'm convinced that moving to Captain's Point was one of the best decisions I've ever made. My life here is so filled with excitement and new opportunities."

CHAPTER XIII

So Susan Carlisle had a child – a four-year-old boy. Who would have thought it? Anderson turned the key in the ignition of the seen-better-days gas guzzler that belied the powerful engine hidden beneath its hood. Allowing the vehicle to roll slowly along the road, he kept pace with the woman and her child, enjoying the unimpeded view of her legs.

He'd known all along there was something more behind the haunted look in her eyes than mere concern for her own safety as she fought to end the messy divorce proceedings that currently filled the front page of evening newspapers across the country.

Bernice would have to pull all the past articles for him to review the next time he was in the office. In the meantime, though, he needed to figure out what game his client was playing – higher child support, restricted visitation, or the most dangerous game of all – possible kidnapping by either her or her spouse.

He needed to learn more about Joseph Carlisle, too. Hadn't there been some mention of possible organized crime affiliation in the one article that he had read?

Suddenly, Anderson wondered if he had named a high enough surveillance fee when he had first discussed taking her case with Ms. Susan C. But then, he always had been a sucker for blonde hair, big blue eyes and long legs.

Edmund Robinson, Manager, hit Save on his computer a few minutes past noon the next day and lifted the receiver from the phone on his desk. "Sheffield Place Inn, Edmund Robinson speaking," he said in his smooth, cultured voice. "Yes, Robin, the renovations on the downstairs rooms should be wrapped up later this afternoon, except for two paintings that will be hung by an expert tomorrow morning. Chase was saying only an hour ago how pleased he is with our progress. Will you still be arriving sometime Saturday afternoon?"

He reached for a pen while listening to the rapid fire response from the woman on the other end of the conversation.

"Between four and five – excellent. We'll look for you then," he confirmed. "Have a safe trip."

Then the caller having cut their connection, he hung up the phone and absentmindedly ran the long, slim fingers of his right hand over his white hair to smooth it.

"That woman!" His middle-aged wife, Marissa, looked up from where she was reading the latest issue of *Innkeepers Magazine*, a hint of her Puerto Rican heritage slipping into her accent. "'Do you know what you're doing?' 'Do you have all the help that you need?' 'Will you be ready?' She goes on and on, and she has yet to lift one little expensively manicured finger, even if she was our lovely Adrianna's suite mate in college."

"I'm sure she's done plenty on her end," her husband stated in his calm way. "Those brochures she sent are top grade as are the individual soaps, the stationery and the write-up in the *Washington Post*. Good public relations will go a long way towards insuring our success."

"As always, you're right my so smart husband." His wife let out a small sigh. "It is only the nerves that are bothering me. All will be okay once we are open, and having Mr. Jefferson as a guest has given us a good chance to practice our routines before the rush starts."

"Yes, I'm glad I allowed him to talk me into letting him stay," Edmund agreed. "He's a nice man, and he hasn't been any trouble."

"Only four more days." Marissa turned to the next page in her magazine. "We will survive."

The object of the final moments of their conversation rang the doorbell at The Cove promptly at six o'clock that evening only to be greeted by a cacophony of barks from inside the house.

"Shoo! Now sit!" A female voice could be heard next, followed by silence as the door was swung open. "Hello!" A pleasant looking middle-aged woman, with auburn hair streaked with gray, greeted him warmly. "Won't you come in? I'm

Elizabeth Chesterton, and this is my husband Anders." She indicated a tall, well-built man whose blond hair and deep blue eyes immediately proclaimed him to be Susan's father.

"Nice to meet you." Anders held out his hand as their guest entered the large foyer.

"John Jefferson." He met the other man's strong grip as they faced eye-to-eye. "Please call me Jack."

"Jack it is," Anders said and then turned to where Susan now stood in an archway that led to what had once been a large formal parlor, but had long since been redecorated and now served as a comfortable family room.

"Don't you look nice!" Jack's face showed his appreciation. "And this is…?" He eyed the four-year-old boy she held in her arms, his head buried in her neck.

"This is my son," Susan said, stepping into the foyer, "but I'm afraid we have a problem. Daniel's ear is hurting him, and I couldn't reach you by phone. They said at the inn that you had left an hour ago, and I didn't have your personal number."

"An earache? Now that's bad." Jack immediately pushed aside all memory of the time he had spent polishing and arranging pieces of his uncle's antique furniture to advantage around the first floor of the Victorian and the fresh flowers that now stood in a vase on the large kitchen table. "Is it your right ear or your left," he addressed his date's son.

"This one." Daniel lifted his head and pointed to his right ear.

"Oh, dear, that's not good." Jack held the boy's gaze as his own right hand slid in and out of his pants' pocket and slipped something into his left. "A right ear always hurts worse than a left one, especially if it has one of these stuck behind it." With a flash, he raised his left hand to just behind the child's sore ear, withdrawing it with a quarter held between two of his fingers, which he pressed into the boy's hand.

"Mama!" Daniel's eyes widened. "Look what was behind my ear – a quarter!"

"I see that." Susan suppressed a smile.

"Have you been able to reach his pediatrician?" Jack asked.

"That's part of the problem," his date filled him in. "I'm planning to register him with the one my sister uses, but there hasn't been a need yet."

"So which will it be – the ER at the hospital or the doc in a box downtown?" Jack asked.

"I know most of the staff at the ER," Susan said.

"Your carriage or mine, ma'am?" Her date smiled at her.

"Oh, but you don't have to..."

"No, I don't, but I'm going to," he interrupted, before once again addressing her son. "I don't suppose you would let me hold you for a minute while your mom gets her purse, would you? You see, I'm a little concerned about the worried look on the face of the oversized retriever over there." He nodded to where the large dog was seated next to a small terrier mix.

"That's Casey," Daniel told him as he held out his arms to be taken. "He won't hurt you, but Terror will eat you alive if he doesn't like you."

Enchanted by this view into the workings of a four-year-old boy's mind, Jack held back a chuckle. "In that case, I'm glad to have you serving as a human shield for the next few minutes," he took the boy in his arms, surprised when the child snuggled his head against his own shoulder. "Perhaps you should tell them both that it's okay and you'll be back in a flash, even better than ever. In the meantime, I've made a mental note to make friends with Terror as soon as possible, since I prefer not to be eaten alive, at least not before I've dined myself."

"Speaking of dinner." Elizabeth chose this moment to speak up. "I was just putting together a pan of homemade lasagna, and it should be ready by the time you three return. I've already set a place for you at the table."

"Mama..." Susan glanced at her maternal parent, embarrassed. "Jack may prefer..."

"Susan!" Her date again interrupted her, his dimples now showing. "Word to the wise, never and I mean *never* stand between a grown man and a plate of homemade lasagna. I bet your grandmother makes good lasagna, doesn't she, Bud?" He addressed the child in his arms.

"It's great!" Daniel nodded his head, still not lifting it off the warmth of Jack's shoulder. "But my mom's is better. Grandma makes the best sugar cookies, though, because hers have icing on them and not just sugar."

"I'll get my purse." Susan met her mother's gaze as she passed, both of them working hard not to laugh.

"We'll need to take my car because of the child seat." Having retrieved her recently rescued, quilted bag from a side table placed just inside the family room, Susan handed Jack her keys as he turned to open the door for her.

"You and I will have to sit down and have a long talk once your ear's feeling better," Jack said to Daniel as he was pulling the door closed behind them. "It's clear to me that you've figured out the inner workings of this household down to the last dot."

"Oh, Anders!" Elizabeth turned towards her husband as soon as the door had closed, eyes shining with joy. "How did Susan find such a wonderful man in so short a time?"

"Now, dear…"

"But did you see how he…?"

"Handled Daniel?" her husband interrupted as he drew his wife to him and brushed her lips with his, effectively cutting off any further words from her. "Yes, there's nothing wrong with my eyesight, and I also saw how he made a complete about face, scuttled his own plans and did everything he could to ease our daughter's burden, something that self-centered jerk she married never bothered to do. But still, you should leave Jack Jefferson alone. He's perfectly capable of roping our Susan in on his own, and I for one wish him the best in his endeavors. Besides, time will tell."

"But, Anders…" Elizabeth tried unsuccessfully to pull away as her husband once again cut off her words, this time with a slightly more passionate kiss.

"If you really want to forward our Susan's chances," he said, letting his wife up for air, "then you should go and slip your main course into the oven. I don't care what our Daniel thinks, I'd pit your homemade lasagna against anyone's, and while it may be trite, it's still true – the way to a man's heart is through his stomach."

"You've hit the nail on its head!" This time it was she who threw her arms around his neck, before she hurried into the kitchen to do what she could to enhance her daughter's chances.

Delighting in the sight of his wife's athletic figure as she made her way along the hallway, even as part of his mind was rejoicing about the man who had now entered their Susan's life, left alone in the foyer Anders whispered beneath his breath, "Besides, I'm starving to death."

CHAPTER XIV

After dinner Thursday evening, Chase and Adrianna carried their wine glasses into the library, where he turned on the gas logs to take away the slight chill in the high-ceilinged room and she flipped on the reading lamps before they settled in for a cozy read at either end of the sofa.

Glancing up half an hour later, Chase was surprised to find his wife with her book closed, her knees gathered to her chest and a faraway look in her eyes as she gazed at the flames in the fireplace. "Adrianna…" He closed his book. "What's bothering you?"

"I'm wondering if maybe we should discuss our finances," she broached the subject so hesitantly that he laughed.

"My queen wishes to inspect her treasury," he joked, but then his expression sobered. "Thank goodness, it's about time!"

"Why?" She looked startled. "Are we having difficulties?"

"Hardly." He chuckled.

"Then what made you say that?"

Sliding his arm along the back of the couch, he leaned closer to her, part of him glad of her knees as they separated them – this being the time of the day when her nearness most called to his desire – part of him wanting to choose his words carefully as he remembered a time before they had become engaged when he had tried to make a point and she had called him heartless.

"Do you remember the week before our wedding, when I asked you to clear your calendar for several hours so we could take care of some legal matters?" he asked, thinking it best to enter this pool of water one toe at a time.

"Yes, I never did understand that," she replied. "It only took me forty minutes to sign everything, and then we had all that time left. Not that I'm complaining. I enjoyed picking out that duet with you on the piano."

"But you signed a two-ream-high stack of legal documents without more than glancing at any of them or asking me a single question."

"Was I wrong not to read them?" She asked with all seriousness. "It was you who had asked me to sign them, and you told me what each one of them was before you handed it to me." She lifted eyes to him so full of trust that the common phrase 'his cup runneth over' ran through Chase's mind.

"No," he said, kissing his finger and touching it to her cheek. "It wasn't wrong of you. You will never find your trust in me to be unfounded as you have in others."

"I do pay attention when I'm with Larry and we're going over things," she referred to their broker. "You and I would both trust him with our lives, but even the best intentioned, most knowledgeable people can make a mistake, and I'm not..."

"A stupid woman," he finished for her, wanting her to be assured that he respected this quality in her. "Larry was blown away by your quick understanding of the state of Martha's affairs when you first inherited Montgomery House and her estate. I believe his exact words when I joined him for a beer at Patrick's the evening after you two first met were, 'That little snippet of a girl put me to shame. I wanted to reach into my pocket and hand her everything Martha would have made on her investments had her great-aunt taken my advice.'" For a moment, he recalled the look of amazement on their friend's face and smiled.

"Did he really say that?" Adrianna grinned shyly. "That was nice of him, but the point is that he is capable of making mistakes."

"So am I."

"But I know you, Chase," she countered his point. "You had already checked every one of those documents backwards and forward two or three times, hadn't you? You will always do that when it comes to anything that pertains to my welfare."

"Actually, it was more times than that." He grinned sheepishly, pleased at her faith in him. "Still, I would be more comfortable if we could sit down and really discuss our situation for two reasons. One, I want you to have a sound idea of where everything stands, and two, because from time to time I'd like to be able to ask for your educated opinion."

"Sure," she agreed, equally pleased by his desire for her input.

"We've gotten off track, though," he pointed out. "What was troubling you when we started this conversation?"

"All that wrought iron and wiring you had installed in the tunnel."

"Yes?"

"I've been a joint general contractor with Otis for months now as we've worked on the Montgomery Properties' renovations, and it cost a great deal of money to get those improvements to the tunnel installed," she pointed out.

"A fair amount," he conceded the point. "Money well spent."

"I agree," she said and moved on, "and what you're suggesting for here at Montgomery House will cost megabucks."

"The cost will be fairly substantial, but our lives and the lives of our children will be enhanced by the changes. I'm still not getting your point."

"I'm wondering if we can really afford them." Adrianna's face reflected her discomfort, even as her heart leaped at his having spoken of their future children.

"Come here." He drew her to him, leaning his cheek against the top of her head where it now rested on his shoulder. "Where is all of this coming from?"

"It's just that you're so generous when it comes to me." She pulled back, and he saw that her face retained its worried look. "Every time I say I like something, you give it to me – the Wilde program, the bronze in the foyer. This is worth a fortune." She held out her hand, and the rose cut diamonds from his great-grandmother's engagement ring sparkled in the glow from the fireplace. "And you didn't stop there. Oh, no. On our one day anniversary, after everyone had left, you surprised me with a complete set of emeralds from Tiffany's – ring, necklace, earrings, bracelet, hair clips, they're all there."

"They set off your hair, and I wanted you to have them." He reached up and replaced a wayward lock amongst her dark waves, then met her gaze. "Don't you like them?"

"I love them, but where will it end?" she asked.

"I would never spend money on anything if it would endanger your future welfare," he sought to reassure her. "Do you realize you've never once asked me how much money I brought to our marriage?"

"I didn't think it was..."

"Your business?" Again, he interrupted her. "Of course, it's your business, and I would have sat you down and told you beforehand, except it meant something to me that you didn't seem to care how much money I had and we now share, thanks to all of those documents you signed."

"I don't care," she stated firmly. "Don't get me wrong, I appreciate all of this." With a small wave of her hand she indicated the house and the surrounding properties. "But I've had to grow accustomed to it since I've come to Captain's Point. The seven years it took me to get my degrees were a struggle, Chase."

"How did you manage to pay for your education?" he asked, suddenly filled with a desire to know this about her as well.

"I got up every morning at two-thirty and worked the first shift at a bakery to offset what the student loans I was accumulating at a horrendous pace didn't cover," she told him, her finger nervously tracing a circle on his stomach in a way that set his own nerves tingling. "It left the daytime clear for me to attend classes and study."

"When did you sleep?"

"On the weekends, and I took naps when I could," she answered.

"And you still earned a Phi Beta Kappa – amazing!"

"There were two quarters when I was working on my MBA that I wasn't sure I'd make it," she shared.

The palm of her hand traveled up his chest to where it finally rested on his shoulder as she snuggled against him, Adrianna unable to see the pleasure filling his face in response to the route along which she had sent it.

"Those were the worst," she admitted. "Basically, I lived on a spoonful of peanut butter in the morning and a yogurt or ramen noodles in the evening, unless someone asked me on a date that included a meal."

"Given your looks, I doubt you were in much danger of starving," he teased, wishing with every fiber of his being that he could have spared her that struggle. "And still, you were able to forgive Martha," he referred to the great-aunt who could've helped her, but hadn't.

"There was one guy who offered to 'keep' me in exchange for my tuition." Her eyes took on a distant look, even as her hand moved back down and along his rib cage until it found a home at his waist, sending a shock wave up his spine.

"What did you say?" he asked, aghast at the prospect that had been presented to him the moment before.

"I declined his offer and never went out with him again." She lifted her head and sent him another shy smile. "He had proven himself to be a jerk earlier in the evening anyway."

"Wise woman," he stated, "and Brad…?" He brought her ex-fiancé into the mix. "Why didn't he help you?"

"He was in the same boat," Adrianna explained. "He would've done, if he had been in a position to do so. Unlike you, Brad was flawed, but he wasn't all bad."

"I'm not perfect, Adrianna," he sought to set the record straight. "I make mistakes."

"I suppose you're capable of it," she considered as if his making an error verged on the impossible, "but you take such care not to when it comes to me. None of us are perfect, but you are a man among men."

Relaxing in his arms, her hand once again took on motion as it traveled across his stomach and she snuggled closer, sending his need for her up yet another notch. "That's why I've never asked you how much you're actually worth, now that you've settled your aunt's estate and sold some of Oliveira's paintings that you inherited. I know that if you had nothing but your hands and your brain, you would do whatever it took to meet my needs."

"That I would, girl." He hugged her closer and then released her, knowing that he would name her a figure when they talked on the morrow that would astound her with its incredible size as much as it had shocked him.

Then he reached over and turned off first one lamp and then the other before standing and drawing her up and into his arms.

"Now, if you're going to continue tracing geometric patterns on my chest, I suggest we combine your obvious need to fondle the muscles of my upper body with some pleasurable, but more athletic endeavors in a slightly more romantic setting," he suggested as he led her to the thick rug in front of the low flames that played in the fireplace, where he stretched out beside her, the soft look she craved in his eyes.

"I love you," he said and kissed her tenderly.

"I love you, too." She felt a tingle run up her spine as his fingers found the buttons on her blouse. "See what I mean?" She slid her arms around his neck, giving herself up completely to the pleasure she knew was to come, releasing a small gasp as his lips barely brushed the hollow of her neck before sliding downwards. "Yet another venue where you are truly a man among men."

CHAPTER XV

"It appears that we already have an applicant for the marina manager position," Chase said at the breakfast table the next morning, having received a text message from Susan. "Apparently, such men have no respect whatsoever for privacy-seeking, honeymooning couples."

"Who is it?" Adrianna looked up from her paper, intrigued. "Someone local?"

"I'm not sure. Do you want me to call and find out?"

"I think we had better pursue it," she replied. "This is the fifth day since Captain Reb gave notice, and we haven't had any other applicants step forward."

Resigned to his fate, Chase tapped his firm's number where it resided on speed dial, as he once again forced aside a strong desire to locate Captain Reb and strangle the reprobate. "Bridgette? Good. Please put me through to Susan."

"Susan Chesterton," his law partner answered.

"You can't give us a moment's peace, can you?" he teased her. "I'm putting you on speaker phone, since it was my bride who insisted we call."

"Who's applied?" Adrianna asked, curious.

"His name's John Jefferson," Susan filled them in. "He's Ivan Lancaster's heir."

"The one Edmund has staying at the inn?" Chase asked.

"Yes," Susan answered. "Billy Spooner grabbed my purse from my shoulder while I was waiting for Larry in front of Chester's on Monday, and John stopped the kid cold, retrieving my purse for me. Frankly, it was amazing. I spoke with him at the house on Tuesday, and we had dinner on Wednesday at The Cove with the folks, which is where it came up in casual conversation that there was an opening. He faxed his resume and a cover letter over this morning, and it's pretty impressive. Bridgette should have already faxed you a copy."

"Did he say when he could make himself available?" Adrianna asked, wishing she could have seen her friend's face as she was describing the time she had spent with this mystery man, her own matchmaking instincts on full alert.

"Anytime today," Susan filled them in.

Chase signaled his bride for her to finalize the arrangements.

"We had set aside some time for something else this morning," she told Susan. "Could Bridgette arrange for him to come here at three-thirty this afternoon?"

"That should work," their friend confirmed. "I'll text you once we know everything's a go."

"Thanks for your help," Chase said and then terminated the call, surprised when his wife quickly folded her paper, picked up her coffee mug and headed for their home office.

"This is impressive." She handed him Jefferson's resume a few minutes later, her voice filled with disappointment. "I'm afraid he won't want the job, once he fully understands what it's all about."

Having glanced through the document himself, Chase wondered if the man would even show up. Wanting the worried look removed from his wife's face, he tossed aside the resume and spread the large sheets that contained his plans for some possible renovations to Montgomery House along the length of the long library table instead.

Promptly at three-thirty, the front doorbell rang. Penny, accompanied by Max, answered it and showed John Jefferson into the library, where the newlyweds were once again pouring over plans for their home that had morphed into two more versions and now required several legal pads to accompany them.

"Chase Sheffield." He strode forward and shook Jefferson's hand, before turning to his bride who had joined them. "This is my wife, Adrianna, who actually owns the marina."

"How do you do?" Adrianna forced herself to say, her breath having been taken away by the sight of the magnificent specimen before her, whom she immediately categorized as perfect for her friend.

Dressed in a blue blazer and khakis that set off their applicant's dark hair and eyes, the man who had just arrived had made his presence felt in the large room immediately almost, but not quite, eclipsing her Chase. And those dimples that had formed when he smiled... A woman could get lost in them, she thought, unaware of her husband's quizzical gaze.

"Why don't we sit over here?" Chase indicated the seating area in front of the fireplace with a nod, surprised by Adrianna's failure to proceed with the interview on her own.

Once settled on the loveseat beside her husband, his wife found her voice. "We've both reviewed your resume, John," she began. "A B.S. degree from the University of Virginia and a stint in the Navy that you followed up with an MBA from Harvard. All of that is very impressive, and yet, you seem to have spent the intervening years moving from one locale to another, primarily employed in lower level extreme sports pursuits." She looked up and suddenly felt very shy as the man she was interviewing held her in his direct gaze.

"First of all, please call me Jack," Jefferson said, and Adrianna shot a quick glance at her husband, relieved to see his face reflected no adverse reaction to the name that she knew held bad memories for him. "I did well at UVA, but frankly, I was bored so I joined the Navy, thinking it would provide me with a chance to see the world. Instead, it left me with a love of flying in addition to my love of boats and a good education in how to get around rules." Here he smiled.

"So I would've expected from what I've heard," Chase interjected.

"Recognizing that I would prefer to be rich rather than poor, I next secured my MBA," their applicant continued. "Still being single, I realized two things – the world was my oyster and I preferred to travel life's road to the beat of a different drummer."

Had Adrianna still been looking at her husband's face, she would've been surprised by his sharp reaction to this statement, but as her focus was once again directed at Jack Jefferson, she missed it.

"Over the years, I've used the skills I learned in the military to earn a fair living enjoying athletic pursuits in various interesting locations around the world," he continued. "Then my uncle's health deteriorated, and I developed the habit of staying with him for a few week's each year – keeping the house in good repair, enjoying his company and learning to love Captain's Point. Unfortunately, Uncle Ivan passed away, and as soon as I could resign from my position and make my way here, I did. I've spent much of the last fifteen years around planes and boats of all types. My MBA has enabled me to increase my earnings enough that, with the house I've inherited paid for, I don't need to work, but an idle lifestyle isn't really for me. This position wouldn't tie me to a desk and would, at the same time, get me out and around people. I believe it would suit me if I would suit you."

"The salary for the position is…," Adrianna named a figure she was embarrassed to present to so qualified an applicant. "Health and disability insurance are provided, as well as a 401K – the terms of which we will discuss with whomever we choose."

"I'm sure your benefits package is exemplary," Jefferson stated in his same calm voice with a straight face, but Adrianna was surprised to see that his eyes appeared to be laughing at her.

At this point, Chase stood, signaling an end to the interview. "If you wouldn't mind waiting for a few minutes, my wife and I can make our decision and let you know," he said. "Would you prefer to wait inside or outside in the gardens?"

"Outside on a day like today." Jefferson sent him a slow smile. "It was nice to meet you Mrs. Sheffield. I look forward to getting to know you better, one way or another."

"Please call me Adrianna." She stood and watched as the two men left the room, before plopping back onto the sofa.

How perfect Jack Jefferson was for Susan! Adrianna's mind took off like a shot. Now, if only Chase liked him, too.

"Thinking of another already, my bride?" Her husband sent his hands down her arms from behind a few minutes later, landing a kiss on the sensitive spot on her neck just below her right ear.

"No, I was thinking of Susan," Adrianna said as he came around the couch and joined her. "I've been worried about her."

"I have been, too, which is why I told her to hire three more associates," her husband reminded her. "Now, what do you think of Jack Jefferson?"

"I like him, and he's certainly qualified," she answered in her thoughtful way. "And he does seem to want the position, despite being so overqualified. Did you notice his shoes? Handmade Italian - probably cost him a thousand dollars if they cost him a euro."

"I wouldn't mind a pair of those for myself," Chase admitted, surprised at her having noticed. "So you're going to hire him?"

"Unless you think it's a bad idea, yes."

"Mind if I tell him?"

"Not at all," Adrianna assured him, glad for some more time in which to spin her matchmaking web undisturbed.

A few minutes later, Chase located their applicant where he stood on the lawn just past the sundial garden, his back to the house as he surveyed the view. "Care to join me?" He asked the visitor as he nodded at the benches that surrounded the obelisk in the garden's center.

"Sure." Jack obliged as his host held out his hands – one holding a canned lemonade, two green bottles suspended between the fingers of the other.

"Pick your poison," Chase said.

"Since you seem to have picked yours, I'll join you in a beer." Jefferson grinned, showing his dimples. "Belgians always have known their lagers, and the sun's bound to be over the yardarm somewhere."

Both men having taken their seats and enjoyed a first cold drink, Chase broke their silence. "The job's yours if you want it," he began. "We'd be fools not to hire you."

"That you would," Jack agreed, his eyes twinkling. "I know my business management."

"I daresay you do." Chase removed a rectangular object from the back of his jean's waistband and placed it on the bench between the two of them.

"Does your wife know?" Jefferson's eyes narrowed.

"No."

"What put you on to me?"

"Let's just say that I, too, identify with the motto the world is my oyster and I also prefer to live life to the beat of a different drummer," Chase explained. "Unfortunately, circumstances didn't leave me as free to roam the world as they left you, so I had to work harder to achieve those goals here in Captain's Point. Frankly, if it hadn't been for Adrianna's arrival on the scene, I might have followed along more in your footsteps."

"And were you able to meet those goals here?"

"Yes." Chase's deep blue eyes met the dark ones of the man next to him head-on. "In the end, I discovered you could be just as successful in that type of a pursuit in a small town as anywhere else in the world, because it's the people around you that matter."

"Good man." Jack sent his host a firm nod. "I may have to call on you to be my mentor. I meant what I said back there. During my visits with Uncle Ivan, I grew to love his house and Captain's Point, and you're spot on when it comes to the people – they're the same all over the world. Still, I'm going to have to shrink some of my skills down to size."

"You'll manage," Chase stated, tapping the object that still lay between them. "I have no doubt of that. On the other hand, you're going to be spending a fair amount of time with my bride, and I wouldn't want to see her hurt by you or anyone else." Again, he met the other man's gaze, one male staking out his territory when faced with another.

"That's right, you two are still on your honeymoon," Jefferson selected the single word 'bride' from the warning as if the rest didn't matter.

"My feelings won't change over time," Chase stated calmly, bringing the topic once again front and center.

"Not if they mirror what mine would be in a similar situation," Jack assured him and then reached out his right hand. "Friends?"

"Friends." Chase shook the offered hand, and then tucked the object back in his waistband before taking another swig of his lager. "Speaking of my wife, she recognized your shoes, and I must say that I envy you those."

At which, Jefferson threw back his head and laughed. "I'm going to enjoy getting to know you and your bride better," he said before pulling a small, gold automatic pencil and a tablet from his blazer's inside pocket. "You're in luck." He made a quick note and tore off the top sheet, then handed it over. "This is the name of the Little Italy shop up in Baltimore where they were made for me a month ago."

"Friends forever." Chase sent him a grin as he slipped the folded paper into his pocket, feeling for the first time in a long while that a huge void in his life had been filled by the arrival in Captain's Point of the man who now sat beside him.

CHAPTER XVI

"You look as if you've stepped from an artist's canvas," Arthur announced when Edwina opened her door just before noon on Saturday, prepared for their luncheon date. "That shade of rose you're wearing brings out the blue of your eyes."

"What a sweet thing to say!" A light blush touched the older woman's cheeks. "Always trust an artist's eye. That's my motto."

The couple headed to the former carriage house to retrieve Arthur's car, the bright August sun shining upon them. "I'm anxious to see what you think of my favorite lunch spot," he said as he held the passenger-side door open for her.

He rounded the front of the car and rejoined her, then drove out of the Montgomery House property towards town.

"How did you hear about the tea room?" Edwina asked once they had turned onto the main road that would lead them into Captain's Point.

"An artist friend from England, Charles Evans, told me about the place. The owner's name is Connie Buckingham whom he knew from a visit he had made to London. She came over to the States twenty years ago and opened her shop. It's tucked away around the corner from the Williams's gallery." Arthur steered the car into the parking lot they sought, where he found an open space. "Once you're inside, you'll feel like you've stepped back into Merry Old England."

"There's nothing more comforting than a good cup of tea." Edwina waited for him to open her door and accepted his helping hand, which he then moved to her elbow as they strolled along the stone pavers to a side stairway leading to the restaurant's second story location.

Over the door on the landing, a finely carved wooden sign proudly announced Tea, Crumpets and More.

"Arthur, how are you?" Connie Buckingham's face lit up as they entered. "It's good to see you. I was wondering what had become of you lately."

"I've been tied up with the opening of my gallery, but now that we're here, let me introduce you to Edwina Foster, a recent transplant to Captain's Point," he said. "I thought I'd let her in on the secret of your tea room."

"Nice to meet you." The shop's owner sent the newcomer a smile. "I hope you find things to your liking."

Edwina suddenly felt like a third wheel as Connie chatted gaily with Arthur as she led them to a table overlooking the hustle and bustle of Main Street beneath them, where she left them with their menus.

"What a lovely view!" Edwina's good manners dictated an upbeat start to the meal.

"I'm glad you like it." Arthur held out her chair, a pleased expression filling his face. "The watercress and pimento cheese sandwiches are delicious. Ah…and the blueberry scones are divine."

"Sounds scrumptious." Edwina took the white linen napkin from her place setting and, draping it over her lap, took a moment to look around.

A section of shelves behind the main counter area was devoted to containers filled with loose teas from around the world, along with teapots of all sizes and shapes. The white linens, soft curtains and yellow carnations in tiny vases on the tables provided a pleasant setting that complemented the aromas of cinnamon and nutmeg wafting from the kitchen.

"Connie serves the smoothest Darjeeling tea I've ever tasted. Would you like to try some?"

"Whatever you recommend," Edwina responded as she browsed the menu of specialty teas, crumpets, scones and sandwiches. "I've never seen so many varieties to choose from in one tea shop."

"I've tried nine or was it ten… But then again, who's counting, right?" Arthur chuckled and continued viewing the menu.

His date kept one curious eye on the shop's owner as he gave their beverage order, something giving her the idea that there might be more on the other woman's mind than tea and crumpets. Perhaps, it was the fact that Connie only made eye contact with Arthur.

"Then, if you'll indulge me, Edwina, we'll try the Queen's selection."

"Marvelous!" She delighted in the thrill of having a man order for her again. All at once the years fell away, and she felt as young as when she had accompanied Hamilton on his first international business trip.

"I'll put your order in straight away." Connie assured them before crossing the wooden wide-planked floor to the small kitchen beyond.

Edwina glanced again at the Queen's selection, wondering at its many components.

The tea leaves having been measured, water having been heated to just below boiling, the pot having been warmed, Connie returned with a piping hot Spode tea service and small silver containers of honey, milk, lemon and sugar. "Cheers!"

"Isn't she great?" Arthur didn't wait for an answer. "Would you care to pour?"

Obliging him with a smile, Edwina hid the twinge of jealously that had crept into the back of her mind.

Minutes later they were presented with an attractively arranged, doily-lined, three-tiered server. Tea sandwiches, tiny pastry-covered warmed brie with honey, miniature quiches, lemon-filled tarts, truffles and an assortment of freshly baked scones served with Devon cream and various jams filled its surface. A sliced seed cake was also set upon their table by a young waitress.

"Sylvia, my late wife, loved having afternoon tea," Arthur shared. "Whenever my schedule at the college permitted, I would rush home to join her."

"What a pleasant ritual. Tell me more about your wife."

"Where do I begin? She was the light of my life for thirty-nine years. We met in Milan. She was studying history abroad for a year, and I was exploring the arts throughout Italy. As we both waited at the station for a train to Rome, our eyes met. Her brown hair cascaded halfway down her back, and her blue eyes reminded me of the sea off Capri.

"Once on board, I took a seat beside her, and we ended up sightseeing around the city for the next two days. Each of us finished our respective projects in Italy, she flew back to New York, and I returned to Washington. We kept in touch - hours spent on the phone, weekend trips, etc. - until her graduation from Columbia and my completion of a Master's at Maryland."

"What wonderful memories!"

"What about Hamilton and you? How did you meet?" Arthur reached for a scone to which he added a dollop of Devon cream.

"My story isn't as exciting, although it's as memorable to me. Ham and I met in Chicago where my family had taken me to see the Art Institute as a treat. A group of college students were attending an art lecture, Hamilton among them. I left my parents, moving to the next gallery room, and as I studied the painting before me, he introduced himself and began reciting fact after fact about various works and artists, explaining that he had chosen me to practice his knowledge on before his exam."

"As good a line as any." Arthur chuckled.

"He took my breath away." Edwina's eyes filled with a faraway look. "I was speechless, which was okay because Ham liked to talk. When my parents joined us, he talked to them, too. He accompanied us to lunch, and six months later, after he graduated from Northwestern, we were married. The next fall, he entered law school."

"How neat that art led both of us to our spouses," Arthur pointed out.

Connie chose that moment to reappear. "Have you two saved room for some ice cream or a slice of cheesecake?"

Arthur looked to Edwina, who replied, "I think another cup of tea will top me off."

"Same here," he agreed.

"Then I'll be back with your check."

Edwina felt full and satisfied as she finished her last bite of seed cake. "This has been lovely. Thank you for inviting me."

"Here's to more tea times in our future." He smiled at her as he accepted their check from Connie.

Having left the shop a few minutes later, they headed back to his car, the sun's warmth feeling good after the air-conditioned café. As Arthur smiled greetings to those they passed, Edwina felt proud to be seen in his company.

Realizing she would remember today as the beginning of another important phase in her Captain's Point adventure, she fought an urge to reach out and take her date's hand as she had done so many times before when walking with her Hamilton. How lucky she was to have another such man in her life!

CHAPTER XVII

Anderson slid his arms into the burgundy coat that proclaimed him to be a concierge desk employee at the Grantham Arms high-rise apartments, the city home of Joseph Carlisle, and let out a sigh. "The sleeves are at least a half an inch too short," he complained to the wiry, grizzle-haired manager who stood before him.

"Trust me, the next size up will hang on you," the other man replied.

"You understand that I only want to deliver to and assist those going and coming from Mr. Carlisle's apartment?" Anderson asked.

"Give me another of these, and you can sing from the rooftop for all I care." The manager slid a C-note into his thin wallet as a sneer flitted across his face.

"Consider me as one who is completely tone deaf." The detective sought to nip the man's hopes for future bribes in the bud. Still, he had placed himself where he needed to be if he were to protect Susan C's interests in the best possible way, and he couldn't complain about that.

As the revolving door of the Arms disgorged its first customer of the evening into the marble-floored, wood-paneled lobby, Anderson knew he had made the right decision in coming to this place at this time and in this way.

Stephen McKinney relaxed in his home office's desk chair, his fingers leaving the keyboard of his laptop behind for a moment. Who would have thought that in a matter of days he would have gone from a struggling accountant working hard to build a small business to the possible new CPA for the Sheffield-Montgomery joint holdings?

Not that everything was settled, of course. He still had to win the account during his meeting with Chase and Adrianna on Tuesday, but he had as much to offer them as anyone, including a growing list of satisfied clients. Larry Chesterton had even made it a point to tell him after the early service at church just two Sundays before that he should feel free to give him as a reference at any time going forward, and everyone knew that Larry and Chase's friendship went back years.

No, it was his contract to lose, something he certainly didn't intend to do. At this point, the only thing that concerned him was the little surprise that was in store for Chase Sheffield on Sunday.

As the accountant's mind settled, the object of his thoughts turned to his bride. "Worried?" Chase asked as he turned their SUV onto the main road and headed to their new inn.

"Not worried, exactly." Adrianna smiled back at him. "I'm more thoughtful and, maybe, just a little sad."

"Can I help?" He steered the car into the long drive of his ancestral home, respectful of her privacy.

"Not with this." She chuckled. "Even you can't stop the passage of time. I was remembering how much fun Robin used to be when we were suite mates in grad school. She was a nut – certifiably crazy, and now she's a hardcore, career-oriented professional who probably hasn't cracked a smile but twice in the intervening years."

"Are you regretting that you recommended we use her to handle the inn's initial PR, because I can say in all honesty that I'm not," he assured her. "She's developed an impressive marketing plan and package, secured advertising in the greater D.C. area, located reasonably priced, upscale stationery and toiletry sources and finalized the details of tomorrow's pre-opening event in a way that will impress and inspire the locals who may recommend us – all to my complete satisfaction."

"Mine, too," Adrianna admitted as he turned off their vehicle, but then waited for her to continue. "It's me that I don't like – not the me that I am now, thanks to my having come to Captain's Point and meeting you, the me that I was when I first arrived."

"And to think that I fell in love with that horrid person almost on sight." Chase leaned over and kissed her cheek before opening his door. "What a desperate fellow I must have been!"

"Now you're laughing at me," his wife said as she disembarked a few moments later, once he had opened her door.

"No, I understand what you're saying." He took her hand and kept her beside him where they stood. "But I don't see why you should dwell on it. Everyone here loved you at first glance, me included. You didn't change in any integral way because of your move to Captain's Point, rather you reset your priorities based on your own recognition that there was a better way for you to live your life going forward."

"You think so?" She looked up with eyes full of trust in his wisdom.

"I know so." He drew her to him and kissed her, unmindful of whether or not someone might see them through one of the inn's windows. "You've always been all that is wonderful inside. You had just allowed the world as most people know it to rub off on you a bit more than was good for you, and as soon as you were placed in a position to compare it to life here, you went for the gold."

"That's true." Her face cleared as hand-in-hand they walked towards the new inn's front door, but then, she held him back. "Before we go in and you show me all the changes that you've had done, answer me one thing."

"Anything." He gave her his full attention, having taken in the underlying seriousness of her tone.

"Now that your childhood home has been put back in order the way that you've always wanted it, do you wish that we had chosen to live here instead of at Montgomery House?" she asked, working hard to keep her face void of her hopes for his answer.

"Not at all." He gathered her into his arms once again. "We have only been married for one week, and yet Montgomery House in my heart is my home, something Sheffield Place never achieved in all of the years that I lived here. Yes, I've managed with Peter Marlborough and Company's help to bring The Place back to what it was in my grandfather's time, and yes, I've enjoyed doing it. Still, I have absolutely no desire to carry you over this threshold, although I will be carrying you up the tower stairs at Montgomery House later this evening." His eyes twinkled.

"Chase really, control yourself." His bride giggled unaware that Edmund had opened the front door, the twitching at the sides of the manager's mouth the only sign amidst his formal expression that he had even an inkling of the subject of their previous moments of conversation, despite the fact that his employer was now passionately kissing his new bride right in front of him.

CHAPTER XVIII

When Chase finally allowed his bride up for air, the couple was surprised by the sound of applause coming from the lawn to their left, a quick glance informing them that Larry and Susan had just arrived on foot from The Cove.

"You know, Cuz, I'm thinking of writing an article for *The Captain's Point Gazette* – working title, *Our Little Town's Shame – Sex on the Streets*," Larry teased as they approached.

"You two trespassers can go on home." Chase's face turned on a stern expression.

"I'll have you know we were invited," his childhood pal informed him with a grin, "and as your broker, I can offer a reasonable explanation to Captain's Point's finest for my interest in your investment here anyway – not to mention the clause in our contract that provides me with carte blanche to invade your territory anytime, anywhere, anyway that I please."

"How did you manage a clause like that?" Susan asked. "I feel cheated."

"You both know that you're welcome in any of our homes anytime," Adrianna stated. "The only codicil being that you can't blame me for any of the actions of my personal attorney here." She indicated her spouse with a nod of her head.

"So, what do you think of the renovations your husband has had done?" Susan asked their hostess.

"I don't know yet," Adrianna surprised the cousins. "He hasn't allowed me to see anything since the demolition work was completed."

"I wanted to surprise you." Her groom attempted a hurt look. "Besides, you kept flirting with me in front of the workers, and it was embarrassing."

"Liar!" His bride turned on him. "That was all about you, and you know it."

"Tell all," Susan demanded. "What has my partner in crime been doing now?"

"Guilty as charged." Chase threw up both hands and grinned. "I'm afraid I've developed a penchant in my dotage for nubile young women who wear white short shorts while sporting a pink hard hat atop their delightfully wavy dark hair."

"Where?" Larry made a show of looking all around. "I could go for one of those myself."

"You'll have to get your own," Chase stated firmly, throwing his arm around his bride and hugging her to him. "This one is taken."

"You two are never going to grow up, are you?" Susan rolled her eyes, but then turned her attention along with the others to the inn's doorway, where Edmund had cleared his throat to make his presence known, just as the first strong notes of Beethoven's *Fifth Symphony* as played on an organ came to them through the front door.

"Mr. Marlborough is waiting for you in the parlor, sir," Edmund stated in his cultured voice as the music shifted to a silent screen tune that sounded as if it would've accompanied a scene where a good looking blonde was tied to the tracks with a train barreling towards her.

"Pete plays the organ?" Chase asked as he led them towards the door.

"Not that I know of." Edmund stepped back out of their way. "I believe that's Mr. Jefferson."

In the house and turned around to await their guests, Adrianna was just in time both to capture the awe contained in the manager's tone as he mentioned the name of the inn's first guest and to note the way Susan lit up at the sound of the new marina manager's name. Obviously, she thought, her instincts had been right – Jack Jefferson was the man for her Susan. Now, if she could only figure out how to bring the two of them together as often as possible.

"You know, I had hoped for a little more reaction," Chase interrupted his wife's thoughts as he waved a hand in front of her face.

"I'm sorry. I was a million miles away." She let out a small laugh, as she quickly took in the newly refurbished foyer. "Oh, Chase, it's wonderful!"

Gone were the floor-to-ceiling mirrors that his mother had installed in an effort to wreak vengeance on his father in the mid-70s, replaced by oak paneling similar to that found in Montgomery House's still original foyer. Black and white marble flooring now lay beneath their feet where a garish carpet had been placed before, and a round mahogany table on which a vase stood filled with roses graced the center of the space. A full-length portrait of her husband's maternal grandmother held pride of place to the left of the arched entrance to the large formal parlor, her dark hair and deep blue eyes that proclaimed so well their connection to one another set off by the blue velvet gown that she wore.

"What a beauty she was!" Adrianna crossed to the portrait so as to take in every detail.

"According to your great-aunt, she was the belle of every coming-out ball she attended in New York that year, and my grandfather was a lucky man to have won her," Chase whispered in his bride's ear as his arms came around her from behind. "I know just how he must've felt when he knew he had secured her love for all time."

"What a lovely thing to say!" She twisted around in his arms, oblivious to those around them.

"There they go again." Larry's strong voice came through to her as her new husband lowered his lips onto hers.

"I don't know why you sound so surprised." Susan's wistful answer came through loud and clear. "Even an idiot can tell they're head over heels in love, and they are on their honeymoon."

As Chase let her up for air, Adrianna swore to herself yet again that somehow she was going to secure Jack Jefferson for her friend if Susan wanted him. After all, it was the least she could do, and somehow she felt it was important to pay being as happy as she was forward.

The organ music having changed yet again – this time to a rich rendition of *Amazing Grace*, the group proceeded into the parlor, where they found Pete Marlborough lounging on one of the comfortable sofas that Chase had retained from his aunt's Beacon Hill home while Jack Jefferson effortlessly coaxed its best from the inn's pipe organ, a holdover from the current owner's great-grandfather's time.

"Sorry we're late," Chase said as he extended his hand to the young architect who had done such a good job with the historical renovation, glad he had given the twenty-seven year old a chance to make his mark with such a large project.

"I've only been in the foyer and this room so far," Adrianna spoke up, "but from what I've seen, I agree with my husband that we may have another major commission for you, if you would have time to fit us in."

"Sure," Pete replied, having shaken her offered hand. "It would be a pleasure to work with the two of you again. Are you thinking of doing some renovation work to Montgomery House as well?"

"Actually, what we're considering would be even more extensive than what was required of you here," Chase filled him in. "Would you be able to discuss it with us when we return from our trip out of state three weeks from now?"

"Absolutely!" The architect's amber eyes sparkled. "Let's set a date now."

Leaving the two men to formalize everything, Adrianna slowly wandered around the large room, pleased with the changes her husband and the auburn-haired architect had made. Silk drapes now hung alongside the tall windows, puddling just beyond the Aubusson carpet on the wide-plank hardwood floor. Thank goodness the carpet had been found rolled up in the house's attic, she thought. It would have cost a small fortune to have replaced it.

Equally pleased with the way her husband had called upon antique furnishings from his aunt's home to fill the room, she paused in front of the fireplace to reacquaint herself with one of the two Oliveira paintings that now hung in this house - a beach scene centered around a family. Once again struck by both the artist's use of color and his careful attention to detail, she was glad that most of the paintings Chase had kept for himself would now grace their own home at Montgomery House.

The music stopped, and Adrianna noted that Larry had joined her husband and Pete, while Susan had taken a seat in a comfortable armchair that sat near enough to the organ's bench to enable Jack to turn around and address her.

"I'm glad you enjoyed it," he was saying. "It's a fine old organ, and it deserved to be brought back to life."

"Chase is quite a musician himself," Susan explained. "He's an accomplished pianist, but I don't know if he plays the organ."

Adrianna could have informed them that he did, but she remained silent, not wanting to interrupt their conversation.

"I want to thank you for arranging my interview so quickly," Jack said. "I'm looking forward to getting started on Tuesday."

"That's great!" Susan beamed at him. "I'm glad everything worked out for you. How are your renovations coming along?"

"Slowly, but surely," he filled her in. "It's like so many things that are worth it in the end – you first have to make a mess to get where you want to go. Some of the upstairs rooms are beginning to come together, though."

Feeling a bit like an eavesdropper, Adrianna was relieved when the doorbell emitted its clear tones, but then she heard her former suite mate's voice carry through from the foyer and realized once again how little she was looking forward to her old friend's visit.

How glad she was that circumstances had allowed her to answer her great-aunt's call to Captain's Point! She looked across the room to where her strong, tall husband was chatting comfortably with Larry and Pete, just in time to have him glance her way, the soft look she loved in his eyes as he sent her a smile. If she hadn't come to this wonderful town, she recognized, she would never have met her Chase, and her life would've ended up all wrong.

CHAPTER XIX

"Robin!" Adrianna pasted a welcoming smile onto her face and hurried forward. After all, it wasn't her friend's fault that Captain's Point had changed her own priorities so much since the two of them had last spent serious time together.

"Did you have a pleasant trip?" Chase asked, always the gentleman.

"I did, once I left the city behind," Robin filled them in. "You're near enough to D.C. to be convenient and far enough away to offer a total change of pace."

"We have put you in the master suite." Edmund took the handle of her suitcase. "Let me show you the way."

"When you've settled in, why don't you join us in the kitchen?" Adrianna suggested. "Marissa has promised to let us sample some of the items she's preparing for tomorrow."

"I thought we were having everything catered by Montgomery's." Robin paused halfway up the steps.

"Those arrangements are still in place," Chase advised her, "but Adrianna, Marissa and I felt that it would be nice to include some additional items that had been made onsite."

"Oh." Robin gave a slight shrug of her shoulder before heading on up the stairs as Adrianna turned to her husband and rolled her eyes.

"Hang in there!" He threw an arm around her. "Let me show you the rest of the downstairs, while it's just us." He headed them into the second parlor, a comfortable sitting room that led into the home's library where a well-equipped, oak desk resided at one end, ready for any guest who chose to make use of it.

"You and Pete have done a marvelous job," Adrianna stated as they made their way next to the dining room, where a Duncan Phyfe table stood ready to act as the central serving area for the next day's event, its three leaves already inserted.

"As you know, this leads to the morning room." Chase indicated a small hallway. "It's set up as a pleasant place to read a book or write a letter, and here we have the breakfast room. The table seats eight so most of the time guests will be served here, which will be easier for Edmund and Marissa."

"Speaking of Marissa, whatever she's cooking in there smells delicious." Adrianna slipped her hand into his.

"Wondered what had happened to you two lovebirds." Larry sent them a grin when they entered the kitchen. "I hope you don't mind that the rest of us law-abiding citizens have started without you." He lifted a pastry-wrapped miniature sausage from his plate and dipped it into a pool of honey mustard sauce before popping it into his mouth.

"Not at all, as long as you left some for us," Adrianna assured him. "You're going to have everyone in here asking for more," she addressed Marissa, giving her a quick hug. "What time do you want Chase, Penny, Otis and I to show up tomorrow to help?"

"Eleven o'clock, if you wouldn't mind going to the early service," Marissa replied.

"Larry and I wouldn't mind pitching in," Susan piped up.

"Not at all if I get to sample the wares," her cousin agreed.

"Count me in, too." Jack lifted a toothpick onto which an olive, a cube of cheese and a cherry tomato had been speared as if signaling a bid. "This kitchen is big enough to handle all of us, and the more hands you have, the quicker the work."

"You, at least, will know what to do," Marissa accepted their guest's offer. "You should have tasted the feijoada he made for Edmund and me the other night – oh-la-la – so delicious. While this one..." She lightly pinched Larry's arm. "He will eat half of what he prepares."

"I can't help it if your food's irresistible and I can't get enough of it," Larry pointed out. "I'm a growing boy." He added several more sausages to his plate.

"You'll be growing in all of the wrong places if you continue like that," Susan pointed out. "We'll have to put you in charge of producing the vegetable trays."

"I'll have you know I've been at the gym working out every day for the past week," her cousin shot back.

"I can testify to that," Jack spoke up for him.

"Help yourself to some of the food." Chase handed a plate to Robin as she joined them. "Do you know everyone?"

"Everyone but this gentleman here," she singled out the new marina manager. "You must be the inn's first guest that I've heard so much about. I'm Robin. I've been helping out with the PR, particularly in the D.C. area."

"Jack, and I'm guilty as charged. Edmund and Marissa have made me feel very welcome during my stay."

"This will sound like a pick-up line," Robin said as her eyes narrowed, "but don't I know you from somewhere?"

"I doubt it," Jack replied, sending her one of his slow smiles. "I've only been in the area for a couple of weeks."

"No, I'm sure I know your face from somewhere," Robin insisted, "and I'm very good with faces. It's part of my job. Have you spent a lot of time in New York? That's my other stomping ground."

"No more than I have to." Jack turned his attention to a new offering of freshly made empanadillas that Marissa had placed on the counter beside him, offering the plate to the others around him before taking one for himself. Glancing up, he found himself locked in Chase's steady gaze and sent the inn's owner an almost imperceptible negative nod of his head, to which Chase responded with a quick wink and a half smile before turning casually around.

Meanwhile, from her vantage point a few steps away, Adrianna had noticed the shy smile that Susan had sent Jack as she added two of the tiny stuffed pastries to her plate. There was no doubt about it, this was the right man for her friend, the self-appointed matchmaker told herself, and the newcomer had easily fit into their group, something that Robin with her high-powered manners had not yet managed to do.

Making a mental note to invite the new marina manager to the Labor Day cookout Chase and she had organized during the past week, Adrianna eagerly accepted a canapé from the plate her new husband was now passing around and sent him a shy smile of her own, once again very grateful for his presence in her life.

CHAPTER XX

Once Larry and Susan had taken their leave of the group and headed to the Chestertons' farm for Lizzie's family birthday party, Chase had surprised Adrianna by turning to Robin. "I appreciate your excusing my wife and me this evening," he had stated in his gentlemanly way, "but we are still on our honeymoon."

Looking forward to a quiet evening together, she was trying to decide which he might prefer, grilling steaks and enjoying the sunset in the kitchen garden or a cozy meal in the morning room. Either way, she knew they would prepare their dinner as a team, this being an off day for Otis and Penny.

"Humor me," Chase said, his eyes twinkling, when he set her down in Montgomery House's foyer, having insisted on carrying her once again over their home's threshold.

"Now?" she teased, assuming he meant to fulfill his plans for carrying her upstairs to their bedroom.

"If you don't mind." He surprised her again by merely guiding her up the stairs and into their room. "Between finding the captain's replacement, preparing for tomorrow's event and pulling everything together for our cookout, we've been fairly busy these past couple of days – all great things, but still… I'd like for both of us to be rested and relaxed for this evening. Why don't you take one of your long soaks in the tub, and then, if you would, put on the sexy black dress that you brought with you when you came to Boston at my request."

"Do I get to know where we're going?" she asked, having sensed his excitement, more than willing to play along with his game.

"Does it matter?"

"Not as long as you'll be with me." She slid her arms around his neck, pleased with his kiss, but once more surprised when he didn't draw her towards their bed, instead plopping down in one of the Queen Anne chairs where he proceeded to give Max a good scratch behind his ears.

"Want some dinner and to go out, Big Guy?" Chase addressed the dog, and then raised his eyes to hers. "I think I'll catch a quick shower myself, and then I'll meet you back here."

"One relaxed bride in a black dress coming up." She sent him a grin and headed towards her dressing room.

A little while later, a warm bubble bath enjoyed, she took care with her makeup and donned the black dress as requested, but then, Adrianna was surprised to hear a tap on her dressing room's partially open door.

"Almost done." She sent her husband a smile where he lounged against the doorframe, looking very dapper in the black suit, white shirt and blue tie he had worn in Boston when they had gone out to dinner, his presence in her 'girlie' space causing butterflies to flutter in her stomach.

"I don't know." He looked at her quizzically. "Something's missing." Stepping forward, he pulled open the drawer that held her jewelry. "Let's try some of these," he suggested as he withdrew the fitted box that she knew contained the set of emeralds he had given her. "Not all of them, you understand, but certainly the earrings."

He lifted them out and passed them to her, and she obliged by removing the simple gold balls she had chosen and replacing them, pleased with the look of pleasure that filled his face.

"They really do set off your eyes," he said his voice taking on a slight roughness. "Why don't we try these, too?" He handed her one of the hair clips and then drew his fingers through her waves on one side, drawing them into an uplift and sending a tingle down her spine. "And here…" He repeated his actions as she held his gaze in the mirror, feeling her knees weakening as he brushed against her.

"I really do love them," she breathed, wanting him to know how much she had appreciated his generous gift, even as she found it hard to talk as her body called out in response to his actions.

"Only one more thing missing." He bent and kissed her neck where it met her shoulder and now lay exposed, withdrawing from the box not the heavier chain of gold encased emeralds, but rather the single emerald pendant suspended from a filigreed chain, which he proceeded to fasten in place before he turned her around. "Perfect," he proclaimed, his eyes filling with so much love and admiration that she reflexively reached her hand up and touched his cheek.

"I love you," she whispered as he drew her to him, crushing her so strongly and kissing her so passionately that one of the hair clips dislodged and had to be adjusted.

"You're so beautiful," he said softly, his voice filled with awe. "I hadn't factored in what seeing you like this would do to me, although I should've known. Being around you all the time this past week has morphed me into some sort of over-sexed, teenaged boy. I've hardly been able to keep my hands off of you."

"Trust me, you perform like a fully qualified adult male," she assured him, sliding her arms once again around his neck and melding her body to his. "Do we have to go?"

"Yes, I've planned something special for our one week anniversary, and the others are waiting." He let out a sigh and then lowered his lips onto hers, completing yet another passionate kiss before continuing. "You should know, though, that I will be ravishing your body later this evening," he stated emphatically, lessening his hold on her.

"Promise?" She looked up at him through eyes glazed with desire, but then pulled away as his words finally registered. "Others? Are you saying that my company alone wasn't enough for you this evening?" she teased.

"Surely you know better than that after the way we've spent a large part of these past few days," he laughed, taking her hand in his and starting them towards the downstairs.

When they reached the foyer, though, instead of heading to the front door, he turned left and entered the dining room where the table had been set with fine china, silver and crystal for two – red roses for romantic love and pink ones signifying perfect happiness filling a bowl and providing a centerpiece.

Pulling back the chair to the right of the head of the table for her, he then seated himself to her left.

"I didn't know what to expect when I summoned you here to Captain's Point last April, and when you entered my office, you took my breath away with your beauty," he said as he reached for her hand. "I had such a hard time pulling my wits together that I fell back on a lot of legalese and probably came across like a real stick in the mud. And yet, I was filled with frustration, knowing that I was responsible for overseeing the terms of your great-aunt's absurd will and the position that might put us both in."

"And I had no understanding at all of the position in which you had found yourself and probably made your life much more difficult," Adrianna said, wishing she could take back some of the things she had said and done to him at the time.

"Then I found Max and you on the beach with the tide coming in so quickly, and my heart leaped to my throat," he continued, a flash of anguish crossing his face. "The next evening, I called on you here to take you to Montgomery's for dinner, expecting nothing more than a business meeting with the most beautiful woman I'd ever seen, and when I looked up the front stairs and saw you standing there in this dress, I knew that I loved you."

"Oh, Chase…" She squeezed his hand unable to finish, a lump having developed in her throat.

"We spent the next several hours in a romantic setting, enjoying a dinner comprised of John Thornburg's tasting menu at your suggestion, and during that time, I learned why I felt the way that I did as well as why I would never be able to live without you in my life," he shared. "In honor of that special evening on this our first week anniversary, John has agreed to provide us with a replay, changing a few items due to seasonal availability."

"What a romantic gesture!" She sent him a watery smile. "It was a wonderful evening, wasn't it? We talked and talked, and I learned to appreciate the special layers that lay beneath your business exterior."

"I hope you don't mind." Her husband sent her a sheepish grin. "But John and I put our heads together over the wine and…"

"You've opened one of my great-grandfather's bottles! You are pampering me yet again, aren't you?" Her eyes sparkled, much to his relief. "This evening is going to be memorable."

"Are we ready?" John asked, having tapped on the door to the butler's pantry before opening it.

"Thank you so much for doing this!" Adrianna sent the chef a grateful smile. "Between my husband and you, our special evening is going to be truly wonderful."

"Don't forget your great-grandfather's contribution," John reminded her.

"How many bottles did it take?" Chase asked.

"Three, but I believe we have a winner," the sommelier replied.

"I hope you'll join us in a toast when the time comes," Adrianna said. "It wouldn't be fair for you not to enjoy a glass as well, especially since you of all people will appreciate it."

"I'm not going to argue with you," John agreed as his face filled with excitement. "In the meantime, let's start with your cream of crab soup." He disappeared into the kitchen to be replaced in a few seconds by a waiter who filled their water glasses and then returned with their soup.

Three hours later, the gourmet meal had been consumed, John had raised a glass of the Lafite-Rothschild Bordeaux in a toast to the newlyweds, and the chef and his staff had said their goodbyes, leaving Adrianna and Chase to linger over the last remaining coffee in their cups.

"I will always treasure you and the memory of this evening," she said, raising eyes filled with love to her new husband.

"As I will always treasure you." He stood and drew her to him, kissing her tenderly.

Then he lifted her into his arms and carried her up the tower stairs as he had promised her earlier he would do, where he proceeded to ravish his bride's body in a way that she found to be most satisfactory.

CHAPTER XXI

Eleven o'clock the next morning found the refurbished kitchen at the Sheffield Place Inn filled with a bevy of activity, Marissa having taken on the personality of a drill sergeant.

"You are on sausage duty." She had pointed at Larry upon his arrival. "We must replenish our supplies. Mr. Chase, he will help you and keep an eye on you as well. Otherwise, you will eat more than you should."

"And here I was looking forward to our time spent together," Larry protested, throwing an arm around the middle-aged woman and dropping a kiss on her cheek.

"Get on with it," Marissa commanded, knowing him too well to put up with his shenanigans.

"You heard the lady," Chase followed through, steering his friend to where a stack of cookie sheets awaited them.

"Ah, my lovely Adrianna, I am counting on you for the empanadillas," Marissa lined up her next victim. "You have such good fingers with the pastry. Do you know how to do it? Let me show you here, and the beautiful Susan will help Jack with the plantains. She will prep, and he will fry. He knows how not to burn them."

Out of the corner of his eye, Chase watched with pride as his bride quickly learned how much of the chicken filling to use and proceeded to amass a fair number of the small turnovers in a very short time.

"I tried to make plantains once, and they didn't turn out," Susan shared quietly with Jack as he got her started. "I see now where I made my mistake. I didn't purchase these dark ripe ones."

"The others can be good, too, but you fry them in corn oil to use as a savory," he explained as he slid the first diagonally sliced coins of fruit into the melted butter in a commercial-sized skillet. "The dessert ones like these are harder to make, because the sugar burns if you're not careful. You'll have to come over one evening when we're not under such a time crunch, and I'll give you a lesson in both kinds."

Wishing Chase and she could be included in his tutorial, Adrianna made a mental note to call on Susan's new found expertise later, envisioning sparks flying between Jack and her friend as they fried plantains in his kitchen.

"You see how quickly Adrianna's fingers move?" Marissa addressed Larry. "You must follow her example."

"Do you have another bowl of filling?" her teacher's pet asked. "This one is almost empty."

"That's all of the chicken. We will move on to the cheese and fruit filling for the rest." Marissa pulled a large bowl from the fridge. "Thank goodness you married our Mr. Chase!"

"I'll second that." Chase reached over and kissed his bride's cheek, pleased when she sent him one of her shy smiles.

Soon, Jack was declared to have been right. With multiple hands on deck, all contributions being prepared by the inn were prepared easily and quickly, and the kitchen was sparkling clean in plenty of time for Montgomery's staff to make use of the facilities.

Their work done, everyone adjourned to the main parlor, where a string quartet was setting up their music stands and tuning their instruments at the far end.

Again, Adrianna was pleased to see that Susan and Jack were engrossed in conversation on one of the couches, obviously enjoying each other's company.

"Let's take one more look around, just to be sure," Chase suggested, taking her hand.

A satisfactory tour of the downstairs completed, they joined Edmund, Marissa and Robin in a receiving line at the front door as the invited guests began arriving.

"Don't you miss being single just a little?" Robin asked an hour later as the two former suite mates once again stood together in the formal parlor, where the new bride had been enjoying the music.

As was her way, Adrianna considered a moment before answering. "No," she replied, her tone indicating certainty. "You see, without Chase beside me, I'm incomplete."

Spotting that Edmund was free in a corner, Robin excused herself for a moment.

Adrianna passed a contented gaze around the room, focusing on anyone who might need her attention. But just as she remembered that the punch bowls in the other room might need refilling, two strong arms wrapped her in their grasp from behind, and the scent of Chase's aftershave wafted towards her.

"I thought I'd stand close to you for a moment, so neither of us would feel incomplete for too long," her new husband whispered into her ear.

"There's certainly nothing wrong with your hearing, is there?" She made a one quarter turn and smiled up at him.

"Not when a compliment floats through the air." He dropped a kiss onto her forehead.

"Everyone's having a good time, aren't they?" she asked as they now stood side by side, his left arm still around her.

"Seem to be," he agreed, "which bodes well for the recommendations we were hoping to get."

The quartet chose this moment to stop playing and take their break as Susan and Robin approached the newlywed couple from different directions.

Adrianna was surprised to note a man coming through the room carrying a snare drum pedestal and a cymbal attachment, followed by Jeff Stuart dressed in his Sunday best, a drum case in one hand and a cymbal case in the other.

Thinking that her husband had planned yet another surprise for her, she determined that it would be best if she acted as if she hadn't noticed the set-up. Deliberately turning aside, she engaged Susan in conversation at the same time that Robin was reporting back to Chase, thus missing the arrival upon the musician's platform of her newly hired marina manager, her dentist David Eskar and her possible new accountant Stephen McKinney.

"Ladies and gentlemen," Edmund's cultured voice addressed the room fueled by the musicians' microphone. "Unbeknownst to the inn's owner, you have a treat in store for you. As a lifelong musician, the one thing that concerned me when I left Boston to accept my new position as the inn's manager was that I might be moving to a musical wasteland. The inn's first overnight guest quickly dispelled this notion as I was blessed to learn almost immediately that he wished to play his violin in his room."

Adrianna noticed that more guests were joining them from the other downstairs areas, drawn by the sense that they were missing something important.

"Imagine my surprise upon learning that not only did John Jefferson play, he was the same John Jefferson whose piece *Alpine Summer* had been recently debuted by String Flings, this phenomenal group long known for providing its audiences with unique musical experiences as they debut works by newer talents," Edmund continued.

"As you'll remember, early Tuesday morning a thunderstorm passed through our area, luckily disturbing Mr. Jefferson in his room. Glancing out his window, he was moved to compose the piece that we now wish to play for you. Titled *Storm at Sheffield Place*, the piece is dedicated to Mr. Chase Sheffield in honor of his ancestral home and calls for the use of the refurbished pipe organ installed in the house by Mr. Sheffield's great-grandfather as well as two violins, a cello, and a percussionist. You should hear first the storm approaching, then its full intensity, followed by its moving on up the coast and, finally, the moon coming out from behind the clouds and spreading its beams over our fair town as a sign that all is once again right in Captain's Point. So, without further ado, I present to you Mr. Jefferson on first violin, Dr. Eskar on second violin, Stephen McKinney on the cello, Jeff Stuart as our percussionist and myself on the organ."

As the musicians took their positions, Adrianna slipped her hand through the crook of her husband's arm and beamed up at him. "How thrilling!" she exclaimed in a whisper as a round of subdued applause encircled the now packed room.

"But they're taking over your event." Their PR expert's face expressed her displeasure.

Adrianna stepped forward and leaned across her spouse, so as to keep her voice lowered. "Robin, I'm sure Chase will agree with me when I say that while Captain's Point is a small town, we are not a bunch of country bumpkins." Then she quickly returned the smile to her own face as she stepped back and glanced up at her husband, pleased to see the pride in his eyes as he returned her smile.

Beside them, Susan forced herself to breathe steadily, surprise and fear vying for position within her as she prayed that her fellow citizens would treat the man she had grown to care for so quickly with the kindness and respect he had so readily shown her.

Then, with a nod from Jack, the Sheffield's part-time gardener whisked his brushes across the drum's head, creating the first hint of windblown leaves and twigs in the air, until deep tones from Stephen's cello marked the distant approach of the actual storm. But then, the organ softly joined in and grew in intensity until all the instruments were engaged, including claps from the cymbals that clearly represented bolts of lightning crashing to earth as the storm passed over Captain's Point.

As quickly as the piece had risen to such heights, the composition gradually began its descent, until a lone violin played a simple melody surrounded by quieter rolls from the organ and the soft brushes against the head of the drum - the magical tones of Jefferson's violin emerging, leaving them and then reemerging. Susan's heart sang along with the music as the room full of people disappeared and Jack's bow drew forth his haunting solo, his dark eyes holding hers until the music ended on a long, soft final note.

As the room around them burst into a rousing applause, Chase gave his wife a quick hug and then strode to the musicians' platform where he shook Jack's hand before raising their arms into the air. The composer, in turn, gave credit to the musicians who had supported him with a sweeping gesture of the hand holding his violin and bow.

"Bravo! Bravo!" The mayor called out from the back of the room, quickly joined by others as the applause continued until Edmund once again approached the microphone and signaled for quiet.

"As I said earlier, Mr. Sheffield was not aware we would be performing today," the inn's manager began. "We are hoping to continue playing at the inn from time to time as the first step towards developing a Captain's Point Chamber Music group or volunteer orchestra, believing as we do that we are not the only committed musicians in the area. So if you know of someone who might be interested in joining us in our endeavors or are a musician yourself, please contact me here at the inn. You will find the inn's number on the brochures and pads left for you to take home by the front door. In the future, when you recommend a stay at Sheffield Place Inn to visiting friends or relations, know that from time to time they will be treated to similar renditions."

Since the hired musicians had been retaking their positions as Edmund spoke, the crowd began to thin as many sought another plate of refreshments or to refill their cup at one of the punch bowls.

"You were right," Robin said to her old suite mate as Chase approached. "This will go a long way towards insuring the success of Sheffield Place Inn."

"And the pavilion that's now part of Montgomery Properties," her new husband reminded Adrianna as Jack made his way through the crowd to Susan's side next to them.

"That was marvelous," Susan greeted him, her eyes shining. "I don't believe I've ever heard anything more beautiful at either the Kennedy Center or Carnegie Hall."

"Don't get too carried away," Jack replied, his obvious pleasure at her words reflected in his dark eyes, "but I'm glad you enjoyed it." He threw his arm around her and gave her a quick hug then just as quickly released her, stepping back to speak with Chase as the three women formed a group.

"Edmund tells me that you and he play a killer dueling piano piece," he addressed the inn's owner.

"We enjoy a good romp amongst the keys now and again," Chase admitted.

"Then you might want to join our group when we practice another composition of mine that's been waiting for the right moment," Jack suggested.

"That I might," Chase agreed, thinking yet again how glad he was that the man beside him had decided to put down roots in Captain's Point.

CHAPTER XXII

Labor Day dawned bright and sunny, a perfect day for a cookout at the pavilion. Having slept in and enjoyed a leisurely breakfast, Chase and Adrianna had begun preparations for their cookout, the guest list including all residents of homes on the Montgomery House property, the Chesterton clan, Edmund and Marissa, Jack Jefferson, Jim Laidlaw, Arthur Stern and Bev Lockhart.

Chase had gathered all the items that needed to be toted to the pavilion except for the food and had hauled in bagged ice that was now waiting in the refrigerated cooler his bride had installed prior to their wedding in the new garage for events such as these.

Adrianna had spent her time baking pans of homemade brownies and making hot fudge sauce to pour over ice cream for sundaes, other toppings already lined up on the counter alongside bags of hamburger and hot dog buns as well as the makings for s'mores.

"I'm glad you suggested this," Chase said, dipping a tablespoon into the oversized bowl of traditional potato salad his wife was mixing together.

"Why don't you help Otis set up the pavilion?" she suggested, pushing him away with a nudge of her hip. "Your tasting is getting out of hand. At this rate, Penny and I will never get enough food put together."

"Men!" Their housekeeper rolled her eyes at them from where she stood at another counter stirring sour cream into an equally oversized bowl of a take-off on ambrosia that her mother had always called Heavenly Hash – a commercial-sized metal bowl of cut-up fresh fruit already standing ready on the counter next to her current work space.

"Yes, and the shame of it is that you and I captured two of the best of them for ourselves." Adrianna laughed as she started working on a second large bowl of lemon dill potato salad built around small cubes of red potato.

"Mine will be having the time of his life today thanks to your suggesting that Daniel and Lizzie be allowed to ride Silver Queen," Penny pointed out. "He always has had a soft spot for that Shetland, ever since he taught you to ride her."

"She's a sweet-natured pony." Adrianna reached for a commercial-sized jar of mayonnaise. "She'll enjoy the time with the children as much as they will, and I wanted to do something for them since they did such a good job as ring bearer and flower girl in our wedding."

Two hours later, the guests beginning to arrive, Chase and Otis headed to Montgomery Farm to retrieve the pony in question, the former surprised when Jack Jefferson rode up to the barn on a 16-hand plus quarter horse of the hunter variety, the mare's palomino coat glistening in the late afternoon sun.

"What a beauty!" Chase greeted him.

"Meet my Goldie." Jack smiled down at him. "I retrieved her from the farm where she's been boarding in Virginia this morning and knew she would need to stretch her legs a bit after the ride. As soon as I brush her down and shower, I'll be over to join you."

"This isn't the Goldie that I…heard about, is it?" Chase asked, his eyes widening.

"The one and only." Jack grinned. "When a horse saves your life, you kind of feel obligated to give them a home, especially when they're as special as this one. You wouldn't believe all the tricks she can do."

"How much…?"

"How much is true?" Jack finished for him, having glanced quickly around. "Just about all of it. I'd taken a group up into the Sierra Nevada range much too late in the season, but the guy who booked the tours had insisted. One of the campers slipped and broke a leg just as snow started falling, and I left them in their tents and tried to return to base so I could bring back some help.

"Coming down the mountain, the side of one of the trails I had walked a hundred times gave way beneath me, and I broke a small bone in my foot when I landed wrong leaping to safety. I managed to crawl into a narrow indentation in the rock cliff that ran along the path as the sun began setting, but it was freezing by then. I didn't hold out much chance for my survival, but I stretched out pressed against the rock with my back facing the opening, covered my face with my arms and hoped for the best. Sometime later, this gal nuzzled my back, probably because I was taking up her space.

"I don't know how long she'd been running wild, but obviously, she had been at least partially domesticated at some point although she hadn't been marked in any way. She was wearing her winter coat when she found me. I reached up and stroked her nose. She let out a sigh, and the rest of the night she stood between me and the cold, turning herself around from time to time. Understand 'warm' is a relative term, but she blocked the wind and her presence kept me warm enough that I was able to ride her bareback down the mountain the next morning, complete with all of my fingers and toes."

"Amazing!"

Having retrieved Silver Queen from the barn, Otis rejoined them. "You'll find the fourth stall on the left all set up for her," the property manager told the horse's owner. "Silver Queen here resides in the third. No wonder you wanted only the best for your mare. She's top grade."

"So is yours," Jack replied with a nod towards the Shetland that sported a series of beribboned braids in her mane. "What's the occasion?"

"Otis taught Adrianna to ride on this pony years ago," Chase filled him in. "We're letting Daniel and Lizzie, both of whom participated in our wedding, ride her as a treat today."

"Would you like for me to bring Goldie over as well?" Jack asked. "The two of us spent the summer after we met working at a camp in Wyoming that specialized in special needs children. Lizzie and Daniel might enjoy seeing some of her tricks."

"Sounds like a great idea to me," Chase agreed.

A few minutes later, those gathered at the pavilion were surprised by the arrival of the now enlarged group. Glancing up from where she was helping Adrianna, Susan thought Jack epitomized her childhood fantasies of cowboys she had watched in B-movie westerns as he rode up on his palomino wearing jeans, a blue and white plaid shirt, boots and a worn Stetson.

"Howdy, ladies." He lifted his hat to the two of them, his dimples clearly showing.

"Mama! Look!" Daniel cried out. "Jack's riding a horse, and the pony has braids!"

"With ribbons in them!" Lizzie added her two cents worth.

"I see that," Susan said as Adrianna and she hurried forward to join Elizabeth and Courtney, who were doing their best to keep the excited children in check.

"I'm going to tie Goldie to one of those trees." Jack indicated the pine woods that lay a short distance away. "After Daniel and Lizzie have ridden the pony, she can show them a couple of her tricks."

"Nothing like a man on horseback," Courtney said, letting out a small sigh of appreciation as horse and rider walked away. "If my Trey hadn't ridden over to bring that message from his father the first time we met, I might not have given him a second glance."

Susan and her mother exchanged meaningful glances themselves, while Adrianna turned away to hide her smile.

A few minutes later, Jack rejoined them, only to be met by a barrage of questions as to why he hadn't mentioned his horse before, explaining once again that he had only this morning brought her to Captain's Point.

"Would you mind spelling Otis for a while with the pony?" Penny asked. "Tell him I could use his help. He won't say anything, but his knee was bothering him this morning."

"Sure." Jack hurried forward and delivered the message, taking Silver Queen's reins and holding onto Daniel's belt as he walked the pony and small rider twice around in a large circle.

"I want to ride your horse," Daniel stated in his firm way as their second trip was ending.

"We'll see if your mother's okay with that," Jack promised. "Why don't we let Lizzie have a turn on the pony now, and you and I can retrieve Goldie?"

"Okay." Daniel leaned too far to the other side as he turned to look around, and Jack easily straightened him in the saddle.

Having brought the Shetland back to home base and turned her reins over to Chase, who was now walking the large circle with Lizzie in the saddle, Jack took Daniel's hand and walked over to his own mount, Susan accompanying them.

Undoing the reins from the tree, Jack stood by the palomino's head. "Would you like to feed her a sugar cube?" he asked the excited child.

"I don't have one." Daniel looked disappointed.

"It just so happens that I have," Jack admitted, pulling one from a bag in his pocket. "Hold it on your palm with your hand flat like this." He demonstrated. "I'm warning you, though, her lips kind of tickle."

"It looks like Chase is bringing Lizzie back in," Susan pointed out.

"Would you like to see Goldie do some of her tricks?" Jack asked Daniel as he handed him another sugar cube.

"Sure!" The boy's eyes widened.

"I'd enjoy a demonstration myself." Susan smiled at him as she stroked the blaze that ran down the horse's nose.

"Goldie's going to do tricks!" Daniel announced to Lizzie as he ran ahead of them. "She eats sugar cubes."

"I imagine Silver Queen would enjoy a sugar cube, too," Jack said, passing them each one. "Show your cousin how to hold her hand, Daniel."

Having taken the pony's reins from Chase, Otis gazed happily at the two excited youngsters as they pampered the pony, petting her nose and stroking her mane.

"Can Goldie do her tricks now?" Daniel turned back to the horse.

"If you want," Jack agreed. "How old are you, Lizzie?"

"I'm four," Lizzie replied holding up four fingers.

"How many fingers do you see, Goldie?" he asked.

Susan followed his lead and raised four of her fingers, the horse struck the ground four times with her right forehoof, and the onlookers offered a brief round of applause, at which Goldie bent her right foreleg and lowered her head taking a bow.

"Do you like children?" Jack addressed Goldie, who immediately nodded her head up and down.

"Do you like flies?" her owner asked, and the horse shook her head side to side and let out a snort.

"Goldie's smart," Daniel pronounced in his firm way, "and I'm going to ride her if my mama says okay."

"If you'll do what Jack says," Susan agreed.

"She's big." Lizzie's eyes widened.

Jack sat on his heels and gestured her over, unaware that Elizabeth, Courtney and Susan were now gathered in a group behind him. "But look at her eyes," he said. "See how soft and warm they are? Would you let me pick you up for a minute? Then you'll be tall like her, and you can pet her. She may be big, but she still wants people to like her. Everyone needs friends."

Shyly, Lizzie shook her head in the affirmative, and Jack lifted her onto his hip, taking her right hand in his and helping her to pet Goldie's blaze, at which the horse nuzzled the child's knee.

Behind him, Courtney placed her hand over her heart and lifted her eyes skyward as Susan merely smiled, impressed by the kind and gentle way in which her niece's fears had been overcome.

"See, she's saying thank you for caring about her, because she likes you," Jack pointed out to the child in his arms. "Now let's put you back down."

"She's a nice horse," Lizzie admitted and then turned to her mother.

"Chase, would you mind lifting Daniel up?" Jack asked as he expertly swung into the saddle.

"One young boy coming skyward!" Chase obliged, and then turned to Adrianna. "Do you miss riding?" he asked.

"Very much." His wife's face took on a wistful look. "We often had horses around us on-site, and my roommate at college had a mare stabled nearby that she allowed me to ride."

"Would you like to go another round on Silver Queen?" he asked Lizzie, having made a mental note of Adrianna's answer.

"Hang on!" Susan commanded her excited son, even as she noted that Jack was holding his arm around Daniel, had run his thumb through one of the boy's belt loops and had a firm grip on his waistband as well.

"We're going to walk first, and then if you're okay with it, we'll go into a trot," Jack indicated for Goldie to move forward across the long stretch of lawn.

"Can she go faster?" Daniel asked.

"Sure, but we'll only go up one more gait today, because this isn't a large field." Jack nudged his horse to a trot and completed two large circles before drawing up a short distance from the pavilion, where Chase waited to let him hand down the excited child.

"Mama, I rode with Jack!" Daniel ran to his mother.

"Susan, catch!" Jack tossed her the bag of sugar cubes, from which she doled out one to each of the children.

"Would it help if I led Silver Queen back to the stable and bedded her down?" Jack asked Otis, who nodded his head with relief and brought the pony over.

"Thank you for making Daniel and Lizzie's day even more special than it already was," Susan said, smiling up at him.

"Goldie loves to show off, and she enjoys the children," he replied as he took the pony's reins and switched to a fine Texas drawl. "I'll be back as soon as I'm done with my chores and have cleaned up a bit, ma'am. I sure hope you and some vittles will be awaitin' me."

"I may be, and then maybe I won't," she teased him back, "but you can count on the vittles."

Somehow, though, he knew that she would be awaiting his return, pleased he could count on her presence beside him - at least, this time.

CHAPTER XXIII

Early afternoon sun bathed the grounds of Montgomery House in a warm golden glow as Edwina looked out of her kitchen window and caught a glimpse of Arthur as he headed towards Paul Lynch's cottage. She had thought that their lunch at the tea shop had gone rather well, but he hadn't mentioned getting together again since. Now it was Tuesday, and she felt foolish for allowing herself to entertain wishful thinking about her future.

Why did she yearn so to spend more time with the artist? After all, Arthur had been frequenting Tea, Crumpets and More much longer than she had been a visitor to, much less a resident of, Captain's Point. She had seen the way Connie, the tea shop's owner, had looked at him. She might be up in years, but she wasn't stupid. There had been an ease of presence between the two of them that had caused her own confidence in her date's interest to wane.

Feeling the need for some fresh sea air laced with a hint of fall, Edwina untied the blue and white print apron from around her waist, hung it on a hook and started out for a stroll. Lost in thought, she soon left the sidewalk, watching for possible rabbit holes as she crossed the lawn towards the gazebo where she was greeted by the object of her confusion.

"Edwina!"

"Arthur? I thought I saw you heading towards Paul's, but…"

"I closed up shop for lunch and thought I'd eat and do some thinking in this beautiful setting. The days will soon be filled with the chill of the season, and I want to enjoy this view as long as possible. My son's wife packed two sandwiches for me today. Would you care to join me?"

"Thank you." She took a seat in the gazebo.

"It's a turkey club on toasted honey wheat," her companion said, handing her his other sandwich. "With a pickle, I might add."

"You're lucky to have such a nice daughter-in-law."

"Indeed."

Sensing he was not his usual cheerful self, she asked, "Is something wrong? Maybe I can help."

"The holiday weekend brought a bevy of activity to my shop, and I sold two more paintings," he replied, his focus on the ocean spread out beyond the cliff. "The sales have energized me, but at the same time, things are happening so fast. Maybe I've leaped before I looked." He returned his focus to her, worry engulfing his face.

"I'm sorry you feel that way." Edwina sent him a caring smile.

"What made me think that now was the time to open such a business establishment? Up until a few years ago, my wife and I did everything together. My business is succeeding, but I don't have her to share it with. Somehow, it doesn't feel right to be going it alone." He shrugged one shoulder slightly. "You probably think I'm crazy."

Instinctively, Edwina took his hand. "Nonsense! I know exactly how you feel. This is the time in our lives when we can do anything we want. We don't have to answer to anyone except ourselves…and our children, perhaps.

"The concept takes some getting used to. You may feel like you're an island surrounded by a sea of happy people living their merry lives, but we're not. We're still missing those who are no longer here - my husband Ham and your Sylvia. Trust me, it will get better with time. Their absence never goes away, but we have to adapt. Understand you're allowed to feel happiness and accomplishment, and Sylvia would want you to do so."

Arthur's faded eyes lingered on Edwina's comforting face, while he marveled at the ease with which she could lighten his heaviest load.

Covering her hand with his other one, he asked, "Would you have dinner with me Friday night?"

Taken off guard, Edwina quickly ran through her mental calendar. "It would be my pleasure to dine with you," she answered, her voice soft. "Could we make it a week from Friday, though? I'm already committed to babysitting Lucy this week."

"I understand," he replied. "The next Friday will work fine." He released her hand and returned to his sandwich. "I feel a hundred percent better. Let's meet here for lunch whenever possible until then."

"I can't think of anything I'd rather do," she agreed, knowing at that moment her relationship with Arthur had taken on a much deeper significance.

A few minutes later, their meal finished, Arthur stood and asked, "If you have the time, would you come back with me to my shop? I should fill the display voids after my recent sales, and your recommendations would be appreciated."

Her smile saying it all, Edwina accepted his extended arm, and the two of them proceeded to his gallery at a leisurely pace.

CHAPTER XXIV

"Those smell good," Chase said as he appeared in the mudroom door just in time to witness Adrianna pulling a sheet of molasses cookies from the oven. "Mind if I have one, or are they destined for something special?"

"Pour yourself a glass of milk to go with them and enjoy as many as you want." She slid the last one onto a cooling rack and then popped another sheet into the oven.

"How much longer will you be with these?" he asked as he took a seat at the island and reached for a cookie.

"About another ten minutes, why?"

"Otis has something he thought we'd enjoy seeing over at the farm." He eyed her white short shorts as she rinsed a bowl in the sink and then placed it in the dishwasher. "He suggested we wear jeans and tennis shoes. Are you game?"

"Sure." She took a cookie for herself.

"It's wonderful seeing you so happily domestic," he said, the soft look she loved so much in his eyes. "Knowing your hands made these makes them all the more delicious."

"What a lovely thing for you to say!" She sent him the shy smile that always filled him with a desire to hold her in his arms and protect her.

The timer choosing this moment to ding, she slipped her hand in a mitt, pulled out the last sheet of cookies and turned off the oven. "I'll leave these for Penny to pack away once they're cool." She indicated what remained on the cooling racks of her efforts. "Give me five minutes to change."

"Take your time." Chase stood and followed along as they left the kitchen behind, having first grabbed another two of the warm cookies to munch on while he waited.

Ten minutes later they arrived at the farm, where Otis could be seen talking with a small, wiry man near the stable's door.

Having parked the SUV and disembarked, Chase and Adrianna approached, at which the stranger removed his blue baseball cap and sent the latter a smile.

"This is Harry Parker," Otis introduced them. "Chase Sheffield and Adrianna Montgomery, the farm's owners."

Adrianna felt a pang of regret at the sound of her name, still not comfortable with Chase's insistence that she retain the use of her maiden name socially, even though she had signed all business documents Adrianna M. Sheffield since their marriage.

"People around here will always think of you as a Montgomery anyway," he had stated, "and it's a proud heritage."

Not a battle she had wanted to fight, she had acquiesced, but it still didn't sit well.

"Nice to meet you." She extended her hand, feeling the calluses on his as they shook. "Chase says you have something you want us to see." She shifted her attention to their property manager.

"Bring her on out," Otis addressed Harry, who grinned and led a chestnut Arabian mare into the sunlight a couple of minutes later.

"What a beautiful lady!" Adrianna's face shone with pleasure as she stepped forward and stroked the horse's neck, receiving a nuzzle in return. "What's her name, and where did she come from?"

"The couple who own her have a weekend place a mile or two up the coast," Otis explained. "They've been paying to board her for the past two months, but World Bank has transferred him overseas, so the mare needs a new home."

"Oh, Chase…" Adrianna looked to her husband, surprised when he responded atypically.

"I don't know, Adrianna, a horse like this requires a lot of upkeep. Would you really have time to ride her regularly with all that you have on your plate? She deserves an owner who'll appreciate her."

But then, she glimpsed the twinkle in his eyes. "You've already bought her for me, haven't you, best of all husbands?" She grinned.

"Her name's Jenny, ma'am," Harry filled her in, "and you won't find a sweeter-natured lady anywhere."

"I can believe that." Adrianna moved to the horse's head. "What about it, Jenny? Would you like to make your new home with us? Our dog Max will give us a good recommendation."

"Harry was the owners' groom, and he's agreed to stay here with her," Chase spoke up, throwing his arm around his wife. "I'm hoping against hope that you'll let him accompany you on your rides, when I'm not available to be on rescue duty."

At which, she threw back her head and laughed. "You see how I'm treated, Harry? I have a feeling that you and I are destined to become fast friends."

Used to a complete lack of consideration, the groom immediately lost his heart to his employer's lovely bride, silently pledging to keep her as safe and sound as a new babe in its cradle, satisfied that Fate had blessed both Jenny and him with the best of all homes.

"May I ride her now?" Adrianna asked.

"She came with tack including an English saddle, but if you would prefer a new one or a Western style, we'll get whatever you want once we wish to reappear before the general public," Chase told her.

"English is fine," his wife assured him as she accepted Jenny's bridle, enabling Harry to retrieve the necessary saddle. "But what about you?" She turned to her husband. "Do you know how to ride?"

"I rode a few times when Susan and the rest of them were growing up on the farm," Chase stated, failing to mention the box of dressage ribbons he had won as a boy. "I'm glad you think I need a horse, too." A sheepish grin appeared on his face.

"Are you telling me that Jenny brought a friend with her?" The edges of Adrianna's mouth turned up in a smile as her husband checked the girth on her saddle and then, taking her left ankle in his strong grip, hoisted her up.

"Might as well bring out The Black." Chase winked at Harry. "Our secret's out." Then he turned to his wife. "He has a long pompous name on his registration papers as does your Jenny, but his previous owner referred to him as The Black and I'm sticking with it. He is, as you'll see in a moment, one of a kind."

"You always did sit well in your saddle." Otis looked up at Adrianna while they waited, pride on his face.

"Remember, I had the best of all teachers." She smiled down at her old tutor as Harry led from the stable the most magnificent Arabian stallion she had ever seen, already saddled.

Obviously fresh, the horse's black coat shone in the sun where it stood tossing its head. For a moment, she was filled with awe, but then fear struck her heart as the realization hit her that this was her new husband's mount, glad when the frisky mare required her attention.

"How're you doing, fellow?" Chase amazed her as he took the bridle from Harry's hand and approached the animal's head, meeting The Black's gaze as he reached into his pocket and produced a couple of sugar cubes, which the stallion haughtily accepted as his due.

Having already seen the horse's new owner in the saddle, Harry stood at ease next to Otis.

"Ready to take me up?" Chase kept a firm grip on the bridle as the Arabian nodded his fine head and then pawed at the earth with his right forehoof before poking his owner's upper arm with his nose as if to say, "Let's get on with it."

From her position on Jenny's back, Adrianna thought with relief that the two males appeared evenly matched.

"I'll take that as an affirmative." Chase ran his hand along the stallion's muscled neck and then swung himself into the saddle with an ease that immediately confirmed him to be an expert. "We should be back in an hour or two," he addressed Harry. "Thanks for your help."

"Believe me, sir. It's been a pleasure."

The stallion picking this moment to rise up on its hind legs, Chase shot Adrianna a glance. "Ready?"

"Ready."

"Follow me then, and I'll show you the way." He led them towards a broad expanse of open land as Otis held the gate open for them, calling out as they passed through, "The whole area is free and clear, except for a few cows by the pond on your left."

Starting at a trot as the horses warmed up, Chase then allowed The Black to break into a canter, satisfied that his wife was indeed an accomplished rider, but soon gave the stallion his head.

As they galloped forward, Adrianna was filled with a complete sense of exhilaration, thinking she had never seen a more impressive sight than her strong husband seated upon his powerful stallion. The surrounding woods coming into sight, Chase reined in The Black and instigated a wide circular cool down.

"You've been holding out on me," Adrianna stated as he slowed until they were positioned side by side. "You're forgiven, though, that was wonderful! I can't thank you enough."

"I beg to differ, ma'am." Chase sent her a knowing look. "Be forewarned that I'm expecting payment in full as soon as the sun's set."

"Rogue!"

"Compliment accepted." He grinned and then steered them towards the pine trees that marked the side of the open fields.

"I spent hours riding through these woods when I was younger," he shared, and Adrianna wondered at the face of the boy Chase who looked back at her for a moment, only to be replaced in a flash by that of her handsome, mature husband. "These trees are riddled with bridle paths, and I'm looking forward to sharing them with you."

Two hours later as promised, they returned to the stables – a wide grin on Chase's face, a look of pure pleasure on Adrianna's.

Watching them coming across the field, obviously in love with each other and so thrilled with their mounts, Harry Parker knew he would never see a more beautiful sight, even if he lived to be two hundred.

CHAPTER XXV

"Susan will be right down," Anders greeted Jack when he arrived at The Cove. "If you'll excuse me, I'm producing what will be, if I don't remove it from the oven soon, a very rubbery chicken for our dinner. Make yourself comfortable in the family room, although watch out for toys before you sit in any of the chairs." His host indicated the archway with a wave of his hand before hustling along the hall to the kitchen.

Entering the large room, Jefferson first thought it to be empty, but then he spotted Daniel and Casey hunched over a coloring book in front of the fireplace, the latter sending him a half wag of recognition.

"Jack!" Daniel leaped to his feet, ran forward and threw his arms around the newcomer's knees, when a creaking floorboard revealed their visitor's presence.

"Whoa, Charger!" Jack picked the boy up and tossed him lightly in the air, before giving him a quick hug. "You're liable to knock me clean over."

"Not someone as tall and strong as you are," Daniel declared in his firm way. "You're like my grandpa. Both of you know how to hold your ground and stand firm on your pins."

Once again amused and amazed by the boy's seeming wisdom as he quoted out of context phrases the adults around him had uttered and the child's open, innocent acceptance of this new acquaintance in his life, Jack was not unhappy to have another opportunity to interact with him. "So what were you working on when I disturbed you?" he asked as he took a seat in one of the armchairs, having first heeded Anders' advice and checked it out for possible booby traps.

"Want to see?" Daniel didn't wait for an answer, but quickly retrieved the coloring book, spread it across Jack's knees and remained standing himself as he pointed to what had started out as a simple outline of a hill with a stream flowing down its slope. "I didn't want a plain old mountain, so now there are trees, a house and a goat."

The trees were recognizable, the house was way out of proportion and the goat looked more like a dog. "Much better," Jack stated firmly. "There's nothing worse than a plain slope. Who lives in the house?"

"Mama and I will," Daniel stated as if there was no doubt. "That's why it's so big. Big houses are happy, and small ones are sad."

Quietly watching the two of them from the archway, Susan felt guilt once again wash over her at the pain her son had endured while they had lived with his father in the D.C. condo. At least, she thought, The Cove had been good for him.

"How big is your house?" Daniel lifted his eyes to her date's, the boy's face filled with hope.

"It's on the large side," Jack filled him in, "as big, if not bigger, than this one, although right now the second floor is all torn apart so I can make some improvements. When they're finished and I've moved in, you'll have to come take a look."

"Could I really?" The boy's eyes widened. "I bet you have neat stuff lying around, and I know how not to break things."

"I have a few things you would probably enjoy seeing," Jack acknowledged, "but you know, Daniel, it isn't the size of a house that's important or even the things that are in it. It's the people who fill it. One of the happiest homes I ever knew was no bigger than this room and barely contained anything."

"The whole house? Here in Captain's Point?"

"No, the home I'm talking about was a Mongolian ger or yurt, clear on the other side of the world," Jack explained. "They're bigger than most tents, but you can take them down and reassemble them anywhere else that you want in just a couple of hours. Seven people lived in the one I mentioned, and while they worked hard, their home was filled with laughter."

"Maybe Mama and I could get one of those," Daniel again raised eyes full of hope to this fascinating adult. "My piggybank is this big." He held his arms wide. "And it's almost full."

"I'm not sure a yurt would have enough closet space." Susan forced a smile onto her face and ended the discussion before her heart broke. "Grandpa almost has dinner ready, so it's time for you to wash your hands. Give me a kiss now, and I'll check on you in your bed when I come home."

"Casey will be asleep, but I'll still have my eyes open," her son assured her, before kissing her cheek and receiving a hug as her date stood. "Will you be checking on me, too?" he asked their visitor.

"Not this time, Charger." Jack was surprised by the disappointment that filled the small face before him. "But we'll have to get together again soon."

"Promise?" Daniel's face cleared.

"Promise," their guest stated in all seriousness.

"Now you and Casey run along," Susan admonished her son. "You know Grandpa doesn't like it when his dinner grows cold."

"I'm going to be the envy of every man at the marina." Jack gazed at her with frank appreciation as Daniel left them. "That shade of blue really suits you."

"Thank you." She suddenly felt as awkward as when she had dated the first boy in college who she hadn't known since grade school. "I hope Daniel didn't talk your ear off."

"Not at all," he assured her as they walked to the front door. "I find his conversation very illuminating and, frankly, refreshing. There isn't a hint of guile in him. He says what he means, and he means what he says."

"Which can be both good and bad, depending on the topic of conversation he has chosen." Susan chuckled. "The last time he saw his paternal grandmother, he asked her why she had those three white hairs sticking out of her chin."

"I can see where a little discretion here and there might not hurt." Jack grinned as he held open the door and then escorted her to the Mercedes SUV that awaited them, its interior still exuding a new vehicle smell. "Do your ex's parents take much interest in Daniel?"

"Not much before the divorce and none at all since." Susan was glad when the SUVs door closed and provided a neat ending. "I'm really looking forward to touring the house," she switched to a new topic when her date rejoined her.

"I should explain that only the downstairs is in good shape at the moment." Jack headed their vehicle along the drive. "I've installed a new boiler, and all the radiators have been refurbished. Foam insulation has been sprayed under the roof in the attic and covered with dry wall, and now that the solar panels are in place on the roof, I'm having central air installed throughout."

"You are doing extensive renovations."

"I plan to live here a long time." Jack held her gaze for a moment, having brought the SUV to a stop at the main road, then steered them in the direction of his own home.

Enjoying a comfortable few minutes of silence, Susan wondered how much all of this was costing him. Even allowing for the fact that he had done some of the work himself, the house was large, and the cost of the kinds of upgrades he had described would've escalated quickly. How much had Ivan's estate been worth? She felt a sharp stab of guilt as she realized she had access to this information at the firm. The question now was should she look?

"Here we are," Jack stated the obvious as he turned off the engine. "My home, sweet home."

Susan was surprised a few moments later to see that he had installed a security system as he paused to key in the code.

"The footprint of the downstairs is a little unusual for a Victorian," Jack explained, "due, I imagine, to the original owner's desire to take advantage of the view." He opened the front door, revealing a wide foyer divided at the back by a stairway on the left that rose straight up to a landing and then right to the second floor and a comfortably wide hallway on the right that led to the formal rooms at the back of the house. "Notice the cranberry glass in the windows going around the door and in the transom," he pointed out with pride. "It isn't as obvious from the outside, unless it's dark and the light shines through it."

"You're right," Susan agreed. "I've never noticed it before, but then I've always been here during the day. What a beautiful bombe chest." She ran her hand lightly along the edge of the top.

"Do you like antiques?" Jack asked, and for a moment his face reflected the same degree of hope that had filled Daniel's only a few minutes before.

"More than anything." Susan nodded towards the room that could be partially viewed through the open pocket doors to her right, not having noticed his expression. "May I?"

"Certainly." He smiled. "That's why we're here."

"I notice that the woodwork is still all original," she said and then paused. "What a wonderful room!"

"The library." He joined her in the wide doorway. "As you can see, I'm using it as my home office as well, but it's large enough to serve two or three people and still hold a seating area. The original owner was the proprietor of the dry goods store and sold tin ceilings as well, so you'll find them throughout the house. He had also acquired a share in a local lumber mill, so the ceiling in the round breakfast room across the hall is comprised of wood as are two of the ceilings upstairs. According to my uncle, the family conducted their business ventures from this room for many decades, which is why it houses a large safe."

"And you're retaining all of these historical details?" Susan's eyes ran over the built-in shelves and under cabinets in the library, as well as the richly carved fireplace with its matching framed over-mantle mirror.

"Wouldn't you?" He tried hard not to hold his breath.

"Definitely." Her blue eyes when they met his were full of appreciation. "So this is the breakfast room across the foyer?" She turned towards the opposite pocket doors.

"Yes." Jack followed her. "As you can see, it has built-in bench seating that also acts as storage in the curve formed by the mock Queen Anne tower you see from the outside. The one on the opposite side of this floor forms one end of the formal parlor, and I'm using it as a music nook."

"Not surprising with all of your talent." She smiled at him and then headed through the smaller door that connected the breakfast room with the kitchen. "Oh! It's just like I always imagined it would be!" She turned excited eyes in his direction.

"The table came with the house," he filled her in. "My uncle bought the property from the granddaughter of the original owner, who was ninety-two at the time. She had never married and needed to move into an assisted living situation."

"It's perfect!" Once again, Susan ran her hand along the edge of the table's top, relishing the feel of the oak as she noted the fresh wildflowers displayed in an aqua-toned Mason jar in the middle. "Can't you imagine all the wonderful memories that must have been made in this room?"

"And all the ones I'm looking forward to making in the future." Jack was pleased with her obvious approval so far of his choices.

"And this?" Susan pointed at a swinging door.

"Leads to the butler's pantry and then into the dining room." He gestured for her to go ahead.

"Look at all of this storage," Susan marveled at the floor-to-ceiling drawers, counters and cabinets, most with glass panels, that lined the surprisingly large pantry, noting that a stainless steel sink and fair-sized wine fridge had been installed – the latter already well-stocked.

"Oh, my!" She once again paused inside the dining room. "How many people does this table seat?"

"Fourteen as you now see it, but I believe twenty-four with the leaves are in."

"And the built-in hutch is gorgeous as, of course, is the view." She strode forward to one of the large windows, through which the ocean could be seen - the tide rolling in, absent of whitecaps in the calm evening air.

"And this is the parlor," she stated as she headed through the connecting pocket doors into the vast room, a grand piano on display in its rounded corner, tall wainscoting ranging around its perimeters as in the other main rooms. "And you can see my view from everywhere!" she exclaimed without thinking.

And at that moment, Jack's heart filled with hope that, with the house's help, he might actually succeed in winning this skittish mare for himself.

CHAPTER XXVI

Their tour of the Victorian's downstairs completed, Jack and Susan had left the house behind and were now walking along the side of Montgomery's at the marina towards the short wide pier that held the restaurant's less formal, outside annex. Japanese lanterns and tiny twinkle lights ranged overhead, and the white wrought iron tables and chairs were arrayed in bright cloths under glass and seat pillows. At the far left end a small stage sat one step up, now hidden by a canvas curtain suspended from a thick braided wire on metal grommets.

"Jack Jefferson," he gave his name to the hostess, and Susan was surprised when they were led to the opening on the left of the curtain and shown to a single table for four set for two on the stage, out of sight of the other diners. "I hope you don't mind my arranging for a little privacy," he said as he held out a chair for Susan, both of them set so as to maximize their view.

"Of course not," she assured him, touched by the gesture and the rose bowl filled with white roses that atypically graced their table. "I'm surprised by how much further along the coast you can see from here on the stage, because the boathouses don't obstruct the view."

"Your server will be right with you." The hostess handed each of them a menu and then left them to choose as soon as she had filled their water glasses.

"As a regular over the years, do you already know what you want?" Jack asked.

"I usually get a lobster roll, because they're so good," Susan said.

"Let's make that two, although I'm going for the grand," he agreed, "and to drink?"
"Lemonade, please."

"We'll have one lobster roll platter, one grand lobster roll platter and two lemonades." He handed their young waiter, who had just arrived, their menus.

"I'm glad we were finally able to agree on an evening," Jack renewed their conversation once their waiter had left them. "Between my quick trip to Virginia, your late appointments and Lizzie's birthday party, I was beginning to think we would be sitting here sometime around Christmas."

"Me, too." Susan smiled back at him. "I had been looking forward to the tour, and this is lovely." She gave a small wave of her hand, encompassing the ocean before them and the sky above that was just beginning to be tinged by streaks of light rose as the sun set somewhere behind the main restaurant. "As is your house and all the antique furniture you've retained from the previous owners."

"What did you keep from your marriage?" Jack asked.

"Daniel."

"I meant furniture wise." He sent her a kind smile.

"I saved Daniel." Her blue eyes filled with such pain as she met his gaze that he instinctively reached out and took her hand.

"You saved the best," he made his position clear.

"I wouldn't have wanted any of the furniture anyway," Susan shared. "Bill was into ultra-modern, and while I can appreciate it when it's well done, I wasn't comfortable living with it."

"No, having seen the furnishings in The Cove, I'm sure you wouldn't have been," Jack acknowledged, still holding her hand lightly in his. "What was it like growing up there?"

"I didn't," she filled him in. "When Andy, Courtney and I were growing up, we lived on the farm next to Ivan's, where Courtney and her family now live."

"And your brother?"

"He's an accountant and lives with his wife and two teenaged children in Georgetown," she told him. "Andy works with homeland security, but that's all any of us know about what he does."

"Is he happily married?"

"Why did you ask that?" Susan pulled her hand back and then unwrapped her silverware from her napkin as an afterthought.

"I'm not sure." Jack considered. "Yes, I am, now that I think about it. I've had so many diverse experiences over the years that sometimes I've learned a lesson and filed it away, only to have it ring a bell later on in an odd way."

"So what caused you to ask about Andy's marriage and not Courtney's?" she asked. "Both of which, for the record, are happy ones."

"One of the first jungle tours I took was in Borneo, which has the oldest rain forest in the world," Jack began. "Four guides were with us, and I was in the lead with the oldest guide, while a much younger fellow who fancied himself a ladies' man was right behind me. Suddenly, the largest king cobra I've ever seen reared up in front of us. The younger guy grabbed my arms and used me as a shield, while the older guide attacked the snake, his desire to protect the group overriding his own instinct of self-preservation. A few weeks later, when I knew him better, I asked him why that was, and he answered that I could've been his son."

"Amazing!" Susan was struck both by the story and by her date's calm telling of it, the smooth flow of his words enhancing the tale.

"Two lobster roll platters and two lemonades." Their waiter reappeared with a large tray. "Will there be anything else?" he asked after setting their condiments on the table.

Jack glanced at Susan who indicated that she was fine. "We should be good for a while," Jack assured him, "although we'll want to see a dessert menu when the time comes."

Once again, they enjoyed a comfortable few minutes of silence as each sampled their meal.

"I'm going to have to join you in your addiction," Jack reopened their conversation. "These rolls are delicious. To finish my answer to your question, when you live the kind of life that I've lived, you find yourself judging another man's willingness to watch your back, because your life may depend on it. It's been my experience that a happily married man will often do that best, because his instincts are geared towards protecting those around him."

"Interesting." She met his gaze, and he once again reached out and took her hand.

"I wasn't commenting on your marriage, Susan. I don't judge you for that. Your jerk of a husband, yes, but not you – never you. There is no doubt in my mind that you're a very capable, loving woman, who did what she could both to be a good wife and a good mother to Daniel. He's the only proof anyone could possibly need of that."

"Thank you." Embarrassed, she looked away for a second as she blinked back tears, then faced him again. "I feel so guilty about Daniel."

"But why?" He turned in his chair, leaned forward and shielded her hand in both of his. "You have provided for and loved Daniel with all of your heart. As soon as you realized the truth of your situation, you had the guts to do what needed to be done and to bring him here to Captain's Point, where he is surrounded by people who love and care for him as much as you do and will do him no harm in the bargain. Anyone can see that he's a happy, well-adjusted little boy."

"He would still like more of my time."

Jack laughed as he released her hand and returned to his dinner. "What normal, well-adjusted male wouldn't?" he asked, and as Susan took another bite of her lobster roll, she felt a little bit of her dark shroud of guilt lift.

How comfortable it was to be with this new man in her life, and how comforting! Still, Daniel must be her first thought, not her second, and she didn't want him ever to be hurt like he had been again.

A few minutes later, having put in an order for two chocolate mousses and two Irish coffees, Jack stood and pulled her chair over closer to his, settled back into his own chair and laid his arm along hers, stretching out his long legs beneath the table as the sunset provided them with its breathtaking splendor, enhancing the view.

"Now answer my question," he brought their conversation back around. "What was it like growing up on the farm?"

"Wild, crazy, happy, fun – a complete, never-ending zoo." Susan chuckled. "We were loud, rambunctious and, sometimes, completely out of control, although only within certain strict boundaries. My father, as you probably have noticed, has a strong dramatic streak in his nature, and we were often called upon to participate in amateur theatricals. Then, of course, there were the animals. We had a cow, chickens and horses – not to mention the dogs and cats that found their ways to us over the years." She looked over at him. "I'm surprised you don't have a dog."

"I do." He surprised her yet again. "An extremely well-trained German Shepherd. She hasn't made it through customs yet. Daniel will be as delighted by her as she will be with him."

"I sometimes worry that he's going to grow up thinking he's part of a pack." Susan laughed, and her date was glad that she seemed to have recovered completely from their earlier discussion.

"No more than you did, from the sound of it," Jack reminded her.

"That's true." She took a last bite of her mousse and settled back in her chair, welcoming the feel of his arm across the back of her shoulders. "Although for a while, I pictured myself as a young Dale Evans."

"Not with your gorgeous blonde hair." He played with one long wave, sending a tingle up her spine as he unknowingly brushed it against her neck just below her right ear. "You didn't mention you rode at the cookout the other day. You'd be doing both of us a favor if you would give Goldie some exercise as often as you want. I promise you won't come to any harm on her."

"I'll consider it," she said, once again struck by her date's generous nature.

"We'll have to go sailing one of these days soon," he changed the subject.

"I'd enjoy that." She was surprised at how pleased he looked by her response. How fair was she being to him allowing him into her life, knowing that he couldn't be given first place no matter how much she was drawn to him?

"Whenever you're ready, sir." Their server placed a small folder on their table and Jack immediately handed him a credit card, relieving her of any thought that she might be expected to contribute.

The sun now having set completely, Susan was sorry to see their evening ending. It had felt good to be treated so special by someone who was as much of a gentleman as Jack was, and if she was truthful with herself, part of her needed that.

"I assume you're still planning to attend the box luncheon at the Animal Shelter this weekend that you all were discussing at the cookout," Jack commented as they strolled back to the SUV a few minutes later.

"I don't think Larry and Jim are likely to let me out of it." She grimaced.

"I'll see you there then." He placed his hand on the small of her back as he held the SUV's door open, and she felt her knees weaken.

What was it about this man's calm, quiet strength that called to her so? Susan fastened her seatbelt.

"Tell Daniel I said he should dream with the angels when you tuck him in," Jack said a few minutes later as he walked her towards the front door of The Cove, pausing and taking her hand before she stepped onto the porch.

"I had a lovely evening." She gazed up at him, her wide eyes once again filled with their haunted look, but he surprised her again, merely throwing an arm around her and drawing her to him in a brotherly way and planting a kiss on the top of her head.

"I did, too," he said into her hair and then released her to walk the last few steps on her own, only turning back to his vehicle once she had closed the house's door behind her.

Inside the dimly lit foyer, Susan leaned her back against the same door, glad for its firm support, and let out a long, slow sigh. How part of her wished that Jack Jefferson had drawn her into both of his strong arms and swept her away with a kiss!

CHAPTER XXVII

Blue suited her, Anderson thought as he looked across the café table at his client – blue and the platinum that comprised her earrings and the part of her ring that held the largest aquamarine he had ever set eyes on. Now, if only he could get her to relax and enjoy herself, but always there was this tension residing just beneath the surface – a tension that he hadn't as yet chased away.

Still, she was a good listener. He would give her that. So far, she had listened to two fish tales, the story of his team's little league win, and a complete replay of his most recent bear hunting trip to Canada – all as they had waited for her to finger Skinny Jones. Never had he met such a woman.

Anders glanced up from his computer screen as a movement in the doorway of his study in what had once been The Cove's library caught his attention.

"Do you have a minute?" Susan asked, remaining where she stood until he motioned her forwards.

"For you, certainly." He sent her a smile. "How was your dinner with Jack last evening?"

"Lovely." For a moment, the tension left her face as she briefly glowed from within while she took a seat in the chair on the other side of his desk, but then just as quickly, the crease reappeared between her brows. "He told me some stories about his travels."

Resigned to his fate, Anders settled in, long ago having learned that it was an utterly useless exercise to request that any of the women in his life come straight to the point.

"I imagine they were quite interesting," he replied.

"They were," Susan agreed, her face maintaining its serious expression, "and one of them got me thinking."

"Yes?"

"When you make the acquaintance of a man, how do you determine how to categorize him in your mind?" she asked.

"I'm not sure I'm following you." Anders considered that his current state of confusion might well resemble that of someone who was drowning.

"Jack was explaining to me that in some of the lines of work he's pursued over the years, it was important that he recognize who would and who wouldn't watch his back, because his life actually depended on it."

"I see," her father stated, still feeling as if he were groping in the dark. "You mean how do I judge whom I can trust?"

"Among other things." Susan toyed with a pen that had been lying on her side of his desk.

"Generally speaking, I try not to judge other people," Anders started out slow, "but occasionally, it can be important to know whether or not you can trust someone even here in our little part of the world. Over the years, I've found that a man's actions usually are a better indication of his true worth than his words."

"Can you give me an example?"

"Would it be helpful if I used Jack?" he asked, thinking it might bring the matter to a close sooner if he did.

"If it would help you to do so." Susan's relief at his having made the suggestion was palpable.

"I was impressed the first time I met him with the way Jack switched gears and helped you, the way he handled Daniel, the way he held him, the way he opened the door for you, the way he smiled at you and treated you and your needs with respect." Anders paused and took a breath.

"And since then?"

"When he and Chase were helping Daniel and Lizzie to ride Adrianna's pony, I was impressed with both of them," he humored his daughter, realizing this discussion was somehow much more important than he had originally thought. "Even though there was a lot going on around them, both of them never took their hands off the child they were watching out for, part of their attention always focused on that responsibility, so that when Daniel shifted too far to his left and would've fallen off, Jack easily pulled him back into position without scaring him."

"And?"

"I appreciated the way Jack understood your needing to keep your appointments with your clients and Lizzie's birthday party, when he was trying to reschedule his date with you," Anders continued, hoping he was somehow assuaging her fears. "As far as I know, he didn't pressure you in any way to either belittle your career by shifting your clients' appointments or to disappoint your niece by missing her party."

"No, he was very understanding," Susan agreed.

"How did he treat you last evening?" her father turned the table on her.

"Like a queen." His daughter smiled back. "He had reserved the stage at the pier, so that we were secluded from the rest and enjoyed a better view than I had realized you could get, and he had arranged for roses to be on our table. And even at his house before, there were fresh flowers in vases on both the kitchen and dining room tables that I'm sure had been put there for my benefit."

"So he planned ahead for your enjoyment right down to the last detail," Anders pointed out.

"Yes."

"And in point of fact, you did enjoy yourself," he stated.

"Very much."

"What more could you want?"

"I don't know what I want," Susan admitted, and her father realized at that moment that they had finally reached the crux of the matter.

"Well, I know what I want," he told her, having decided to risk all. "I want a man like Jefferson in your and Daniel's lives - someone who will watch over, care for and respect you as you deserve long after I'm gone. Whether or not that someone is Jack, only you can tell when the time comes."

"Thank you." Susan rose, came around his desk and kissed his cheek as she hugged him. "You always have been the best father in the whole world."

And with that Anders found he would have to be content as she left him and he returned to his keyboard, knowing that there weren't all that many men like Jack Jefferson in their small part of the world and his Susan would be a fool not to accept him if he offered for her.

CHAPTER XXVIII

Edwina looked at her kitchen clock as the hour hand struck noon. Arthur would be waiting for her at the gazebo for their now regular, but by no means routine, luncheon date. She hastily filled her small wicker picnic tote with carefully wrapped lobster salad rolls and containers of dilled potato salad along with spicy coleslaw. Dessert consisted of homemade blonde brownies drizzled with chocolate. After all, what man could resist chocolate?

Packing a carafe of fresh iced tea and two plastic glasses in her summer canvas bag and grabbing the picnic tote, she left on her short walk to the gazebo overlooking the ocean. Here, she discovered she wasn't late at all, Arthur being nowhere in sight, although something else caught her attention.

Behind Paul Lynch's cottage, two young children were playing with a handful of balloons as their dutiful parents looked on. Laughter and squeals abounded, and the widow's mind drifted back to memories of her son playing on the beach as a toddler - jumping waves, flying kites and chasing balloons.

"Penny for your thoughts," Arthur said as he came up behind her and gently rubbed her shoulders.

"I'm sorry, I was mesmerized by the sights of the children playing and remembering years ago when Hamilton and I took our son and then our grandson on happy vacations to the beach."

At that moment, the older couple witnessed a bunch of balloons lifting towards the sky and a young boy chasing after the multicolored pack as the wind drew it up and over the Atlantic.

"What a shame!" Edwina's heart sank as she remembered the same thing happening to Ham, Jr.

"Well, hopefully, that airborne bunch doesn't have a ring attached."

"A ring? I don't understand?" She was at the same time puzzled and intrigued. "Do tell."

"I'll make you a deal. If you'll show me what scrumptious things you've concocted for us today, I'll tell you a story that you'll never believe." He lifted the picnic tote from her hand as he guided her towards the gazebo.

"Today, I felt the urge to make lobster salad served in rolls," she told him as she began unpacking their lunch.

"Sounds great! I'm starving." He took a round yellow cloth from the tote and spread it over the surface of a small table.

Edwina poured two glasses of tea. "Well, I'm waiting."

"It's rather bizarre, but one has to find the humor in it. At the time, we could laugh or cry, and Sylvia and I choose to laugh."

"Go on." She took a sip of tea.

Arthur sampled his tea as well and then began, "Sylvia and I decided we would get married at her parent's home on Long Island. The setting was beautiful with the ocean as our back drop. Her family went all out, and we had a full wedding party, including a flower girl and ring bearer - Sylvia's brother's twins. They were about five years old at the time. Instead of throwing rice, we were going to release balloons into the air to float out over the ocean with beautiful sentiments attached since it all began for us across the Atlantic."

"How romantic!" Edwina sent her gaze out over the horizon, as if she could envision the picture her luncheon companion was painting.

"Howie, the ring bearer, was a curious little boy. He wanted to know if one of the helium-filled balloons would be strong enough to lift the rings. Right before the ceremony was to begin, he took three balloons from their holding room, managed to take Sylvia's and my wedding rings out of their boxes while others were occupied, tied them to the silk ribbons and let them go."

"No way!"

"Yes! That thing took off like a rocket. Howie was screaming in amazement, his twin sister was crying as was their mother when she realized what had occurred. We improvised, and the ceremony went on. We were too much in love to let it ruin our day. Despite the fact that the symbols of our love for each other were gone, the love in our hearts had, of course, not diminished one bit. I didn't even want to know the consequences given for that misbehavior."

"Sylvia was a lucky woman to have you by her side."

"What a sweet thing to say! Thank you, Edwina. Now anytime I see a balloon, I think of that incident." Arthur finally took a man-sized bite of his lobster roll. "Delicious! I'll have to have you come over to the house. You can meet my son and daughter-in-law, and we can cook lobsters."

"I'd love that." His companion finished her share of the slaw and potato salad while he caught up.

"While you were telling me that story, it spurred a memory of an unexpected event Ham and I shared at our wedding - nothing nearly as romantic or dramatic," Edwina told him. "It's kind of funny, I have to admit, although our moment occurred after the ceremony. Ham and I had decided that we'd like to take a nice drive across the country for our honeymoon before he started law school. We had planned it all out and wanted to make a clean getaway once the bouquet had been tossed and the rice thrown."

"It's a must." Arthur reached for the brownie in front of him.

"Ham's sports car was decorated with streamers attached and 'Just Married' written on the back windshield. We got into the vehicle to make a dash out of the venue's parking lot, and we ran out of gas. Everyone was waving and watching us, and the car just stopped. One of the groomsmen was supposed to fill the tank while we were getting ready to leave. Everything happened faster than anticipated, so he estimated we could at least get to the first gas station as we left town."

"Wrong!" Arthur finished for her. "My word, we have both had our share of strange occurrences at our weddings. Maybe, the third wedding is a charm."

And, at that, a warm feeling rose within as Edwina smiled at her companion and, unbeknownst to him, pictured how dashing Arthur would look in wedding attire.

CHAPTER XXIX

Relaxing against the back of the red leather banquette, Anderson drummed his fingers on the wooden table in front of him, impatient for Susan C to return with her son from the ladies' room.

Now that Skinny Jones was on his way to the slammer, wearing a pair of steel bracelets for good measure, there was nothing for it but to get her and the boy out of town. Thank goodness his sister and her husband had gone on that road trip with their kids, leaving behind their big rambling farmhouse that was crying out for him to make use of it.

Hadn't his client mentioned the other day that she boarded her horse somewhere on Long Island? Well, there were three mares in the barn that she could ride, and he wouldn't mind showing her some of the bridle paths from atop his brother-in-law's black stallion. If he remembered right, there was even an aged pony for the boy if he was old enough.

Visions of his client standing in front of the big cast iron, wood burning stove in a blue shirtwaist dress and a crisp white apron filled his mind. He had just finished mentally unhooking the top three buttons when she and her son reappeared, their eyes filled with fear that called to his protective side – the one he tried so hard to hide.

A week or two with the pair of them wouldn't be all that bad, he laid a ten beside his glass to cover their tab plus a large tip for the overworked waitress. The kid was well-behaved, and Susan did things to him that no other woman had done in a while. If things turned out the way they had been going, this could end up the best assignment of all time.

Jack Jefferson glanced up from his laptop just in time to see a white SUV pull into the long driveway and head for the rambling

Victorian. Pleased to see that his old college friend had made such good time on his drive from Baltimore, he hurried onto the front porch to greet him.

"Jack!" Kurt pumped his offered hand. "Good to see you!"

"You, too, you old windbag! Now, what have you done with my girl?"

"She's in the carry cage you left with Pat and me," his friend hurried around to the back of his vehicle. "I imagine she's about ready for a good run, but she did fine last night."

A sharp bark from the back announced that Jack's German Shepherd, Lady, was indeed ready to be let out of the confined space, and he hurried forward to welcome her to her new home. Released from the cage, the excited dog ran rapidly around in circles for a few minutes before jumping up on the man she hadn't seen for several weeks.

"It's about time you got here, Old Girl." Her owner gave her a good scratch behind the ears. "I've met a little guy who you're going to love as much as I do." Then he returned his attention to his friend. "Come on inside. Lunch is almost ready, and then you can get back on your way since you insist you can't stay."

"Wish I could take you up on your offer to enjoy a spot of deep sea fishing, but duty calls," Kurt said as he followed his host into the house. "Nice place you've got here."

"Next time you come, bring Pat and the kids," Jack said as he led their way into the kitchen. "There's plenty for them to do around here, and it's not too far for a weekend getaway."

Two hours later, a couple of fine ribeyes having been consumed and a long stream of over-exaggerated tales having been shared, Kurt took his leave, and Jack called Susan's number at work.

"Bridgette? Jack Jefferson here. I wondered if I might have a word with Susan." Stroking the Shepherd's back where she sat beside him, he waited.

"Susan Chesterton," she answered in a professional tone.

"I hope I'm not disturbing you," Jack began, "but Lady has just arrived. I wondered if Daniel and you would be available to join us for supper at the house this evening. It's such a nice day I'll probably toss something on the grill."

"I won't get away from here much before five-thirty, and I would want to change into something more casual," Susan filled him in. "Would six to six-thirty be okay?"

"Lady, the grill and I will be waiting whenever you can make it," he promised and then cut their call short, knowing that her work calendar was always full with Chase on his honeymoon.

At six-thirty exactly, Susan's car turned into the drive, and Jack hurried onto the porch where he indicated for Lady to sit and stay before making his way down the steps.

"Jack! We made it!" Daniel ran towards him as soon as he was out of the car. "I'm learning to hurry because my mama was eager to get here."

"As long as you aren't in any hurry to leave." Jack hoisted the child into the air as Susan's cheeks took on a pink tinge.

"Why isn't your dog moving?" Daniel asked once his host had given him a bear hug and set him back on the ground.

"Because I told her to sit and stay," Jack explained. "She'll stay there until I release her, because it's part of her training as a hospital visitor dog." He turned to Susan. "Lady and I visited the children's ward regularly at the hospital near where we lived in Switzerland. She'll be fine around Daniel."

"I had no doubt that she would be," she assured him.

"Why don't you give her one of these little dog biscuits like you gave the sugar cube to Goldie?" he once again addressed Daniel as he handed him the treat. "Then I wondered if you would do me a favor and throw that orange Frisbee around here in the front yard for Lady to catch and bring back to you. It's one of her favorite games, and she's been cooped up quite a bit on her trip here."

"Sure!" Daniel's face lit up as Jack called Lady over.

Dog and boy having bonded immediately and then headed into the yard with the Frisbee, Jack threw his arm around Susan's shoulders, surprised and pleased when she relaxed against him.

"Hard day?" he asked as his blood coursed through his veins at the nearness of her.

"Not really hard, just busy and a little bit tiring," she filled him in. "Things are getting better, though, now that the two new associates are getting more up to speed, and it won't be too much longer until Chase is back in the saddle. Frankly, I'm glad I've been able to give him a rest. He'd been carrying a horrendous load for years, although he won't need to do that going forward."

"I hope you don't mind, but I've made some changes in our plans," Jack said. "I realized after we spoke that we have a pretty stiff breeze off the water today, and then I remembered having found some old kites when I cleaned out the laundry room. I've checked them out, and they look like they'll still fly. I thought we could at least get one up for Daniel and then eat afterwards, if you think that would be okay."

"I think that would be marvelous fun!" She smiled up at him.

"I've switched gears on the grilling and eating outside as well, because I was afraid it might be too chilly for the little guy outside once the sun sets. My friend who brought Lady down from Baltimore left me a wedge of prosciutto as well, so I thought we would start with some melon and prosciutto followed by fresh pasta that's waiting to be cooked and topped with some sauce I thawed out."

"Sounds delicious, and Daniel loves pasta as you saw when you joined us for lasagna at The Cove." She marveled at his thoughtfulness as he retrieved the kites from the front porch and then headed to where the Frisbee players had established themselves.

"You really do have a way with animals," Jack addressed the boy as he approached. "That's a gift you should make use of over the years. See how Lady already trusts you? You can tell by the way she's putting her head under your hand, so that you'll pet her."

"She's a good dog, like Casey," Daniel stated in his solemn way, "and she can jump really high. What are those?" He changed direction and pointed to what the dog's owner was carrying.

"These are some kites that I found when I moved here. Which one would you like?"

"This one." Daniel pointed to one designed to recall an American flag. "And my mama will want the pink and white one."

"Have you flown a kite before?" Jack asked, moved by the way the little guy had taken care that his mother's needs would be met as well.

"Grandpa helped me fly one at The Cove."

"Susan, if you'll hold onto these, I'll see if we can get our buddy here started with his." Jack passed the two extra ones to her, and then proceeded to show her son how to launch his and allow it to fly higher on his own.

"Mama, mine's in the air!" Daniel yelled back at her in his excitement.

"I see that." She smiled at Jack. "I want to say thank you for encouraging and helping Daniel like you just did, but you must be tired of hearing me say thank you all the time."

"I'll never tire of hearing your voice say anything," he replied as he took the other kites from her, dropping the Frisbee on top of the remaining one on the ground and then letting out some string on the pink and white one. "Would you like me to get yours started?" he asked.

"Please, I've never been very good at getting them up."

"That should do for you." Jack joined Susan from behind a few minutes later where she stood watching her son enjoying himself, bringing his raised arm around her right shoulder.

And as she lifted her hand to take the ball of string from his larger one, for just a moment, Susan believed that if she were to relax against him, with his strong arms around her, all the concerns she carried within her would somehow be lifted from her in the same way that the kite had risen so easily for him.

CHAPTER XXX

Their breakfast plates now slid into the dishwasher, Chase glanced at the retro cat clock on the kitchen wall and then pulled his bride to him, indicating the timepiece with a nod.

"I see that it is time for my Lady Guinevere's morning walk in her gardens," he said. "Let's pour the rest of the coffee into travel mugs and take them with us."

"I fear Lancelot that you have some devious plot afoot." Adrianna prepared herself with a sense of anticipation for yet another one of new husband's games.

"You wrong me, madam, you have nothing to fear at this early hour." He sent her a knowing look. "Such concerns should be reserved for what I have planned for later this evening."

Laughing in spite of herself, his bride accepted her container of coffee from the fair Lancelot's hand, pleased when he snapped a leash onto Max so that the dog could accompany them.

While the sun shone from a blue sky, a light breeze coming off the ocean provided for a pleasant temperature as they made their way through the kitchen garden. Once on the main path running through the formal gardens beyond, Chase turned to the right, and Adrianna spotted Otis and Jeff Stuart where they stood beside a sundial garden that surrounded a granite obelisk.

"I thought it was time we put our own stamp on the place, on this our second week anniversary," Chase stated in a soft voice.

The two men chose this moment to step apart from one another, revealing that a second stone now rested next to the one that commemorated the betrothal of Chase's great-uncle to Adrianna's great-aunt, under which it had been discovered that those two lovers had buried locks of their hair.

"What a lovely idea!" Adrianna expressed her pleasure as the initials CS + AM and the date of their own betrothal revealed themselves to have been carved into the new addition.

"Good job, guys," he thanked Otis and Jeff. "It looks great."

"You two enjoy your walk." Otis indicated with a nod for Jeff to follow him. "We've got some mowing over by Paul's cottage to take care of."

"I've been meaning to replace the locks of hair we uncovered. Could we do the same with locks of ours?" Adrianna looked to her husband.

Chase cleared his throat as if he had swallowed wrong, a pang having hit his heart at the mere thought of cutting off even one lock of her gorgeous hair. "Certainly, my queen." He threw his arm around her shoulders and hugged her to him, then gathered a handful of her waves in his hand. "We may have to tie a blue string around mine and a pink one around yours to distinguish them, although I think your hair may be a tad darker than mine."

He took a seat on one of the benches that ran around the obelisk, set his travel mug down and patted the place on the other side of him, putting an arm around his bride once again when she joined him.

"That was thoughtful of you," Adrianna said, "and it does make this seem even more like our house."

"Anywhere is our house when you're there with me," he shared. "Even more important, though, is that together we've made this wonderful old place into our home."

"I have to admit that I was pleased when you insisted we live here instead of at Sheffield Place." She snuggled her head against his shoulder. "I have so many good memories here now, including those from our courtship. I fell in love with you in this house, and when you were called to Boston when your aunt died, it was to here that I wanted you to return."

"And I did," he reminded her. "I couldn't wait to get back to Captain's Point, call a halt to your great-aunt's will's requirements and declare myself."

"It's a good thing that you did," she chuckled. "At the rate you were sending me flowers and gifts from Boston, Montgomery House would've filled up fairly quickly."

"Speaking of things, do you realize you have never spent any of our joint funds for anything?" Chase's voice took on a serious tone. "You're not still worried that somehow we'll go overboard are you? Because, as we move forward with the renovations to the house, I want you to feel free to buy whatever furnishings and other items you want."

For a moment, Adrianna gave serious consideration to what he had just said, knowing that the size of their joint estate hadn't really dawned on her. Then she sat up straighter and turned to face him. "I promise you that, when and if I really want something beyond what my salary from Montgomery Properties can provide me, I'll make you aware of it so we can jointly decide if it's a purchase we should make."

"No, that's not good enough," he pressed his point. "I don't want you to feel that you have to ask me to spend our money. Ours means yours, just as much as it means mine."

"I hear what you're saying," she assured him. "It hasn't all sunk in yet, and frankly, there hasn't been any big ticket item that I've wanted. If something does come along, then I promise I'll buy it as long as you're prepared to accept a large portrait of a plucked chicken hanging in the foyer, since you don't want to voice any opinions."

"Okay, I admit there may be a middle ground," he chuckled. "Plucked chickens might be where I would tend to wish to draw a line, but please keep what I've said in mind."

"I will," she agreed, "although I'll probably look to you much of the time merely because I value your opinion."

"That I'll accept as a compliment." He once again drew her to him, planting a firm kiss on her lips, before standing and taking her hand to hold as they completed their morning walk along the cliff, neither of them giving a single thought as to whether or not Captain Reb might have his binoculars pointed yet again in their direction.

CHAPTER XXXI

Saturday noon found the sun shining and a soft breeze blowing – a perfect day for the Animal Shelter's box lunch auction.

Taking an empty seat in the back row of chairs that had been arranged under a large tent behind the animal shelter, David Eskar was relieved to have made it on time as he located the pretty face that he sought amongst the ladies sitting on the stage waiting. Five hundred dollars, he patted the money clip in his pocket. It was a lot of money, but his Karen was worth it.

How long he had waited for Fate to give him such an opportunity, knowing that her father would never accept a mere student or even a qualified dentist for his daughter unless he owned his own practice! With his father's death, the practice now belonged to him – the dental supply firm no longer knocking like a wolf at his and his mother's door. Even so, he would've returned to life as before if his father could've been brought back to them.

"Testing…Testing…" Pearl Winslow, the Animal Shelter's manager tapped her finger on the microphone attached to the podium. "Sounds like we're up and running," she announced as the sound system emitted an ear-offending squeal. "You all know Bev Lockhart, I'm sure. As this year's president of our volunteers' group, Bev has been responsible for organizing today's box luncheon and has done a wonderful job. Let's give her a round of applause."

Immediately, the audience obliged, as Bev approached the podium and Jim Laidlaw let out a wolf whistle from where he sat next to Jack Jefferson a few rows back from the stage.

"Thank you all for coming here today to support the Captain's Point Animal Shelter," Bev said. "Please tour our kennels after lunch, and feel free to take one of our friends home with you."

"Got any kittens?" a woman called from the back row.

"Kittens and puppies," Bev assured them, "but remember, it's first come, first served. Now let's get started, because I'm sure some of you gentlemen can hardly wait to part with your money for a chance to eat lunch with one of these lovely ladies behind me. We will start with those who have done us the honor of participating today only, and then we'll move on to our regular volunteers, finishing with myself. As stated on the posters around town, bidding in each case will begin at ten dollars. When making a bid, please raise your placard with your number on it, so we can keep track of the bids. We are set up to accept cash, checks and most credit cards."

Sitting next to Susan Chesterton, Edwina allowed her gaze to once again land on Arthur where he sat on the end of the third row. How handsome he looked in his white shirt and blue tie! She straightened her shoulders as he glanced in her direction and sent her a smile.

Next to her, Susan searched those seated beneath the tent, still not finding her cousin amongst the crowd, her worst fear being that no one would bid on her box. At least she could count on Jim to come through for her, she thought, but then maybe not. Why had she allowed herself to be talked into this? She wondered at her own stupidity, even as she met Jack Jefferson's calm gaze.

"The first box lunch to be auctioned was brought today by Becca Tate," Bev started the ball rolling. "Becca is a student at the junior college and is currently completing an internship with Dr. Elizabeth Chesterton as well. Do I hear a bid?"

"Ten dollars," a tall, skinny young man, who Edwina recognized as one of the bag boys from the local chain grocery, called out.

"Fifteen dollars," a more Ivy-League looking contender raised his placard.

"Twenty dollars." The original bidder stuck out his chin.

"Twenty-five," Ivy-League accepted the challenge.

"Do I hear another bid?" Bev asked. "No? Going once. Going twice…"

"Thirty dollars." The audience turned as one to see who had entered the bidding, finally locating Jeff Stuart where he held his placard high at the back of the tent having just arrived.

"Bless his heart," Edwina whispered into Susan's ear. "That's a lot of money for him."

"Thirty-five," Ivy-League raised the ante.

"Forty." Jeff's placard once again was held high.

Catching a glimpse of Becca, Edwina thought a look of relief had flashed across the girl's face.

"Forty-five." Ivy-League refused to be deterred.

"Fifty." Jeff held his ground, at which his opponent shook his head to indicate a negative in response to Bev's questioning look.

"I have fifty dollars going once, going twice…," Bev raised the gavel. "Becca Tate's box lunch sold to Jeff Stuart for fifty dollars. What a wonderful start!"

Slowly, but steadily the box lunches were auctioned off, Arthur starting the bidding for Edwina's at two hundred and fifty dollars, effectively precluding any other bidders in a single stroke.

"Oh, dear, I wish now that I'd made lobster salad instead of fried chicken," Edwina admitted to Susan before standing and joining Arthur where he waited to walk with her and find seats at one of the tables.

"The next box lunch was brought today by Susan Chesterton," Bev announced. "Do I hear ten dollars?"

"Fifty dollars!" Larry Chesterton grinned at his cousin from the back of the tent, having been held up by a client. "I understand this box comes with a homemade lemon meringue pie."

"One hundred dollars." Jack Jefferson held up his placard, his pilot's eyes smiling at Susan where she sat on the stage.

"Two hundred." Jim Laidlaw's placard shot up.

"Three hundred." Jefferson met the challenge.

Bev looked to where Larry had stood in the back, but discovered that he was now deep in conversation with one of the city councilmen.

"Five hundred." Jim held his placard up again.

"Seven hundred." A slow smile revealed Jack's dimples.

"Eight-fifty." Jim grinned.

"One thousand dollars." Jefferson evened the amount.

"I'm out," Jim leaned over towards his opponent. "I was just forcing you up on behalf of the shelter. I already enjoy Susan's company as often as I want merely for the price of a meal at any of our local restaurants. Besides, I've got my eye on another prize."

"I should've stuck you with the bill," Jack chuckled, "but you see, I've always been inordinately fond of homemade lemon meringue pie."

And with that having been said, he rose from his seat and strode forward to claim his prize, as Jim's eyes traveled from Susan to Bev where she was efficiently auctioning off the next lunch. Fifteen years to pay for a youthful misjudgment had been long enough, he determined as his hand tightened on his placard.

"Humor me," Jack took Susan's arm when they reached the last row. "Let's sit here for a moment." He indicated two empty seats, gesturing for her to go first. "I want to have a little fun with my veterinarian."

"You men never grow up, do you?" Susan teased, noting the twinkle in his dark eyes.

"Bidding on anyone special?" Jack leaned forward and addressed the dentist.

"Possibly," the soft-spoken younger man acknowledged. "Although, I'm not prepared to go quite as high as you did."

"It was the lemon meringue pie, you see." Jack sent Susan a sheepish grin. "I've always been a slave to it."

"Oh, go on." Susan rolled her eyes and tried to focus for a minute on the bidding.

"Now we'll proceed to the lunches brought by our own shelter volunteers, the first one having been provided by Karen Zobel."

Next to her, Susan noted that the quiet dentist sat up a bit straighter and gave him a closer look. Dark hair and eyes, the latter filled with an innate kindness – Karen could do worse, she decided and silently wished him good luck in his bidding.

"Do I hear ten dollars?" Bev asked.

"Ten dollars." A young man a few rows up from where Jack and Susan sat raised his placard.

"Twenty." Another man on the other side of the tent spoke up.

"Thirty." The first man went for a second bid, at which the second signaled no further interest.

"Forty." Beside them, David Eskar raised his placard.

"Fifty."

"Sixty."

And so it went until the quiet dentist raised his voice and called, "One hundred dollars."

"One hundred dollars going once. One hundred dollars going twice…" Bev raised her gavel and sent the bidder a grin. "Sold to David Eskar, the best dentist I've ever been to, for one hundred dollars."

Relieved that no one else in the room valued his Karen as much as he did, David rose and moved forward to settle his tab, firm in the knowledge that while he had been forced by circumstances to set a limit on what he could bid, he would have given the world if he could have.

Having made quick work of the remaining meals up for bid, Bev passed the gavel to Pearl, who announced, "This has already been our most successful event to date, but we have one final lunch up for bid, brought by our own Bev Lockhart."

"Come on." Jack took Susan's hand, balancing the pie she had brought in his other one. "This is what we've been waiting for."

The two moved into seats in the row right behind Jim Laidlaw, one of the few men remaining, where they sat quietly waiting by unspoken agreement, Susan's blue eyes laughing back at Jack's dark ones.

"Do I hear a bid for ten dollars?" Pearl asked.

"Fifty dollars." Jim raised his placard.

"Sixty." The owner of the local organic market raised his.

"Seventy-five." Jim's placard rose up again.

"One hundred." The market owner stayed in.

"Two hundred," the veterinarian called out.

"Two hundred going once. Going twice…" Pearl raised her gavel, having received a negative shake of his head from the store owner.

"Four hundred." Jack raised his placard and winked at Susan.

"Five hundred dollars." Jim's head jerked around as he raised his placard.

"I'll let you off easy this time," Jack said, grinning back at him, "but I had to get at least a little of mine back. Why don't Bev and you join Susan and me at that table for four, once you've written your rubber check?"

"Should've known you wouldn't be that easy to take for a ride." Jim accepted his medicine. "Save our places, and we'll join you in a minute."

"You don't mind sharing a table with them, do you?" Jack asked Susan as he rose and stepped into the aisle. "I should've asked you first."

"Not at all," she assured him, finding herself suddenly shy in his presence. "Bev was my BFF in high school, and we've kept in touch ever since."

Taking Susan's elbow, Jack steered his prize towards the table where he set down the lemon meringue pie to await their pleasure and then held out her chair. "Susie, that pie of yours looks almost too good to eat." He flashed his dimples as he took a seat himself. "We may have to start with dessert."

Surprised by his use of the diminutive form of her name, Susan's heart glowed at the sound of it rolling so comfortably off his tongue. Still, she was relieved when Jim and Bev chose this moment to join them, afraid that her face might reveal her response too clearly to the man who had paid so much for the pleasure of her company.

CHAPTER XXXII

After dinner on Monday, it being a pleasant evening, Jack decided to return to the marina to have an informal chat with the security guard who was on duty in an effort to get to know this seldom seen employee a bit better. Striding along towards the marina's office, though, he was surprised to see Susan and Daniel approaching him from the opposite direction.

"Jack!" Daniel broke loose from his mother's hand and ran towards him. "I knew you wouldn't break your promise to see me again soon!"

"Hey, Kiddo!" Jack picked the excited youngster up in defense of his own knees. "How've you been?"

"Casey and I have been fine, but Terror ate something that made him sick," Daniel filled him in as his mother joined them. "Are you going to have a gelato cone, too?"

"Daniel…," Susan started to object, but Jack interrupted her with a wink.

"Surely you're joking." He smiled at the boy in his arms. "Don't you know that I'm treating?"

"My mom and I both want chocolate," Daniel immediately placed his order, "and we always get plenty of napkins."

"A necessary evil I would imagine." Jack's face filled with a grin, revealing his dimples.

"I really can't allow you to…," Susan once again attempted to object.

"Woman, how many times do I have to remind you that it simply isn't done for a mere female to place herself in the path of any man who has a beloved food item in his sights?" Jack threw his free arm around her and headed them in the direction of the candy store. "Am I right that we will need one small and two large?"

"Yes." Susan let out a small sigh of resignation even as she sent him a smile, feeling very girlish in his strong masculine presence.

"Three chocolate gelato cones - one small and two large - and one bottled water," Jack gave the teenaged girl behind the counter their order. "With a double order of napkins, please." He passed a twenty dollar bill across the glass counter and then accepted his change, dropping it into the tip bucket. "Inside or out?" He turned to Susan.

"Outside, if you don't mind," she suggested. "It's such a nice evening."

Finding an empty table for four on the boardwalk, they were soon settled – Daniel having insisted on being allowed to sit on Jack's knee and then having been admonished by his mother not to drip from his cone onto their friend's jeans.

"So how was your day?" Jack addressed Susan as soon as Daniel's gelato had been reduced to a safe level.

"Busy, productive, hectic, glad it's over," she replied. "Don't get me wrong. I love my work, but I wish there was some way I could put in shorter hours or, at least, do more of it from home."

"Is that something you might be able to arrange once Chase returns from his honeymoon?" Jack asked, wishing he could wave a magic wand and make it happen for her.

"Possibly, we've already hired two new associates, and a resume for a third candidate arrived on my desk this morning." She took another bite of her gelato. "It's something I believe Chase would be open to for both of us, once things settle down a bit. How do you like working here at the marina?"

"Fine." He bit off some of his cone to buy time, thinking it best not to mention the mess he had discovered in Captain Reb's wake. "All of the staff welcomed me on board, and I enjoy working around boats and the water."

"No regrets?"

"No regrets. It gets me out and around people, most of whom are enjoying a good time, and I will spend a minimal amount of time at a desk." He separated three napkins from their supply, moistened them with some of the bottled water, efficiently wiped Daniel's mouth and fingers, and then asked the now presentable child, "Have you colored any more pictures in your book?"

"The next page was a big plant in a pot, and I've done that," the boy shared. "Casey and I weren't sure what color to use for the camel, though."

"I might be able to help you there," Jack offered. "The camel I rode was about this color." He pointed to a stripe in the boy's shirt.

"You rode a camel?" Daniel's eyes widened. "Jack rode a camel," he told his mother excitedly, in case she might have missed this extraordinary news from her seat a full three feet away.

"So I heard." She smiled at her son.

"Actually, I've ridden several of them over the years," Jack admitted, "but that was the color of most of them."

"Have you ridden any other animals besides horses and camels?" the boy asked.

"An elephant or two." Jack turned twinkling eyes to Susan who rolled her own in return. "I was once asked if I was training to work for a circus."

"I liked riding Silver Queen and Goldie," Daniel stated in his firm way, "but someday, I'm going to ride an elephant – a big one."

"I hope you do." Jack was pleased when the child laid his head on his chest and snuggled against him. "You should always have goals."

"Like learning to read bigger books all by myself?"

"Definitely like reading big books all by yourself," Jack agreed. "Books can take you anywhere in the universe."

"I'm going to Mars," Daniel whispered, his eyelids drooping.

"I hope this won't mess up his schedule for you," Jack said in a soft voice to Susan a few minutes later, when it was obvious that her son had left them for Dreamland.

"Not at all," she replied. "Once he's asleep, he's out for the night. He won't even wake up when I put him in his pajamas."

For a few minutes, they shared a comfortable silence as they watched the boats coming in.

"Would you be free tomorrow evening?" Jack asked, keeping his voice soft. "I've bought a new grill, and you could help me break it in, if you would join me at the house after work."

Susan hesitated, thinking of how she had planned to spend a longer evening with Daniel, but then she realized how happy this man had made both her and her young son, who was even now being held in his strong arms. "My last appointment is at three-thirty tomorrow, and it shouldn't run too long. What time would you want me?"

"Why don't you come between five-thirty and six, since it's a work evening?"

"I'll look forward to it." Susan rose from her chair and put out her arms to take Daniel, but while he stood as well, Jack retained the sleeping boy in his arms.

"Let me carry him to your car," he said. "Is it that way?" He nodded in the direction from which they had been walking when he had spotted them.

"Thank you," she agreed as they began strolling along. "Not just for carrying Daniel, but for making the evening so nice for both of us."

"It was truly my pleasure." He smiled down at her. "You must know that my evening was enhanced by spending it with the two of you."

"I have so many memories of nice times at this marina," she shared, surprised by the number of people they passed who greeted Jack as well as her with a smile or a lifted hand in greeting as they walked by. How quickly this newcomer had made himself a welcomed part of their community!

"Here we are." She unlocked her car as they approached, pleased to see how easily Jack settled Daniel into his child seat and fastened the safety belts around him. "Thank you again."

"Thank you." He took her hand and gave it a gentle squeeze as he opened her door for her. "Could you use some help getting him up the stairs to his room?"

"No, I'm fine. If Dad catches me coming in, though, he'll insist on carrying Daniel up."

"I'll hope that your father is listening for you to get back then, and I'll look forward to seeing you again tomorrow evening at my place."

And with that, he closed her door and stepped back, waiting to wave goodbye as she drove slowly away, wishing with all of his heart that he could've taken them both home with him.

CHAPTER XXXIII

Susan arrived at Jack's home for dinner the next evening promptly at five-thirty, having stopped by The Cove and changed into jeans and a casual top on her way there after work. As she approached the front door, her thick blonde hair that had been pulled back into a ponytail bobbed back and forth in time with her light steps.

"Susie, you get prettier each time I see you!" Her host said, his dimples in evidence as he swung open the front door before she could turn the old-fashioned doorbell.

"Thank you." She stopped herself from responding in kind as she took in how nicely his striped golf shirt showed off his broad chest. No wonder Daniel always wanted to snuggle his head against it.

"You're right on time." Jack stepped back and gestured for her to come in. "I saw you drive up through the breakfast room windows." He led their way into the kitchen where the aroma of baking potatoes filled the room. "Would you be up for a glass of wine?"

"That would be nice," she agreed, noting he once again had fresh flowers arranged in a vase on the table. "What can I do to help?"

"You can sit down and decorate my kitchen with your lovely presence." He disappeared into the butler's pantry, returning a few moments later with a bottle of chilled chardonnay and two glasses. "This should go well with our dinner." He made quick work of the cork and poured them each a glass. "We're having a fairly simple meal, because I didn't want to spend all of our time together cooking."

"I'm sure whatever you're making will be delicious." She accepted her glass and then watched as he pulled a baking dish from the large fridge and removed marinated pork loin chops with tongs, placing them on a plate where they waited to be taken to the grill, after which he put some corn on the stove to boil.

"This is a meal that I first had in Brazil, although they served it with beans and rice as well as the roasted potatoes, adding even more carbs," he explained. "Now let me show you what I've been up to." He indicated for her to follow him through the mudroom, where he held open the door to the outside. "My new patio area stands ready for your inspection, ma'am."

"Oh, my! You said you had bought a new grill!" Susan exclaimed as she caught her first glimpse of a brand new outdoor kitchen and covered patio, complete with a large grill, a smoker, a sink and a small fridge tucked beneath a granite countertop as well as a fire pit and seating area off to the side. "You have been busy."

"I like cooking and eating outdoors whenever the weather permits," he pointed out. "Do you approve of the way I've had it done?"

"Very much!" She raised smiling eyes to his. "You'll enjoy having this as much as we enjoy the pavilion my uncle installed on our beach at The Cove."

"That's what I thought." He busied himself at the grill. "These won't take but a couple of minutes. As you can see, I've set the table out here, but if you would rather eat inside, it won't take me but a moment to switch gears."

"This is fine," she assured him, once again struck by his willingness to change his plans in deference to her, something her ex had never even considered. "It would be a shame to waste such a nice evening. What's in the marinade?"

"Oil, vinegar, fresh herbs, salt and pepper," he shared. "You relax and put your workday behind you, while I stick some biscuits in the oven."

Settling into her comfortable chair at the large rectangular teak table that sported fresh wildflowers in its center, Susan once again wondered how much all of these improvements were costing her host. Not only were they extensive changes and upgrades, but as far as she could tell, everything had been done utilizing high end appliances and countertops – all reflective of Jack's obvious good taste.

The scent of the pine woods to her left blended with the sea air in a way that she had come to love over the years and had missed so much during her time in D.C. Pleased, she noted that the patio and kitchen had been designed in such a way as to maximize the ocean view from this side of the house. She wouldn't have changed a thing.

"Let me turn these one more time, and then we should be about ready," Jack said as he rejoined her. "Yep, they're almost done."

"Are you sure I can't help?" she asked, feeling quite lazy as she watched him bustle around.

"Absolutely not." He held his ground. "You've worked a hard day, and frankly, I haven't. Fishing a little girl's doll out of the drink was the hardest challenge I had to face. That and having to rid myself yet again of Captain Reb, who seems to be having some trouble cutting the umbilical cord."

"I feel sorry for the poor captain." Susan attempted to keep a straight face. "Tiny probably expects him to actually work."

"I believe you have just hit the nail on its head." Jack chuckled as he set a plate of perfectly grilled pork on the table. "I'll be right back."

A minute later he returned with a baking dish full of roasted potatoes and a bowl of buttered corn, followed on his next trip with a basket of biscuits and the bottle of wine. "You're welcome to eat yours however you wish, but I was taught to do this." He cut one of the loin chops in half, split open a biscuit, buttered the latter and then placed the pork in it, before repeating the process once again.

"I think I'll try one your way," Susan said, intrigued, and proceeded to assemble one of her own as he served her some potatoes and corn. "So have you picked up a lot of recipes from your travels?"

"Tons of them," he told her between bites. "Frankly, I would've starved to death if I hadn't learned to at least cook some basics early on, and then I switched back and forth between not being willing to eat someone else's badly cooked food and wanting to learn from a true master."

"This meal is perfect." She helped herself to another biscuit as the sun slipped a few degrees closer to the horizon and the birds settled down for the night. "Remind me when we are inside again, Daniel sent you his camel picture. Understand you aren't to keep it, only to pass judgment on whether or not he got the color right."

"Bless his heart that boy's a charmer." Jack chuckled, and Susan couldn't help but feel pleased by his reaction to such a strange request. "I'll certainly take a look at it before you go, and give you my honest opinion."

Having finished their meal, Susan insisted on carrying the leftovers into the kitchen as he gathered their dishes and glasses onto a tray. Once inside, though, she again found herself relegated to a kitchen chair as he put away the food and loaded the dishwasher, after which he brewed a French press full of coffee and served each of them a bowl of vanilla ice cream drizzled with Kahlua. "In here, back on the patio, or on the porch in the rockers watching the sunset?" he asked.

"On the porch, if you don't mind," she indicated her preference, following him through the house where soft lamplight here and there illuminated their way with a warm, welcoming glow.

Placing the tray he had carried onto the rough-hewn table, he passed her a bowl of ice cream and set her coffee mug within reach, as she once again marveled at how comfortable it was to be with him and not because he was waiting on her hand and foot. Somehow she knew it would be just as comfortable to work alongside him or even to meet one of life's challenges, his quiet strength being more than enough to pull them through.

"Before the sun gets any lower, you should probably pass judgment." She handed Jack the folded picture that Daniel had sent along with her as soon as they had both finished their desserts, surprised when her host actually took a few moments to study her son's coloring.

"He took some real time over this," Jack commented and then turned the picture her way. "See how much better he's stayed within the lines? Tell him the color is perfect, and that it's really good work since he seems to value my opinion."

"I will," she assured him. "He'll be pleased."

For a few minutes, they sat in silence, enjoying their coffee as Susan rocked slowly back and forth and Jack built up his courage.

"I have a little something for you as well." He held out an envelope, retaining his hold on it once she held it in her fingers. "Please let me explain completely before you open it."

"Okay," she agreed, curious. Already aware that whatever was in the envelope carried some weight, she set it on the table and prepared to listen, not surprised when he reached over and took her hand, even as he turned in his rocker and looked out over the water.

"I've already shared with you why I started on my travels," he began after a few moments. "While leaving our homes in Virginia was the right thing to do for both my uncle and me, it wasn't always that easy for either of us. At least, not at the beginning."

Susan again noted the pain that ran beneath his words.

"The first time you visited me here, you mentioned that you had been in the habit of using this porch as a quiet place to think, and I can understand your need to do that after all you've been through. It took a lot of courage to leave your husband and strike out on your own with your child, even knowing that you would have your family's support." He turned and faced her. "I want you to know that I admire you for that."

"Thank you." She felt the prick of tears and fought them back, thinking Jack Jefferson must view her as a regular crybaby at this point.

"Your friend may well have been right," he continued. "You need time by yourself in which to process your divorce – to grieve for your dashed hopes for your marriage, pack it away and find a place for it in your heart."

"Yes," she agreed, not quite sure yet where he was taking them.

"This was your place long before it was mine," he went on, once again facing the sea spread out before them, "and I understand, perhaps more than most, how much a place or a view can speak to you and allow you to tap into a healing energy that we mere mortals don't yet understand. Uncle Ivan made you welcome here for many years, and he would want you to feel free to use this as your place to come to terms with what's happened to you."

"But…"

"Please hear me out, Susie." He turned and once again faced her, his voice soft, his expression filled with kindness. "Most weekdays I'm at the marina until six, and even if I'm here, you are always welcome to come and sit on this porch, to rock back and forth and lose yourself in the view as you clear your mind for a good think. You don't even have to knock on the door or speak to me, if you'd rather not. You need this, my uncle would've wanted you to have it and I do, too. Remember, I have Paint Clan blood in my veins, and we're all about healing."

"But I couldn't…"

"Yes, you could, and what's more you're going to – not just for yourself, but for Daniel as well. The sooner you can get that part of your lives completely behind you both, the better. This envelope contains a key to the house and the security code that I'll show you how to use before you leave. I'm giving you the latter so that you can have access to the house, because I want you to be able to pour yourself a glass of lemonade or grab a bottled water to drink if you've walked over. When you no longer need the key, you can return it, although it wouldn't hurt for someone other than me to have a key and you, as a senior partner, are my attorney. Please let me do this for Daniel and you."

"I don't know what to say." She knew that once again her eyes were awash with tears.

"Say, yes." He held her gaze. "Say that you will allow me to be here for the two of you. Say that you will let me be your friend."

"Put like that I can hardly say no, can I?" She sent him a watery smile.

"There's no reason why you should." He released her hand, picked up a napkin from the tray, stood and then sat on his heels in front of her rocker, gently drying her wet cheeks, fighting the urge to take her into his arms. "Don't you think you've hurt long enough for something you didn't cause and couldn't change, Susie?"

Embarrassed by her inability to control the tears that continued to come in the face of his kindness, she merely nodded her agreement, loving his use of the diminutive form of her name. "I feel that I have so much to thank you for – your kindness to me and to Daniel, all the things that you've done for both of us," she finally found her voice.

"That's what friends are for." He stood, placed another napkin near her on the table and returned to his chair, allowing her some space. "I thought you understood that having grown up in a small town. Don't most of the folks around here leave their doors unlocked, so their neighbors can drop off fresh picked vegetables from their gardens or a jar of homemade preserves whenever they want? All I'm asking of you is that you let me lend you my porch."

"You're right." Wiping her eyes one final time, Susan managed a small laugh. "I guess I'm a little out of practice, having lived in the big city for so long."

"Well, then, you'll just have to relearn." He smiled back at her, reaching across the table and once again taking her slim hand in his strong one. "Because, at the very least, we're going to be friends for a long time to come."

CHAPTER XXXIV

Later that evening, Susan entered Daniel's bedroom and placed his colored picture of a camel on his bedside table where he would see it in the morning. Jack had been right, she realized as she kissed her finger and placed it gently against her child's cheek, her son did respect and value their new friend's opinion in a way he had never done with his own father. The new man in her life had become important in more ways than one to her Daniel.

As she returned to her own room, she remembered her son's excited cry the evening before on the boardwalk at the marina and the way he had run to greet Jack, as well as the honest pleasure at having spotted them that had been reflected on their friend's face. In some ways, she recognized the two of them were much the same – both being in the habit of saying what they meant and meaning exactly what they said only, thankfully, Jack used more discretion.

Her mind too full of thoughts to allow her to sleep, she dropped onto the chaise lounge in her room that allowed her a view of the moonlit lawn and the ocean beyond. Jack had meant what he had said to her this evening. He intended for them to be friends for a long time to come.

How much more did he hope for from their relationship, and how far was she willing to take it? A man didn't pay a thousand dollars for a picnic lunch, a lemon meringue pie and an hour of your company merely to throw his money around, nor did he go to so much trouble to provide special settings and additional touches for times spent together.

For a few moments, she attempted to clear her mind, but soon found the task to be an impossible one. Alright, she told herself, what were the pluses and minuses of allowing this relationship to develop further?

On the plus side, Jack was a genuinely nice person. He had exhibited nothing but kindness to both Daniel and her. He recognized, understood and cared about her innermost needs – evidence his amazing offer this evening. He was gentle and soft-spoken, and yet there was an inner presence and strength that could not be denied. He had felt great pain in his life, but had survived it a better man than when it had found him. He was open and friendly, and he had already become a welcomed part of the community she loved and had indicated both by his words and his actions that he intended to make Captain's Point his permanent home.

If he didn't yet care for Daniel, he certainly had been open to her child's presence in their relationship. Her mind sifted through memories of their trip to the emergency room, his strong fingers gently removing all traces of gelato from her child's sticky ones, his insistence on carrying Daniel to her car and the ease with which he had settled him into his child seat, and the time and respect he had taken in responding to Daniel's request for his opinion of the colored camel. Everything in her being told her that Jack would make a good father, but did he wish to be one?

Even her friends and her family liked this man. Both her father and her mother at one time or another had made their positions clear. Larry had taken an instant liking to him and had continued to sing his praises after he had gotten to know him better. Chase, Larry and Jack had been like The Three Musketeers at the Labor Day cookout, and all of the musicians who had played with him at the inn's pre-opening event had obviously liked and respected him.

So, if Daniel hadn't been part of the picture, what would she have wanted from this relationship? Sure she valued Jack's friendship, but how much further would she have wanted them to take things?

Suddenly, she found it more difficult to be honest with herself, the feelings that he aroused still being touched by the pain caused by the dissolution of her marriage, and yet, she recognized at the same time that she needed to know and understand her feelings as they pertained to this man.

Again her mind recalled past events – the way he had taken her breath away as he had returned her purse, his music calling to her, the way her body cried out to be taken into his strong arms, his efforts both to meet her needs and to please her, the gentleness with which he had wiped her tears. And yet, for all the ways in which he both spoke and called to her, he had never smothered her, he had never diminished either her legal work or the parenting demands imposed upon her by Daniel. Around him, she could breathe freely. Even their silences were comfortable.

Love, she had long since come to realize, was a two-way street, and she had never really known it, even within her marriage to a man who had said that he wanted her but had never given the slightest part of himself to her. Jack Jefferson had already shared more of his inner self with her than any man before him, almost always in aid of her own healing. So, did he love her, and did she love him?

Yes, the answer came back clear and strong in her head, she did. Now only two questions remained – how did Daniel fit into this picture and what were Jack's overall intentions?

Rising from the chaise lounge, she picked up from her bedside table the envelope Jack had given her after dinner, taking care that she knew how to enter the security code on his front porch before allowing her to leave and then drawing her to him and holding her close.

"I would do anything to release you from the pain that you feel," he had said softly before dropping a kiss onto the top of her head. "Thank you for allowing me to do this small bit."

And then, her tears had come once again, and he had held her tightly to him, filling her with a need to remain in his strong presence even as he demanded nothing from her in return.

Finally, she had withdrawn herself from his grasp, uttered another quick thank you almost under her breath, and hurried to her car where she had wiped the tears that remained on her cheeks as she had driven carefully away, knowing that he had watched her from his porch.

Slipping beneath her bed's covers, she slid the envelope beneath her pillow and then turned off the bedside lamp, before trying to recapture the feel of Jack Jefferson's strong arms around her as she drifted into a deep, peaceful sleep.

CHAPTER XXXV

"That's the last of them." Bridgette passed the firm's female senior partner yet another document to sign.

"Finally!" Susan made quick work of her signature, initialed six other pages and clicked her pen closed, before glancing at the time on her computer screen. "If I hurry, I'll be able to spend a couple of hours with Daniel before dinner."

But, when she entered The Cove a few minutes later, she found the normal hub-bub to be missing. Perhaps, she thought as she made her way through the quiet downstairs rooms to her mother's home office, her son was still napping.

"You're home early." Elizabeth removed a pair of black-framed reading glasses, placed them on her desk and greeted her daughter. "What a nice surprise!"

"I was hoping to spend some time with Daniel before dinner, but I guess he's still asleep." His frustrated mother plopped into a leather upholstered visitor's chair.

"Actually, he's out with friends," her mother said.

"Oh? Who?" Not for the first time, Susan felt a stab of guilt at not being more involved in her son's day to day life.

"Jack Jefferson." Elizabeth absentmindedly tucked a stray lock into the loose coil of hair on the back of her head.

"Jack?" Her daughter didn't hide her surprise. "You let Daniel go off with Jack?"

"Why not?" Her mother met her gaze head on. "Jack's a nice man, and they were going to meet up with Chase at the farm. The two of them are taking Daniel out riding with them. I found it to be a kind and generous offer, and it won't hurt your son to spend time in the company of two men who are younger than your father."

"No…," Susan admitted, "and if Chase is there, too, Daniel won't come to any harm."

"Are you telling me that he could've come to harm if Chase hadn't been included in the plans?" Elizabeth asked, her eyebrows lifting in surprise.

"Of course not..." Susan groped for words to explain something that she hadn't yet thought through completely herself. "Jack's a good man, and he's been wonderful to Daniel."

"And..." Elizabeth gave her no quarter.

"It's more about me than about Jack," Susan said, finding it hard to explain. "How did you do it, Mom? You worked, and there were three of us. Still, you were always there watching over us, playing games with us, reading to us, giving us our baths and tucking us in for the night."

Elizabeth laughed. "I'm glad that's how you remember it," she said, her face sobering. "Your brother might tell a much different story, while Courtney's memories would more closely approximate yours. It took me some time and a great deal of practice to find the right balance between career and motherhood, and believe me, your father often despaired that I would. And yet, all three of you turned out just fine. Children are really quite resilient, you know. They need to be fed, clothed and, most of all, loved. They also appreciate some level of routine and a clear understanding of their boundaries, but that's about it."

"Grandma, I'm home!" An excited young voice called to them from the foyer.

"Speak of the devil." Elizabeth rose as the sound of running feet could be heard approaching.

"Mama!" Daniel burst into the room. "You're here! I had the bestest time. I rode Silver Queen and then Jack let me ride Goldie in the saddle with him and Chase rode The Black. We went into the woods and found a pond and Chase brought molasses cookies Aunt Adrianna made and Jack put our drinks in the water to get cold and The Black snorted at a squirrel and..." Here the small bundle of energy was forced to take a breath.

"One young rider returned safe and sound, ma'am," Jack stated calmly from where his tall frame and broad shoulders filled the doorway.

Susan looked up from smoothing Daniel's hair with her fingers, noting the twinkle in his benefactor's eyes. "Thank you." She sent the man before her a heartfelt smile. "I haven't seen him this excited in a long time."

"Jack said we could all three go to Chester's," Daniel announced.

"Now, Partner, that's not exactly accurate," Jack corrected him. "I said we would ask your mother if she would enjoy an early supper at Chester's in our company."

"That's right," the four-year-old agreed. "Gentlemen have to ask the ladies' permissions to escort them." Then he paused, before continuing, "It's a bother, but there it is."

"Yes, well…" Jack had the grace to look sheepish. "I didn't intend for you to quote me quite so accurately."

For a moment, Susan met her mother's gaze as both fought the laughter welling up inside of them.

"Will you, Mama?" Daniel tugged at his mother's hand. "Will you give your permission for us to go to Chester's?"

"I'd need to pop over to the inn for a shower," Jack added his two cents worth. "I could pick you both up in about an hour if that would work."

"You'll need a bath, too." Susan glanced down at her son's eager face, but then met Jack's gaze. "We'd be delighted to join you for supper," she accepted his invitation, pleased by the look of pleasure that flashed across his face.

"Thank goodness that's settled!" Elizabeth sat back down at her desk and reached for her reading glasses. "Now, if you three party-goers will excuse me, some of us need to work."

CHAPTER XXXVI

Time flew by for Edwina. Between babysitting Lucy, helping Arthur several times in his gallery and lunches enjoyed with him in the gazebo, Friday night was soon upon her. Having just returned from the beauty salon, she now attended to her final preparations for an evening with the new man in her life.

A royal blue silk dress waited inside her closet. Noting the time, she opened the velvet lined jewelry box that Ham, Jr., had given her long ago as a Mother's Day gift, revealing a matching set of fresh water pearls and earrings she had selected to complement her outfit.

Filled with a growing sense of anticipation, she hoped it would never go away. At least for tonight, all the uncertainty of her course was gone as she delighted in the prospect of what was to come. Slipping into her dress, she made sure that her hairstyle had remained in place and that her make-up concealed all tell-tale signs of age, feeling twenty-one again in her heart.

At precisely six o'clock, the dependency's doorbell rang announcing the arrival of her date.

"Don't you look handsome tonight? Please come in." She breathed in the enticing aroma of Arthur's spice aftershave, thinking he looked very dapper in his blue suit and dress shoes, his eyes sparkling with warmth as he presented her with a small bouquet of white roses.

"These are gorgeous." She smiled at him. "Roses are my favorites."

"I'm a little out of practice in this area, so my daughter-in-law made a few suggestions." He sent her a nervous smile of his own. "Tonight, the restaurant features dancing under the stars on their outdoor pier. I thought we could give it a whirl after dinner."

"I haven't danced in years," Edwina stated. "Sounds like fun, but I must warn you that I may be stepping on the toes of your shoes all night."

"No worries." He lifted one shoulder in a slight shrug. "Dancing is like riding a bike. Once you learn, you never forget. Shall we go?"

Edwina gathered her shawl and purse from the loveseat, and then Arthur took her hand as they walked towards his car.

"I want this evening to be unforgettable," he remarked as he held the passenger door for her.

Feeling giddy as a school girl, Edwina lost herself in the moment, surprisingly relaxed as they strolled hand in hand towards the entrance to the restaurant.

"We're lucky this evening," Arthur winked at her. "Chase and Adrianna have other plans, so I've reserved the restaurant's best table."

Edwina nodded as they followed the maitre d' past other diners, then settled into the private banquette as chef-owner John Thornburg approached.

"Nice to see you again," he greeted them. "Ms. Montgomery suggested that I offer you a tasting menu this evening with special wines selected for each course. How does that sound?"

"That would make our evening unforgettable!" Arthur beamed at his date.

"Marvelous! This is quite exciting!" Her blue eyes twinkled back at him.

"If you'll excuse me then, we'll get you started." John returned to his kitchen.

"We'll have to thank Adrianna and Chase." Arthur placed his napkin in his lap. "This is amazing, and I'm starving."

"Oh, good, we're still starting with the cream of crab soup." Edwina smiled up at their waiter as he set a cup in front of each of them. "It's my favorite item on the menu."

"And I see that John has paired it with a dry California Riesling," Arthur pointed out. "This wine reminds me of a trip Sylvia and I took to Napa in late summer about twenty years ago. I'd love to show you the family-owned vineyard that we discovered there. At one time, I toyed with the idea of buying one myself, but my better half prevailed."

"Sometimes we must wait until the timing of our dreams is right," his date replied. "Ham and I always talked about visiting the wine country, but he traveled so much for his job that after he retired all he wanted to do was stay home and paint."

"Can you blame him?" Arthur took a sip from his glass.

"Not now that I've moved to Captain's Point and am having the opportunity to experience so many new and exciting things, but there was a time after he passed away when I felt somewhat cheated."

"It's all about balance in a relationship, isn't it?" His eyes filled with understanding.

"Now, though, you own Artful Soul - the shop, gallery and teaching space you had always dreamed of," Edwina strove to lighten the moment. "That's pretty special, too."

"Again, you're so right, my sweet Edwina," Arthur said.

Course by course, the delicacies spanned from tastes of true classics like Caesar salad and Lobster Thermidor to cutting edge molecular gastronomy, foams acting as sauces and enhancing the assortment of frozen mini desserts.

The couple ate leisurely, admiring the twinkling lights of the pier below and the boats beyond as movement of instruments to the outside restaurant for nighttime dance festivities created a flurry of activity juxtaposed against the serenity of the night sky.

Arthur told story after story as his natural ability to make his date laugh and find the amusement in life dominated after-dinner conversation. Both diners lingered over their coffees, savoring each second of their extraordinary meal, not wanting it to end.

"Waiter," Arthur signaled for their check, then faced Edwina with a smile. "The night has just begun!"

"I can't wait!"

A few minutes later, the couple exited Montgomery's as soft romantic tunes flowed towards them from a well-laid temporary dance floor. Strings of soft white twinkle lights hung suspended in neat rows, and above the sky filled with the sparkle of stars further adding to their evening's enchantment.

"Shall we?" Arthur inquired of his date.

"Of course!" Edwina responded laying her shawl down on a nearby chair.

Taking her hand in his and leading his companion to the dance floor, he assumed the classic position as he placed his right arm across the middle of her back, the musical tune dictating the pace of the couple's footwork as they matched it beat for beat.

The salt air blended with the aroma of Arthur's cologne into an intoxicating mix that Edwina found hard to resist. Having glided along through song after song, the couple and the band decided to take a much needed break.

"This has been a wonderful evening." She smiled up at him.

"And it doesn't have to end yet, does it?" he asked, with a hint of desire.

"No, it doesn't." Realization filled his date's face.

As they waited for the musicians to return, Arthur continued them along their path towards an unforgettable evening by ordering champagne, and the couple toasted Adrianna and Chase and then each other.

"To the future!" Arthur made his wishes clear.

Edwina added an additional toast to her former flight mate. "Here's to Adrianna!" The two clanked glasses again. "Meeting her on that plane from Chicago was fate."

"I second that!" Her date took another sip of the bubbly before taking her hand and guiding her back to the dance floor as the band played a final waltz.

Arthur drew Edwina in closer to him, and she felt herself melt into his arms before she glanced up briefly, gazing into his eyes knowing that all was right with the world and then laying her head once again against his chest.

Having parked his car in front of the carriage house a little while later, Arthur retained his date's hand in his once he had helped her from the car.

"Humor me," he said as he surprised her by heading them towards the gazebo where it stood bathed in moonlight.

"I've had such a wonderful time." She raised her face to his.

"You'll never know how much this evening has meant to me." He drew her close. "Because of you, I'm finally beginning to understand that my life isn't over."

And then, he kissed her with a tenderness she had known only once before, and for the first time, Edwina understood the full measure of the possibilities that lay before them.

CHAPTER XXXVII

Anderson looked over the top of his book to where his client was curled up reading in the chintz-covered armchair next to the fireplace, the glow from the flames dancing there highlighting her golden hair.

For the past three days they had been living a dream - riding horses, flying kites, watching her small son pet all of the animals. They had eaten great food, laughed at bad jokes and she had cried on his shoulder.

Tomorrow they would be heading back to town, and he would see them safely through the lobby of their apartment building and to their front door, where he would have to leave and turn away. How had he allowed himself to get so involved?

Suddenly, the peaceful scene turned to chaos as something burst through the window behind him, and Susan screamed. In one fluid motion he pulled her off the chair and onto the floor, checking to make sure she was okay before he began crawling towards the bedroom from which sounds of her child calling for his mother could be heard.

In one fell swoop, the dream had changed into a nightmare!

Larry Chesterton clicked on Save just as his phone indicated a call from Susan.

"It's about time you called me back," he answered. "I'm driving over to Montgomery House in a few minutes with some papers for Chase and Adrianna to sign before they take off for Maine. Want to tag along?"

"It must be the day for signature lines," she replied. "I have a stack to take over there myself. I'm dropping Daniel off at a party on my way, though, so I'll see you at their place."

Thirty minutes later, Susan parked her car behind her cousin's in the circular drive in front of Montgomery House and disembarked. Hopefully, Chase would sign the papers she carried with her fairly quickly and allow her to continue to her destination – the porch at Jack's house where she hoped to spend a little more time alone.

"We saw you drive up," Adrianna welcomed her from the doorway as she approached. "Chase and Larry are in the library."

"Work, work, work…" Her law partner gave her a hard time as she entered the room, even as he rose from the seating area where he had been visiting with her cousin and approached the library table. "Hand them over, and I'll get these out of the way before my friend over there fills my head with a bunch of figures."

"And this is the thanks I get for all of the hard work I've put in helping you to get your aunt's estate settled." Larry pasted on a hurt look that made no impression whatsoever on those around him.

"That should do it," Susan said as she gathered the legal papers into a neat stack. "I hope you both enjoy a fun and safe trip."

"I'm going to walk over to the farm and touch base one more time with Otis about the remaining renovations to the carriage house, while you two men discuss dollar signs," Adrianna tossed over her shoulder as she accompanied Susan to the front door.

"How is Jack working out as your new marina manager?" Susan asked once they were standing on the front porch.

"Great!" Adrianna sent her a smile. "I've been meaning to thank you for sending him our way. He's had some wonderful ideas and…" She paused for a moment and considered. "It's more than that. I don't know quite how to put it, but he exudes that same kind of quiet competence that Chase and Larry have."

"Oh, that." Susan grinned. "I figured that quality out years ago."

"Well, explain it to me please," Adrianna said, more than willing to delay her conversation with Otis for a few minutes.

"One day when I was about ten, Andy, Larry and Chase decided to build some sort of clubhouse in the woods behind the house," Susan began her story. "Andy was the oldest and should have been the leader, but instead he led them along several false starts. Now there's nothing wrong with Andy's mind, he's brilliant in his own way, but Larry and Chase will always outshine him. If you put each of them in their own locked room and said figure your way out, Andy could do it, but it would take him much longer and you would have to slip him a computer, a pad of paper and a pen through a window. Larry and Chase would both pull a paper clip and a piece of string from one of their pockets and be out in a jif. Jack's the same way, and he takes over a room in the same way that Larry and Chase do, too. I was almost relieved when the three of them were together at your cookout that we were outside and not confined in a small space with all of that energy."

"I know what you mean," Adrianna agreed. "Chase always fills a room with his presence, and when Jack walked into our library for his interview, I was immediately struck by the fact that he filled the space, too. But then, I realized that while they both had that kind of effect, their essences didn't compete any more than Larry's and Chase's do, if you know what I mean. Jack is like Chase and Larry in another way, too. When he leaves and takes that energy with him, you know that you would welcome it back – anytime, anyway – because the world will always be a better place for it."

"Exactly." Susan felt reassured as she took leave of her friend and returned to her car. Her instincts had been accurate in her assessment of Jack Jefferson, beyond what her hormones had been telling her. Adrianna was too focused on Chase in that regard for any such thing to have affected her initial judgments of a new acquaintance.

And with a light heart, she turned her key in the car's ignition and headed along the drive, at the end of which she turned left towards the one place in the world that felt most like home.

CHAPTER XXXVIII

Returning home Wednesday evening, Jack had brewed a cup of coffee and taken it onto the porch to enjoy the soft evening air. Placing his mug on the rough-hewn table before sitting down, a slow smile had taken shape on his face. The rockers on the chair Susan always used, which had lain horizontal to the porch's floorboards that morning, now sat on them slightly askew. Certainly squirrels playing on the porch could have caused the change, but somehow he didn't think so. Susie, he knew in his heart, had found her way home if only for a few minutes.

Friday evening, when he had entered the kitchen, he had known immediately that she had been there, the scent of her light perfume still lingering in the air. A quick examination uncovered that the dishwasher, which had been empty when he had left earlier that morning, now contained one rinsed out tumbler and the level in the pitcher of homemade lemonade he had gotten in the habit of keeping on hand had lowered slightly.

This morning he had worked a few hours at the marina and then returned home. Deciding to make use of the opportunity to play some music in the main parlor after he had let Lady out for a run, he had first played a Rachmaninoff prelude and then some Debussy. Now, though, as he rose to switch to his violin, he noticed a flash of blue outside the window, recognizing Susan's Chester's T-shirt where she sat in her rocker. Taking a chance, he strode to the door onto the porch and opened it.

"I have no idea how long you've been here," he began when she looked up, "because my back was to the window while I was playing."

"I enjoyed the Debussy, and I caught the end of the Rachmaninoff as I came around the house." She smiled back at him.

"For some reason, I've had Debussy's *The Girl with the Flaxen Hair* on my mind for the past couple of days. I can't imagine why." He flashed her a grin. "Will it bother you if I switch to my violin?"

"Not at all."

"Am I right in thinking that Daniel must be engaged elsewhere?" he asked, knowing that she valued her weekend time with her son.

"Yes, he's quite in demand right now on the four-year-old birthday party circuit, often filling the role of the token male," she explained with a straight face.

"Glad to hear that he's holding up the side." He chuckled. "Do you like salmon?"

"Immensely."

"Then you may be in luck." He dove in. "What would you say to my continuing my musical interlude with some violin, after which I'll pack us a picnic? There's a spot on this property that's begging for us to enjoy it before it begins to get cold. You take as long as you want out here, and when you're finished come in. If I'm done packing the lunch, you'll find me across the foyer in my study."

"Sounds too good to resist," Susan accepted his offer. "A concert, a picnic and a good companion, what more could a woman want?"

"Lady and I aim to please," he replied, choosing to keep things light. Then he closed the door and gave her the space that he recognized she needed before he returned to the nook where he waxed his bow and began playing – first his own piece that she had heard at the inn's preopening PR event and then Massenet's *Meditation*.

Out on the porch, Susan rocked softly back and forth as he played. These visits he had arranged for her had allowed her in a few hours to come to grips with her past experiences, to toss out what she no longer wanted and to pack away the rest, leaving only a blank slate. As the haunting strains of his violin floated through the open windows, it was as if they encircled her and then somehow entered her very being, softly etching a new story in place of the old one.

Did the man in the room behind her have any idea how much she loved him? She wondered. Leaving his home and returning to The Cove was becoming more and more difficult as she was forced to decide between staying with him or returning to her Daniel, and yet, there was no way she could choose between the two of them, loving them both the way she now recognized that she did.

As Jack switched from his own piece to the *Meditation*, she felt her heart might burst from the sheer beauty that surrounded her – the ocean spread before her, the house behind her, and his music filling her as the light breeze carried to her the mingled fragrance of the pine woods and the salt air that signified home.

Then the piece came to a close, and she heard him return his instrument to its case, feeling the need to hear more of his song calling to her. True to his word, he didn't disturb her, but rather headed to the kitchen to prepare their lunch as told by the diminishing sound of his footsteps along the hardwood floor of the hallway.

Part of her felt that she should join him and offer to help, but part held her on the porch, relishing the thought of his hands doing this for her, knowing that whatever he was preparing would be put together with care, her tastes and pleasure in mind. How long she had gone without that kind of respect in her life! How hungry she was for it now!

And yet, she wanted to do for him, too, to find some way to ease the pain that she sensed he still carried deep down inside, his need to come home and belong to a family that loved him in the way he deserved - unconditionally. Could Daniel and she fill that need for him? Would he even want them to? These were the questions that would require her attention during future visits to this porch, now that her marriage had been left truly behind her.

Realizing that she was beginning to feel hungry and he probably was, too, she rose from her rocker and entered the house, hearing him discussing with Lady in the kitchen whether or not the dog had been a good enough girl to deserve a treat or two of her own being slipped into the basket.

"What can I do to help?" she asked from the kitchen doorway.

"You can carry this smaller basket that contains the wine and the glasses." He handed it to her. "I'll carry the food." He pointed to a much larger picnic basket. "Give me a minute to close the windows, and then we'll be on our way."

A few minutes later, they stepped off the front porch accompanied by Lady who happily chased a late season butterfly along the paving stone path that led to the other side of the house from Susan's family's farm. "I've never walked in this direction," she said.

"We're not going far," he explained, "but I'm glad it will be your first time to experience this particular spot. It isn't the same as the ocean view, but it's pleasant in its own way."

At the edge of the woods, the rock path morphed into one topped only by a deep layer of pine needles, and Jack indicated for her to go first. Here and there, Susan could see evidence of recent trimming, not for the first time acknowledging to herself the care her companion took of his property. Would he take such good care of a wife and child? Absolutely, the answer came to her mind immediately. It wasn't in him to half apply himself to anything to which he had made a commitment.

"Our destination is just beyond this next bend," Jack filled her in, and she felt her heart quicken with anticipation.

Then their way widened, and he moved alongside her on the path, taking her free hand in his as Lady led the way, apparently familiar with where they were going.

"So what do you think?" He brought her to a stop at the edge of the woods.

In front of them, a large meadow filled with low growing wildflowers sloped gently down to the shores of a lake on which three mallards floated blissfully. Off to their right, two white egrets stood still on their stick-like legs, watching for their own lunch to swim within range. A patio had been laid out in thick brick-colored pavers near the shore, grounded by a surround of small boxwoods, and on it a picnic table and benches sat as well as two Adirondack chairs waiting in the shade of a group of trees.

"It's lovely!" She smiled at him. "I had no idea this was here."

"Lady and I completed the patio during the past week, and Jeff Stuart helped me haul in the furniture," he said. "I've contacted the county extension service about stocking the lake, and I'm hoping you'll allow me to teach Daniel how to fish."

"He would love that!" Susan was touched by his inclusion of her son in his plans. "He always enjoys the time he spends with you. I'm afraid you've become quite a hero."

"Then I'll have to make sure that I live up to his expectations," he said in his steady way, his gaze holding hers. "He deserves better than to be disappointed."

He stepped from the shade of the woods into the meadow, and she kept pace beside him, marveling again at how wonderful it was to be contained in his sphere of influence.

Setting the large basket on one of the benches, Jack opened it to reveal a red and white checked cloth that he spread across the table, anchoring it in place with two large white plastic plates, silverware that included two tiny spoons each, and a number of containers and packages.

Susan noted that he had set both places on the side of the table that would allow for a view of the lake as she took a deep breath of the flower-scented air.

"How far does your property extend?" she asked.

"Originally, my uncle owned this half of the lake, but since his death, I've bought both of the farms that shared the shoreline on the other side," he replied. "I don't want this view or the habitat it represents to be destroyed. I've leased part of the original two farms, including the houses that lie closer to the main highway as it approaches Captain's Point, but the part that accesses the lake is now fenced and protected."

Having glanced at the file pertaining to his uncle's living trust, Susan knew that Ivan's estate had amounted to the house and surrounding property, including a working farm that in recent years had been leased out as well. Approximately two hundred thousand in monetary assets had been included, but these would have been required to complete the upgrades and improvements Jack had made to the house. Obviously, he had brought into play some of what he had acquired during the course of his travels. Certainly, money appeared to be no object as he had set about to create the property of his dreams.

"Have a seat." Her host indicated a spot on the bench, and she obliged as he joined her. "I'll pour us some wine, and then we'll dig in."

Expertly removing the cork from what she recognized from Montgomery's as a rather expensive chardonnay, he then proceeded to surprise her with the menu for their picnic.

"I hope you don't object to my informal presentation," he stated as he placed an egg holder on each of their plates. "These are for the soft-boiled eggs," he explained as he opened an insulated container that held four eggs carefully packed in crinkled paper towels. "And here's our topping." He withdrew a sufficient quantity of Volga Reserve caviar packed in ice. Having opened the container, he scooped the roe into a crystal dish set in ice and added a small sterling spoon. "I've had this on order since before I returned to the States."

"This is amazing!" She placed a warm egg in each of their cups. "What a treat!"

"I knew you would appreciate it." He grinned at her. "The trick was going to be getting you and the weather to provide me with the opportunity to share this with you here within the limited timeframe allowed by the caviar." He reached for another container. "We also have smoked salmon and some lamb dolmades that I whipped up last evening as well as cornichon pickles, Kalamata olives, cheese straws, and goat cheese for after the first course."

"I'm going to have to arrange for Daniel to have a regular Saturday birthday party engagement," Susan stated.

"Glad you're enjoying it."

"I want you to know how much I've appreciated the use of your porch." She focused her eyes on the cracker she was spreading with cream cheese and garnishing with crumbled salmon a little while later. "It's really helped me to get a handle on things. I believe it would now be possible for me to complete an entire evening of conversation without tearing up."

Jack reached over and gave her a quick hug. "I'm glad to hear it. I was considering the purchase of a napkin or tissue factory as a cost-cutting measure," he teased. "You continue coming for as long as you need, though."

"Thank you." She took a bite of her last cracker and then helped him to repack the basket once he had removed one other, fair-sized container.

"Here you go." He handed her a plated wedge of cheesecake. "A friend of mine in New York keeps me supplied."

"Delicious," Susan proclaimed after her first bite.

The cheesecake having been appreciated, Jack packed everything away except for two travel mugs that he filled with coffee from a large thermos, and they adjourned to the Adirondack chairs where they enjoyed the breeze and the view while Lady napped at her owner's feet, conversing comfortably as he shared some of his more humorous experiences at the marina.

"I'm afraid I'd better be going," Susan announced after some time had passed. "Courtney was going to drop Daniel off at The Cove, but Mom will be worried about where I am."

"All good things must come to an end," Jack said, immediately rising from his chair, "but I'm glad this worked out well." He slipped both of their travel mugs into the main basket.

"I am, too." Susan raised her eyes to his as he took her hand.

For a moment, they stood in silence in the shade of the trees as he carefully studied her face, reading only warmth and hope in her eyes, and then he drew her to him and kissed her in a way that filled her heart with a sense of at last having come home.

"I want to create many more memories like this one, here in this place with Daniel and you," he said softly as he held her close.

Not trusting herself to speak, she merely nodded her head in agreement where it lay snuggled against his broad chest, directly over the strong beat of his heart.

"I recognize quality when I see it, and they don't come any better than the two of you," he continued. Then, gently, he lifted her face and kissed her once again before releasing her. "Now let's get you back to civilization."

But she surprised him by taking his hand. "I, too, recognize quality when I see it," she said as she met his gaze with a clear conscience, "although it took me a while to get the trick of it."

"The important thing is that you've learned the lesson." He smiled and then handed her the wine basket and took the larger basket himself, again taking her free hand as they started across the meadow.

Arriving back at his house, he set the basket he was carrying on the porch, took the other one from her, setting it down as well, and then drew her once more into his arms. "You've made me very happy today." He brushed her lips with his. "Time spent with you by my side is a gift."

"I feel the same way about time spent with you," she said lifting her face to his, glad when he once again kissed her as if she would break before walking her to her car.

"Thank you again for everything." She smiled up at him from her seat, and then started the car's engine as he closed her door, trying not to look at him in her rearview mirror as she forced herself to drive away.

CHAPTER XXXIX

Taking their time on their drive to Maine, Chase and Adrianna arrived at the rustic cabin during the late afternoon on Sunday, collected the key from the caretaker and asked for directions to the best place that served genuine lobster rolls. Feeling the need to stretch their legs after the drive, they took a long walk, pleased to find that while the cabin was situated in a way that allowed for privacy it was in actuality right at the edge of town.

Beginning to feel hungry, they located the recommended restaurant and then enjoyed the lobster as they eavesdropped on the conversations around them. Purchasing two large slices of cherry pie to go, they window shopped until dusk and then returned to the cabin where they started a fire in the large hearth to take off the evening chill.

"So what do you think of your real estate?" Chase asked as they relaxed on the couch, Adrianna curled up beside him, her head resting on his shoulder.

"I like the rustic feel, and the town is picturesque," she replied.

"But?"

Adrianna took a minute to gather her thoughts. "I'm not sure that we'll use it that much since it's so far north," she stated. "It's already much colder here than it is back at Captain's Point, and I don't see that we gain much by having driven all the way up here. I'm glad I've seen it and shared the trip with you, but looking forward, I believe it would be in our best interest to realize from it as much rental income as possible."

"I agree now that I've seen it." Chase stood, added another log to the fire, and returned to her side, once again gathering her to him.

"In a way, I'm disappointed," she continued their conversation. "Part of me would like for us to have some place not too far from Captain's Point where we could go and get away from the work that surrounds us at home. The beach house in Key West may prove to be more of an answer, but it's a lot farther from home than I was thinking would be optimal."

"Augustus used to go to the house in Key West as Martha's guest for two weeks every winter, so you may be right."

"May I ask you a question?" Adrianna asked, surprising him as she pulled away to better see his face.

"Of course."

"I've been thinking about our discussions about 'our' money as you put it," she began.

"Yes." His mind traveled back over the merchandise they had viewed in the little town's store windows, trying to think of anything she wouldn't have bought without a second thought if she had wanted it.

"It has occurred to me that, while you have organized everything you brought to our marriage so that we now own it jointly, you have left everything that I inherited from my great-aunt, including Montgomery House and Montgomery Properties, in my name alone," she pointed out. "Basically, what we have now is our money and my money."

"Ah…" He drew her to him. "I wondered when you would catch on to that."

"So you did it deliberately?" Again she pulled away, this time turning to face him. "But why?"

"If it bothers you, I'll do whatever you want, but I had it in mind that, once we have children, it would be nice to put what you brought to our marriage into a living trust situation for our heirs," he explained. "That way, it would bypass me who will never need it, and there could be situations where it would have tax benefits."

"But that's a wonderful idea!" She beamed at him, not sure which part she was more pleased with, his recognizing a way to protect as much as possible from the tax man or his already planning ahead for their children. "Until then, though, I should have something in place leaving everything to you. Will you see to that for me as soon as you're back in the office?"

"I'll get it started and check everything out," he assured her, "but we'll let Susan actually be the attorney of record and your administrator."

"Perfect!" She snuggled against him once more, not at all displeased when he drew her closer.

"Do you have any idea how sexy you are when you speak money," he asked, his voice having taken on a rough edge.

"No, but I could list for you the way my 401K is invested if you think you would enjoy it," she teased, not surprised when his lips next sought the base of her neck, which she gladly arched in a way to make his job easier for him.

Both waking just before dawn the next morning, Adrianna quickly brewed mugs of coffee while Chase pulled thick blankets from a cupboard – one to spread on the ground and one to be shared for warmth against the morning chill.

Now sipping their hot coffee from travel mugs, they sat on the slope awaiting the first burst of green light on the horizon that would signal the coming sunrise and the fresh start of a new day, as the waves lapped softly against the shore so different from the cliffs back home in Captain's Point.

"Have these first weeks of our marriage been all that you wanted?" Chase asked in a soft voice, and Adrianna searched her mind, sensing that he would prefer an honest, thoughtful answer.

The memory of their wedding night came first – his kissing away her giggles until her body had cried out for him and then making love to her with a sweetness she hadn't known possible as he had taken her as his mate for the first time per their common agreement. But then, as the night had progressed, their lovemaking had become ever more intense, until she had cried out with the sheer joy of it.

The everyday moments slipped in next – Chase licking a drop of ice cream off her chin before kissing her, watching him toss a blue ball for their dog, and the laughter that had filled their time together. But then, her face sobered as she remembered the day it had come time for supper, and she had been unable to find him, knowing he was somewhere in the house.

It had been Max who had led her to where her new husband had sat in an armchair in one of the spare bedrooms they had been using to store boxes from his aunt's home, slowly emptying them one at a time. A large carton had lain open at his feet, and she had been appalled by the ravaged look on his face as he had sat in the dim evening light and gazed down at its contents. Softly she had approached until he had become aware of her presence and had reached out his hand and drawn her onto his lap.

"Aunt Ruth had kept his room just as Jack left it," he had explained, referring to his deceased cousin, mentor and friend whose death during a naval rescue mission, she knew, had left the teenaged Chase devastated. "It's all in these boxes somewhere – everything, his things, all of his treasures. They sent back the part they thought was him from what was left after the explosion in a closed, flag-draped box, and we were supposed to say goodbye to it. Jack should've made love to his bride as I have with you and held his firstborn in his arms as we both will."

Sensing the depth of his anguish, she had silently kissed his forehead and then wrapped her arms around his neck, holding him close while his body had shaken with dry sobs until she had thought his emotions spent. Whereupon he had proven her wrong, carrying her to their bed and making love to her so powerfully that she had reached her fingertips to his cheek after his passion had been spent and said, "Chase, it's me, Adrianna. I'm here."

"Thank God you came to Captain's Point." He had cupped her hand in his, pressed his lips to her palm and placed it over his heart, holding it to him. "I love you and need you beside me so much," he had whispered as if in awe of it. Then, as he had struggled to go on, he had lifted his eyes to hers, so full of pain that her own had felt the prick of tears.

"Jack…" The single word had been torn from his throat as he had drawn her to him so tightly that she had feared for her ribs - the grief and tears he had held in for far too long finally pouring out of him.

Hours later she had awakened to find the bedside lamp turned on low and Chase propped on the pillows beside her, satisfied to just watch her sleep.

"I want to remember every nook and cranny of you at this moment," he had explained as he had traced the line of her jaw with his finger.

In response, she had reached for his hand and snuggled it against her cheek before transferring her gaze to the spot where three stitches had recently been removed from just below his left temple and, raising her lips to it, had kissed it gently.

Drawing back the sheet, he had revealed a tiny scar on her right knee, the result of her having fallen on a sharp rock in the woods behind the gazebo as a child, and bending his head, he had brushed it with his lips as he had slid his hand along her left leg to her ankle.

"And this?" He had pointed to a tiny star shape that resided there.

"A piece of Minoan pottery that slipped from an overfilled workman's basket on a site," she had explained, and it, too, had been kissed, sending a shock wave up her leg.

Sliding her hand along the smooth skin of his stomach, she had found with her finger the pockmark left by an attack of chicken pox when he was seven. As she had touched it with her lips, he had drawn her into his arms, and they had melded their beings in a way so gentle and poignant that it had made her heart sing.

And in the morning, they had slept in, but when she awoke, she had been greeted by a man reborn, with a lightened step that reflected his new inner peace so much dark baggage had her new husband discarded alongside their joint path.

So now, as they sat wrapped together in the rough blanket, his long legs extended towards the ocean on either side of hers, his arms wrapped around her from behind, warm and strong, she could honestly turn, lift her face to his and say, "I wouldn't change a single moment of our past weeks together."

Tomorrow they planned to go to Cadillac Mountain and watch the first sunrise as seen from any point on the eastern United States shore, but in her heart of hearts, as her new husband brought his lips down to hers, Adrianna knew that this would be the sunrise she would treasure forever.

Holding his wife in his arms, breathing in the soft scent of her hair, waiting for the sun to rise, Chase was filled with a sense of immense gratitude. How far his life had come in only a few months, as it had shifted from a lonely, never ending struggle merely to make ends meet to a world made complete through the presence of Adrianna and awash with new opportunities!

His mind traveled back through their past weeks together – waking to her in his arms each morning, the trust in her eyes, her gentle touch and shy smile. And yet, as much as he now owned, he would give up every bit of it merely to spend a single moment with her in their love-filled home, holding her close and keeping her safe.

The sky above the horizon lightened and lifted his spirit still further with it, and as the tiny flash of green light announced the sun's approach, Adrianna turned her face once again to his and, drawing her to him, Chase gave himself up to the sheer joy of her.

CHAPTER XL

Approaching Artful Soul, Edwina saw that Arthur was locking the door.

"I'm sorry." His face took on the look of a scared rabbit. "I don't have time to visit right now. I...I have an appointment."

Having raised a boy, she knew immediately that there was no appointment and, this being so unlike her Arthur, was concerned.

"I may be back sooner than the hour." He indicated the sign hanging behind the door. "If you'll be home, I could stop by when I return."

"Certainly." She forced a smile. "Although it was nothing important, I was just going to keep you company for a while, if you weren't busy."

Slowly, she walked along the sidewalk until he had cleared most of the drive and then quickened her pace towards the garage, still watching his progress until she saw that he turned to the right just as she opened her car door. Reaching the main highway, she put the pedal to the metal, as her at the time teenaged son had once said, and almost executed the first wheelie of her life.

Arthur's Buick quickly came into view up ahead, and she continued to follow him at a fair distance until he slowed and signaled a right turn, passing between the two granite posts connected by an overhead wrought iron arch that proclaimed he was entering Captain's Point Cemetery. Continuing straight ahead, she turned into a gas station, paused without turning off her car, and then drove back to the cemetery where she parked her vehicle next to his.

Disembarking, she immediately located him up and over to her left and, allowing him his privacy, took a seat on a nearby bench and prepared to wait – in sight of both cars, but with her back to him.

Soon the peace and quiet of the cemetery washed over her, and she let out a small sigh as her mind took her back to the cemetery in Chicago where she had said her goodbyes to Ham before moving to Captain's Point. In her heart, she had known that he wasn't there, but even though he had been dead for many years, it had seemed for the first time at that moment that she would never see him again.

A bright red cardinal landed on a marker up ahead, and she watched as he groomed himself. Off somewhere in the trees, a mockingbird trilled his song, and above her head, a gull let out a sharp cry. A fresh bouquet of flowers had been left on a newly closed grave a few feet away, and she noted with sadness a tiny, weather-marked lamb that recalled the short life and premature death of a long ago child.

Then she saw motion out of the corner of her eye and realized that the man she had followed was approaching.

"Arthur," she called quietly.

With a start, he turned in her direction and halted.

"Won't you please join me?" She indicated the place beside her.

His face a blank slate, he obliged her.

"There's something I feel I must say." She took his hand. "It is not in my nature to follow you like this. It is not in my nature to put a bit in your mouth and hold the reins, but your obvious discomfort in front of your shop troubled me."

"Edwina, I…"

"Please let me finish," she interrupted him in a soft voice. "I know what it is to mate for what you think is a lifetime. I did it and so did Ham, but inevitably life chooses which one of such a couple will be left behind. Half of you from before you met me is buried in this cemetery, and believe me, I understand. I also understand that from time to time you are going to feel the need to revisit that part of you.

"I have no wish to deny you that comforting pleasure, nor do I want to keep tabs on it. I never thought I would have a man in my life again," she continued. "God has given me a great gift, but I do want both of us to be comfortable at all times in our relationship going forward no matter what our pursuits."

"I did you a disservice." Arthur took her other hand in his and shifted his weight, so that they were positioned to better face one another. "I thought you might be jealous."

"On the contrary, I rejoice that you had a wife like Sylvia and I had a husband like Ham, each of us for a very long time." She blinked back tears. "Both of us will bring lessons learned at their hands into our relationship."

"My sweet Edwina…" Arthur gathered her into his arms and kissed her so tenderly and then with such obvious passion that the new cemetery worker who had, unbeknownst to the two of them, been raking a flower bed some paces away, dropped his rake at the mere sight of it.

CHAPTER XLI

Adrianna and Chase had agreed the evening before that they would prefer to head home after visiting Cadillac Mountain, so he headed their SUV south along the coast once they left the park.

"I do love living on the water." His new wife let out a contented sigh, and he reached over and squeezed her hand.

"I do, too," he agreed. "I wonder…"

"Yes?" She turned towards him in her seat.

"Part of me thinks it may be rubbing salt in old wounds, and part of me would like to see," Chase began. "What would you think of our detouring to the Cape on our way back, since we have this extra day?"

"Are you planning to revisit some of the spots you enjoyed with your cousin Jack and your aunt?" she asked.

"How crazy is that, right?" He sent her a wry smile.

"Personally, I found coming back to Montgomery House very rewarding even though, at first, it retained some bad memories," she pointed out. "Don't you think it would be better to see for yourself than to always wonder whether or not we should have revisited the area now? At the very least, we'll enjoy some wonderful seafood and great views, and at the most, you will have recaptured part of your childhood."

"When did you get to be so smart, wife of mine?"

"I think some of you must be rubbing off on me." She sent him a grin. "Should I reset the GPS?"

"Sure, go ahead," he agreed. "Set it for Harwich. That should get us close enough."

A few hours later, as they stood on the shore behind his aunt's former beach cottage, which Adrianna now recognized was truly a house and a fair-sized one at that, she knew she had been right to encourage her husband to return. He had eagerly pointed out first this landmark and then that as they had approached, including the restaurant a short distance along the road where Jack and he had once eaten so many pieces of pie that they had both gotten sick. Now, though, as they gazed out over the bevy of sailboats that he had told her was a constant on this stretch of water, she felt he would benefit from a few minutes alone.

"I'm going to wait for you back at the SUV," she said, withdrawing from his arm. "Take as long as you want. There's a nice breeze, and I'll enjoy it and read some of my paperback."

Once rounding the house, though, she drew up with a start at the sight of a man a year or two younger than she, who was preparing to pound a For Sale sign into the ground.

"Excuse me." She hurried to his side, noting the name of a real estate agency running along the driver's door of his car. "Could you wait a minute please?"

"Are you interested in buying?" he asked.

"I might be," she said as excitement rose within her. "This property used to belong to my husband's family. We're on our honeymoon, and we only stopped by so he could share some of his memories with me. Are you the realtor?"

"Yes, it's my first listing." He sent her a shy smile. "I'm working for one aunt, and the house belongs to another."

"Well, won't they both be surprised when you make your first sale on your first day?" She plunged in. "I'll pay you a holding fee if you'll agree to put the sign away and join my husband and me at that restaurant on the corner in two hours. That will give me time to see what he thinks over lunch, and you can order yourself a steak while you're waiting. How much is your aunt asking?"

He named what seemed to her an astronomical figure and then informed her, "It's a bargain at that with all the property that goes with it."

Pulling her wallet from her purse, Adrianna lifted an inner flap and removed some bills that Chase had insisted she carry with her in case of emergencies once they were married, trying not to show her shock at the home's value.

"There, that should do it." She handed him the money. "My name is Adrianna Sheffield, and my husband's name is Chase.

His aunt's name was Ruth Stanford, and he had a cousin named Jack."

"I'm Chuck Miles," he introduced himself as he carefully placed the bills in his wallet. "I met your husband a couple of times when I was a boy and Aunt Gertrude brought me with her to visit. She bought the property from Mrs. Stanford after Jack's death. They were old friends, and my aunt only bought the place because she thought Mrs. Stanford might regret having sold it. She passed away, though, earlier this year so there's no need to hold onto it any longer, but you would know that." He looked at his watch. "My cousin owns the restaurant you mentioned. I'll head down there, eat my lunch and hang around until you've had time to discuss this with your husband. That way, if you have any questions, I'll be handy, and I have a key with me if you want to look the place over."

"Thank you, Chuck." Impulsively, Adrianna reached out and squeezed his hand. "I believe you're going to be very successful in real estate."

The realtor's car headed along the street just as Chase appeared around the corner of the house, and his new wife felt a lump harden in her stomach. But then, she chided herself. After all, hadn't her husband told her to feel free to buy anything that she wanted?

"You'll never believe what's just happened!" She hurried to meet him. "Come sit in the SUV with me for a few minutes. I have a bit of a surprise for you, and then let's get some lunch at the restaurant where Jack and you ate too much pie."

Three hours later, they were back on their way towards Captain's Point. Chase had agreed that, yes, he would like to share his childhood stomping ground and stories of his cousin Jack with their children, the healing that had begun earlier in their honeymoon being enough for him to look ahead now.

Chuck had called his aunt, who had joined them in time for pie and coffee. The asking price had been reduced to a much lower figure, which the seller had stated would cover her initial purchase price as well as the intervening taxes and upkeep that she had paid for, and she wouldn't accept a penny more from a member of Ruth's family.

They had agreed to drive straight through no matter how late it was when they arrived home, and Adrianna was now spelling her husband at the SUV's steering wheel, a smile on her face as she remembered Aunt Gertrude's surprise at how tall the youngster she remembered had grown.

Beside her in the passenger's seat, Chase lounged with his eyes closed, remembering all of the good memories of times past that had rushed back and his cousin's face no longer darkened by loss, even as he was filled with gratitude towards his new wife. Thanks to her thoughtfulness and understanding, he would now pass that legacy on to their children.

Straightening, he leaned over, planted a kiss on her cheek and then said, "Thank you, my queen."

CHAPTER XLII

His new wife attending a surprise brunch Susan and Courtney were having in honor of their mom's birthday, Chase found himself at loose ends and was pleased when his phone rang, displaying Jack Jefferson's number.

"Larry suggested I go ahead and give you a call," Jack explained once the two men had exchanged greetings. "Something came to my attention while you were out of town that needs immediate action if we're going to forestall what the two of us believe would be detrimental to Captain's Point. Would you be willing to go for a ride and let me show you something, if I dropped by and picked you up in a couple of minutes?"

"Sure," Chase agreed, intrigued – ready and waiting when Jack showed up a few minutes later.

"A friend of mine in D.C. called me Sunday evening and alerted me to the activities of a development group that has been trying to buy up a number of farms in the area from financially stressed farmers," Jack explained as he headed his Mercedes along the drive and then turned right onto the main road, heading away from town. "I had inadvertently squelched their original plans by buying up two properties that connected to mine right after I first arrived and retaining part of the land that I wanted kept undeveloped both for my view and as a small nature preserve."

"Way to go!" Chase sent him a grin. "What are they planning to develop?"

"Another huge theme park, which the area doesn't need and will completely change the complexion of Captain's Point," Jack filled him in. "According to my friend, these folks have a record of mowing down the landscape, using shoddy construction and then, when the project goes under, declaring bankruptcy their having syphoned off investor money into offshore accounts, leaving a huge mess behind."

"So what have Larry and you cooked up?"

"Due to the reconfiguration of their original plans, there are three farms located in such a way that if they can't buy them, it's a no-go for their whole operation," Jack explained. "Larry and I are trying to put together a coalition to undercut them on those three farms, by paying cash and then allowing the owners long term leases with options to buy, part of the rental money going towards possible future repurchase. We're hoping to interest you in joining us."

"I'd want to include Adrianna in the discussion, but it sounds like something I'd consider," Chase replied. "Larry's fairly conservative in his recommendations, and we share a similar viewpoint when it comes to Captain's Point's future as I would imagine you do, too. Where are we going, by the way?"

"Right here." Jack signaled a turn into a small municipal airport. "I trust since you sail that you aren't prone to airsickness."

"Am I correct in my assumption that we are about to test your theory?" Chase sent him a grin.

"That we are," Jack confirmed. "Let me check in here at the office, and then we'll lift off."

"Lift off, not take off?" Chase raised an eyebrow.

"You'll get the best view of what concerns us from my copter with its Rolls Royce engine singing along, which is the way Larry chose to see it." Jack chuckled. "Of course, I could've shown you on a map on your library table, but trust me, this will be a whole lot more fun."

Finding it hard to believe that only a while before he had been bored, Chase prepared to enjoy the rest of the morning, a few minutes later donning the headset Jack handed him – explaining it was a prototype he was testing for a friend - and understanding the coalition's concerns once the properties in question were pointed out to him from the air. All too soon, he found himself back on the ground, stating he had enjoyed himself immensely.

Pulling his phone from his pocket and turning it back on, he was surprised when it rang almost immediately.

"Chase!" Adrianna's voice conveyed in the single word that something was wrong. "It's Daniel!"

"What about Daniel?" He switched the phone onto speaker so the man next to him could hear.

"Part of the cliff at The Cove collapsed out from under him, and he's lying on a ledge fifteen feet down."

"Not on rocks?" Chase confirmed.

"No, on dirt on a ledge, but he isn't moving." The latter had sounded as if she had lowered her voice and cupped her mouth in her hand.

"Have you called 911?" her husband asked, sure they would have.

"Anders has, and they've contacted the Coast Guard. They're not here yet, although I can hear the Rescue Squad's siren."

"Adrianna, this is Jack. Tell Susan and Anders that we'll be there in five minutes. Everyone needs to stay back from that cliff once we're there. Do you understand? I said stay back from that cliff."

"Yes, I understand, but…"

"We've got to hang up so we can come," Chase explained and then turned off his phone.

"Ever done any mountain climbing?" Jack asked as he reached behind the passenger seat and pulled up a worn canvas bag.

"Two summers, when I was college."

"It's like riding a bike if you're game," the copter's pilot flashed his dimples.

"There's a little boy lying unconscious on a ledge." Chase met his gaze. "I'm game." But the other man held onto the bag when he reached for it.

"You should know that my friend's dog partially chewed through one of the long ropes," Jack told him.

"Now I know." Chase began to sort through the bag's contents, first strapping himself into the special force's, full body harness and then quickly, but efficiently testing out the runners, descenders and brake.

"We'll do a flyby first," Jack explained his plan, his voice pure professional, as Chase attached the gear onto the four points within the copter that the pilot had suggested. "You'll have to put on those safety glasses because the blades will kick up dirt. Thank goodness, it's a relatively calm day. What I'm worried about most is the stability of what's left of the cliff and how far it's now sticking over the ledge. It's possible that more is set to come down on top of him, and there's no telling what he'll do if he regains consciousness." Here his voice cracked slightly as he tried not to think that Daniel might actually be dead.

"Got it." Chase strapped himself into his seat as his companion lifted them once again from the ground.

"I won't be able to see you once you're down there," Jack continued, "so keep me informed. Once you have him secured, I'm going to pull you back, then up and over the ground, where I'll set you down. You'll then unhook yourself, and I'll pull on forward, dragging the gear with me."

"Sounds good."

"We can scrap this whole thing at any time," Jack pointed out. "Be careful that you don't hit the landing skid as you're dropping off. I usually lean backwards. Feel free to dump the gloves if you think you can get a better hold on him. You won't need them once you have him in your arms."

The Cove now being in sight, Chase's heart leaped into his throat as he could clearly see his wife, Susan and Elizabeth holding hands, lying spread-eagled, face down at the edge of the cliff – Susan appearing to be trying to keep Daniel in sight. Only the boy's orange Chester's T-shirt, arms and face were clearly visible, his legs being at least partially buried under loose dirt.

"That cliff isn't stable," Jack pointed out. "See how dirt is still sifting down near his feet? That isn't caused by the blades, we aren't close enough."

"Yes, and it's as if it's been carved out somewhat," Chase agreed. "Thank goodness Anders is getting those crazy women away from the edge."

"You do understand that what we're attempting to do is even crazier, don't you?" Jack asked.

"The difference is we don't have a choice but to do it," Chase stated. "That cliff isn't stable, and having it cave in on him isn't going to help Daniel. There's no telling how long it will take the Coast Guard to get here."

"Ready?" Jack held out his hand.

"Ready!" Chase gave it a quick shake. "My wife's going to kill me if this doesn't."

"I would've changed places with you for just that reason if you knew how to fly this," Jack informed him as he brought the copter around. "Go ahead and drop. Once you give me the go ahead, I'll bring you in closer."

Adrianna and Susan now stood with their arms around each other's waists well back from the cliff's edge, but even so, the former immediately recognized her husband's newly purchased Cape Cod jersey as he dropped into thin air from the helicopter's landing skid.

"That's Chase!" She started forward, only to be pulled back by her friend.

"We've got to do what Jack said," Susan insisted. "What they're trying can't be easy, and we have to stay out of their way."

"I think I'm good." Chase's voice clearly came through his headset, and Jack slowly brought the copter in closer.

"Bring me in and down just a little," Chase requested. "Daniel put his hands over his eyes – a good sign. Just a little closer in. Is it okay if I swing, so I can get deeper under the overhang?"

"Don't get too crazy, but yes," Jack gave him the go ahead.

"Keep your hands over your eyes!" Chase shouted at the boy, who was now only a few feet away from him. "This is Uncle Chase. Don't move anymore! Keep your hands over your eyes! Jack is going to give us both the ride of our lives and helicopter us out of here." Then his voice lowered. "He sat up, and his knees are now bent. If I can just… Humph! Hold me steady. Do you hurt anywhere, Daniel?"

"Best I can do," Jack stated, wishing with all of his heart that their roles were reversed as he heard the child answer, "My head hurts and my bottom."

"Got him!" Chase shouted. "Hang on tight, Daniel, and don't squirm. We'll have you back with your mom in a minute. Hoist us off, up there!"

Immediately, Jack pulled the copter away from the cliff.

"You're now going down in history as the only young man ever helicoptered by Jack Jefferson and Chase Sheffield from a

Captain's Point cliff," Chase attempted to make light of their situation for the benefit of the boy in his arms. "They don't even have rides like this at the theme parks."

"I've taken you up forty feet," Jack informed his partner in crime, just as another large portion of the cliff gave way and landed where the boy had lain.

"Did you see that?" Chase asked.

"Yes, thank goodness what we tried worked," Jack replied. "Once you're well over The Cove's lawn, talk me down. I want to lower you slowly."

"That was barely halfway," Chase informed him a moment later. "That much again…Four feet more…There! We're free of you."

Jack pulled forward a short distance and then turned the copter around before landing, giving him a clear view of the Rescue Squad's EMTs and Susan rushing over to Daniel where he now lay on the ground. Then a pink blur caught his eye as Adrianna hurtled forward and flung herself at her husband, the latter almost losing his balance due to her thrust before he could bring his strong arms around his now sobbing wife and hold her close.

"It's okay," Chase stated calmly as he stroked her hair, although his knees felt weak from all the adrenalin. "I'm okay, and Daniel's going to be okay, too. Shh…Shh… It's okay, and I'm here."

"Don't you ever do that to me again!" She looked up, her eyes still awash with tears.

"I won't unless it's absolutely necessary," he promised, "but I've got to tell you, Adrianna, that was an experience of a lifetime."

In the cockpit of the copter, Jack swallowed the bile that had entered his throat as he fought to control his shaking hands, wondering if his legs would even support him – never having felt this way before in all of the years he had been doing rescue work, but this time, it had been Susan and Daniel. What, he asked himself, had he been thinking?

Pull yourself together, man, he told himself as he made his way out of the copter, jogging towards the crowd that had now formed by the Rescue Squad's vehicle just as they were loading Daniel's gurney inside.

Standing two feet away, Susan glanced over her shoulder, searching for Jack in the crowd and finally locating him heading her way, just as the younger EMT told her she could now step inside. Quickly, she mouthed the words 'Thank you!' and then blew her hero a kiss.

Now knowing he wouldn't get to her in time, he responded reflexively, standing firm where he was, a grin on his face as he sent her a quick salute in return.

CHAPTER XLIII

Once settled onto a gurney in the emergency room, Daniel found his voice. "I want Casey and Jack," he stated firmly, his lower lip quivering.

"Casey isn't allowed in the hospital," his mother informed him.

"Jack is," her son insisted from where he lay strapped to a child-sized body board as a young nurse took his finger and pricked it quickly, drawing the blood that was needed to meet regulations. "Ouch! That hurt! I want Jack! He helicoptered me!" His voice became more hysterical as a tear ran down his cheek.

"Do you want me to see if he's in the waiting room?" Bev asked.

"Please." Susan sent her high school BFF a grateful look, thankful that her friend was now the head ER nurse.

"One tall friend as requested," Bev announced when she held back the curtain a minute later.

"How are you doing, Bud?" Jack joined Susan by the side of the bed.

"I want to go home," Daniel demanded. "Helicopter me home!"

"I'm afraid I can't." Jack covered the boy's and his mother's hands both with his larger one. "We left the helicopter at The Cove when your grandparents and I followed that cool ambulance you got to ride in and we didn't. Why don't we see what the doctor says about the walnut you're wearing on your head as long as we're here? In the meantime, I want to say how brave I thought you were on the ledge today and how glad I am that you did exactly what Chase told you to do."

"I was scared," Daniel admitted, averting his eyes.

"So was I," Jack shared with him. "Sometimes being a little afraid is a good thing. It keeps you alert and helps you to think clearly." He glanced quickly over at Susan, needing her assurance that he was filling well the role that was required of him, glad when her eyes shone back at him with gratitude.

"Will you stay here with me?" Daniel asked, a pleading look in his eyes.

"As long as I'm needed," Jack assured him, still holding onto both of their hands even as he put his free arm around Susan's shoulders.

"I see that you've managed to get yourself into trouble again, little fellow." Pug Brownley, the ER doctor on duty and another of Susan's childhood friends, joined them. "First you insisted that I remove a plug of wax the size of an rhinoceros from your ear, and now you show up with an egg sticking out of the back of your head."

"It's not an egg," Daniel insisted. "It's a walnut. Jack says it's a walnut."

"And who am I to contradict Jack, right?" Pug continued his examination in spite of the set down he had received.

"Jack helicoptered me," his patient advised him.

"Are you telling me that this man hit you with a helicopter?" Pug added a shocked expression to his face, even though he knew the true story, and then placed his stethoscope against the boy's chest.

"No, he and Uncle Chase lifted me off the ledge," Daniel explained. "We were all brave."

"Now that I am glad to hear." Pug slowly checked all of the child's limbs. "Do you hurt anywhere besides your head and that place on your hip where you're bruised?"

"No, they saved me in time."

"Good man," Pug said, meeting the other man's gaze with a firm look and a nod of approval.

"Yes," Susan whispered, feeling Jack's arm tighten around her in response, grateful for his strong presence beside her as she fought to control her body's desire to shake from the shock they had all just lived through.

"You've managed to get some dirt in your ears, so I'm going to ask Bev here to wash them out for you," Pug addressed his patient, "and then I'd like for you to let us x-ray that hip."

"Will it hurt?" Daniel's eyes widened. "That other nurse hurt my finger."

"Not at all." The doctor smiled back.

"Have you had an x-ray?" Daniel asked his rescuer.

"Lots of times to my shame." Jack chuckled. "None of them hurt."

"Okay, but Mama and Jack have to go with me."

"Certainly," his amused doctor approved.

The x-ray having shown no cracks, chips or breaks, Pug had recommended that his small patient be admitted for observation overnight.

Jack had found himself swept along by the tide as a room had been assigned and Daniel had insisted that he carry him from place to place once it had been determined that his hip was only bruised, clinging to both his mother's and Jack's hands once he was settled in his hospital bed. Here, as visitors came and went, both Chase and he were treated like heroes, and Jack couldn't help but notice the worshipful glances Susan was continually sending his way, knowing full well that this wasn't at all what he wanted.

Chase and Adrianna had smuggled a bag of Patrick's sliders into the room around six, the latter pleased to be given something to do, when Jack gave them his house's security code and they promised to retrieve Lady and take her home with them. Larry had arrived with a large container of chocolate gelato a little after seven, but even he had now gone. An LPN had made up a mother's bed for Susan a few minutes before, and it was now clearly time for him to go, so he rose from his chair only to feel Daniel tighten his hold on his hand.

"I'm going to leave you and your mom now, so you can get some sleep, Pal." He smiled down at the small, wide-eyed face on the pillow.

"No," Daniel stated in his firm way. "I need you here to be brave for me while I sleep."

"Jack has to go home and get some sleep for himself," Susan explained as her fingers smoothed her son's hair. "It's been a long day for him, too."

"He can sleep here." Their patient remained adamant as he locked Jack in his sights. "Can't you?"

Not displeased when Susan offered no further objection, Jack relented. "I can certainly stay a while longer," he agreed.

"And I could sit in your lap like I did on the boardwalk when we got the cones." Daniel moved the game forward.

Noting that Susan had merely shrugged and sent him a smile, Jack obliged, lifting her son onto his lap where he sat in the room's lounge chair and then setting it to recline, being careful to arrange Daniel so that his weight pressed against his uninjured hip.

"Let's wrap him in this," Susan suggested, folding one of the blankets from the bed in half and then tucking it in around them, before turning the remaining light in the room down to dim.

"We're fine here, so why don't you stretch out and get some rest while you can," Jack said. "You've had a hard day, too, not to mention a shock, and I can tuck him in when he's ready."

"If you don't mind…" Suddenly overwhelmed with fatigue, she took in the fact that Daniel's eyes were already closed.

"Not at all." He took her hand and drew her down to him, brushing her lips with his.

"Jack, it doesn't say all that I mean, but thank you again." She kissed her finger and touched it to the dimple on the right side of his smile, sending his spine tingling.

A few hours later, Susan struggled from her sleep, aware that Daniel sounded as if he were having a nightmare in the bed beside her.

"Shhhh, Tiger." Jack's quiet voice came to her through the remnants of her own dream. "Let's not wake your mom."

"I need to go to the bathroom," Daniel whispered.

"I think we can manage that," Jack replied, "and afterwards I'll tell you about my first elephant ride if you'll go back to sleep when I'm finished."

"Was it a big elephant?" Daniel asked in a whisper.

"Ginormous!"

Recognizing that her son was in good hands, Susan remained where she was with her eyes closed and relished the way Jack had taken over the care of both of them.

Their mission accomplished per the sounds that had carried through the partially open door to the room's bathroom, Jack and Daniel returned, the former settling the latter onto his lap and wrapping him once again in the blanket.

"You understand this was a long time ago." Jack's words came softly to where Susan lay listening. "And while I was half a world away on my own, I wasn't much more than a boy…" Then she heard no more as the stresses of the past day once again drew her to sleep.

"Good morning, beautiful," Jack greeted her several hours later when she opened her eyes, sounds of hospital activity around them having wakened her.

Glancing towards the bed, she noted that her son once again lay there sound asleep, the man beaming at her from the lounge chair appearing to be none the worse for wear.

"Did you get any sleep?" she asked, sitting up.

"Quite a bit actually," he assured her. "Remember, I'm used to camping rough."

"Still, this was beyond the call of duty."

"And I was happy to do it. Besides, I realized when I put the little guy into bed around eleven that the cabs in Captain's Point stop running at ten, and I don't have a car with me." He glanced at his watch. "Otis should be here in about twenty minutes with our breakfast. Penny is sending over fried egg and bacon sandwiches along with some juice. I'm sure he'll give me a ride home, if Daniel will release me."

"Bless Penny's heart." Susan stood and retrieved a comb from her purse. "Better?"

"Smoother, but I had no objections to the sexy, fresh-from-sleep look." Jack stood and gathered her to him, planting a firm kiss on her lips.

"How does it feel to wake up a hero?" She remained in his arms.

"Susan, really, I'm not a hero," he objected.

"You forget that I'm an attorney, Jack Jefferson," she stated firmly. "You risked everything when you attempted that rescue."

"I didn't consciously risk anything," he replied, needing for her to understand. "I merely reacted, and even then, I didn't do anything that I haven't done thousands of times before, flying a helicopter along a cliff's edge on a calm day. Chase is the one who drew on his courage. Believe me, it's hard to let go of a helicopter that's hovering in the air and drop towards the ground, especially the first time. Been there, done that, and I know."

"But…"

He placed a finger on her lips. "You've got to understand, Susie. What Chase and I did yesterday was stupid, foolhardy and downright crazy until the moment it worked. We had improper and half-broken equipment, and the blades could've made everything worse. I didn't have a set of eyes watching Chase up there with me, nor did I have any kind of sight line. We could tell that the cliff wasn't stable, and what Daniel would do if he regained consciousness was an unknown. I'm used to being the only resource available, so I forged ahead. We took a huge chance and chose not to wait for the Coast Guard like we could have and, perhaps, should have."

"And now my child's lying asleep in this bed with nothing permanently wrong with him, believing that he had a wonderful adventure instead of a horrendous experience." Susan reached her hand up and ran her fingers through his hair, straightening it, completely unaware of what this simple action was doing to him. "You were our guide who jumped towards the cobra."

"I risked everything, and I don't mean my worldly goods," Jack stated firmly. "I risked the two of you, and that's all I could think of once I landed the copter and last night when I sat here holding that little guy in my arms, so grateful that I still could."

"Okay, I concede the point." She met his gaze. "You risked…" She hesitated. "Well, everything for us without a single thought for yourself, and in my book that means that Daniel is right and you're certainly my hero."

"Susie…"

"No, hear me out," she interrupted him. "The way I see it, you can do one of two things going forward. You can dwell on what might have happened and didn't, or you can be as grateful as I am that you were there with all of your makeshift equipment and your phenomenal expertise and that both Chase and you had the courage to face the odds and to risk whatever was necessary to save my child."

Susan was afraid that she had gone too far as he gazed down at her, his face filled with a rapid series of emotions, but then he crushed her to him and, sensing that he needed a moment to pull himself together, she merely rested her head against his shoulder.

"Do you have any idea what a great gal you are?" he asked, his voice rough, once his grip on her loosened.

"No, but you're welcome to tell me." She smiled as he lowered his lips onto hers, then held her close for a moment before releasing her.

"Why don't you freshen up, while I stretch my legs for a few minutes?" he suggested.

"Sounds good," she agreed, but then looked up at him shyly. "Pug will probably release Daniel sometime around mid-morning, and we'll both need to clean up and get into fresh clothes once we're back at The Cove. Would you and Lady be available if we were to drive over after lunch?"

"We would," Jack said as his face lit up with pleasure, "although we're both free at lunchtime as well. Why don't we grill some hotdogs and hamburgers for the little guy to share with his newest pack member?"

"Only if you'll let me bring dessert," Susan named her terms.

"You got it." He sent her a grin and then headed from the room as promised.

Appreciating his respect for her privacy, Susan waited until he had closed the room's door behind him, still recognizing as she hurried to put herself back together before his return how much he had done for them, despite his objections, and realizing how much she already missed his presence.

CHAPTER XLIV

Wanting some time alone with his Susie, Jack had asked her to join him for dinner at Montgomery's the next evening, pleased when she had accepted his invitation with no hesitation. Arriving fifteen minutes early, he rang the door at The Cove, glad when it was Anders who let him into the house.

"I want to thank you again for what Chase and you did for our family on Friday," Susan's father stated immediately. "It took courage, guts and expertise on both of your parts, and there's simply no way that Elizabeth and I will ever be able to repay you."

"Actually, there is if I might have a word with you." Jack sent him a smile. "It's why I've arrived a few minutes early."

"Why don't we talk in here," Anders led them into his study, carefully closing the door behind them before indicating his visitor should take a seat.

"I imagine you know what I want to say," Jack began once they were both settled. "It may be a bit old-fashioned, but I've always believed family acceptance is important. The bottom line is that I would like for you and Elizabeth to know beforehand that I plan to ask your daughter to marry me. I've traveled the world for the better part of twenty years, and until I met Susan and Daniel, I never met anyone with whom I wanted to share my life. Now, in one fell swoop, I've found a whole family to love."

"Feel free to proceed," Anders gave him his blessing. "You should know, though, that both of us have hoped for this all along. Elizabeth would've handed them over to you the first night we met, before you had even sampled and approved her lasagna, and I was inclined to think she was right even then. The rescue you pulled off two days ago would have earned our gratitude, but not necessarily our daughter, if you take my meaning."

"Absolutely, I've been trying to convince Susan ever since we reconnected at the hospital that what Chase and I did Friday was crazy until it worked." Jack's face sobered. "It could have ended badly just as easily."

"You might as well stop wasting your words," Anders informed him as he glanced at his watch and then stood. "Neither my daughter nor her mother will ever believe you. As far as they're concerned you two are and always will be heroes."

"I hope to ask Susan this evening," Jack said. "I feel pretty sure that her concern will be for Daniel, and I want to assure you and your wife as I will your daughter that I love Daniel in his own way as much as I love her. He's a great little guy, and he seems attached to me. I'll do everything in my power to make his adjustment to his new situation as easy for him as I can."

"If it wasn't for my daughter's unfounded feelings of guilt when it comes to the boy, she would already see that about both of you," Anders assured him as he opened the door and indicated for Jack to proceed first. "Her mother and I certainly do."

"Thanks." Jack held out his hand, receiving a firm grip in return from the other man.

Two hours later, after giving a candlelit dinner at the Montgomery table its due, Jack and Susan arrived at his home to share dessert and coffee on what she would always think of as her porch.

"That pecan pie was delicious," Susan said as she set her mug on the pine table between them and then let out a small sigh of contentment. "It's always so peaceful here. This view spoke to me as a child, a teenager and a young adult. Even now as I walk through the woods towards this spot, I can feel myself relaxing and touching base with all that's important in life."

"You know that I love you," Jack reached across and took her hand where it lay on the table. "I have ever since that first moment on the boardwalk, and I believe you care for me. There's no reason why you ever have to leave this place for another unless you want to. The inside renovations are completed. All that's needed now is for someone to turn this lovely old house into a home for Daniel, you and me. It even meets the little guy's size requirements," he pointed out with a chuckle, "and with both Casey and Lady in residence, he'll have a familiar pack always around him for support. Say the words, and we can create that home together for the five of us as man and wife whenever you're ready."

For what seemed like hours to him, but was in reality only a few minutes, Susan remained silent - rocking slowly back and forth in her chair, her eyes focused on the ocean spread before them, and like a drowning man clutching the end of a rope thrown his way, Jack hung onto the fact that she hadn't yet pulled her hand from his. Then his lifeline twisted around, and she clutched his fingers in hers, still not looking at him.

"This decision isn't about only me." Her words were spoken so quietly that if there had been more of a breeze he might not have heard them. Then she turned her face to him, and he saw that her eyes were awash with tears, the haunted look having returned to them.

Grasping her hand firmly in his, he stood and drew her from the rocker and into his arms, wrapping them gently around her as he held her to him, swaying slowly back and forth. "Take all the time that you need." His words came to her through the soft evening air. "I will always be here for you and Daniel as will the house. I love you both and want you and need you here with me. I want to hold you and love you and protect you both from the world around you. I want you to know that you can trust me as you've been unable to trust others and that both of you will always receive the respect and appreciation from me that you haven't been accustomed to, but I don't want any of that one minute before you are ready."

"Thank you." She lifted her face to his, and he kissed her, long and deep, filling her with such a feeling of peace, safety and contentment that she almost relented, but then he released her.

"Daniel's waiting for you to check on him," he said, his arm still around her shoulders as he steered her towards the Mercedes, taking her back to the real world of her existence where part of her knew she should go, while the other part wanted more than anything to stay with him.

And when they arrived at The Cove after a silent ride, he opened the passenger side door and saw her up the walk to the porch, where once again he drew her into his arms and kissed her tenderly, holding her close afterwards as he said in his kind, quiet way, "Whenever you're ready." And then, he released her, and she hurried into the house, knowing that if she slowed her steps, her feet would send her back into his strong arms.

Once inside, she listened as he drove his SUV along the drive, recognizing that part of her had left with him, and then she made her way to her son's bedroom, where she found Casey and Daniel both asleep and left well enough alone. Slipping into her own bed a few minutes later, she finally managed to find enough residual peace from memories of Jack's strong presence to fall into a shallow, restless sleep that lasted almost through the night.

CHAPTER XLV

Still not trusting her own ability to make the right decision, Susan made her way through the house the next morning until she found her mother changing the sheets in her parents' bedroom.

Picking up a clean pillowcase, she slid her father's pillow into it as she forced herself to say the words, "Jack has asked me to marry him."

"And did you say, yes?" A warm smile filled Elizabeth's face as she looked up from tucking in a corner of a light blanket.

"I asked him for time to think about it."

"Do you love him?"

"Yes."

"And so?" Her mother held her breath.

"I've decided to accept his proposal." Susan met Elizabeth's calm gaze with fear in her eyes.

"I'm glad, and your father will be pleased."

"It's just that everything has happened so fast," her daughter replied.

"Sometimes, you just know what's meant to be," her mother stated. "I knew the moment I first saw your father that he was the man I would marry."

"Mama, am I...?" Susan started to ask.

"Yes, you are making the right decision," Elizabeth interrupted her. "Jack's a kind and capable man, and he's straight as a die. Additionally, it's clear as a bell that he loves both Daniel and you – nothing will ever get in the way of that, and if you're sure of your love for him, then accept the gift that God has offered to you and your child with a firm mind and a clear heart."

"How did you become so wise in only one lifetime?" Susan asked.

"I always was a quick learner." Her mother laughed as she hugged her. "So, when are you going to tell Jack and put him out of his misery?"

"Probably tonight, maybe sooner."

Feeling better about her decision after this discussion, Susan made her way to her son's room where she found him playing with his wooden blocks.

"What are you building?" She took a seat on the edge of his bed.

"A house."

"Who's it for?"

"You."

"Come here a moment." She patted the bed beside her, putting her arm around him once he had joined her. "What would you say if I told you we might have a wedding?"

"I like weddings." Daniel stated in his firm way. "Lizzie and I get to eat cake and ice cream afterwards."

"Do you have any questions you'd like to ask about our wedding?"

"Can Max come?" he pleaded. "Max helped me when we married Chase and Adrianna. He's a good dog, and he did a good job." He quoted her own words to him at the time.

"We'll see."

"Can he at least come to the party afterwards?"

Realizing that this conversation was not going to yield her the answer that she sought, Susan promised her son that they would discuss including Max's name on the list of perspective guests another time and left him to his blocks.

A few minutes later, she parked her car at the marina where she thought Jack could be found, resolutely disembarked and walked towards his boathouse, thinking as she made her way forward that her mother was right. Jack was a good man. She loved him with every fiber of her being and knew him to return her love in the same way.

But what about Daniel? How could she know that Jack really loved Daniel as opposed to merely being entertained by him and, even more important in some ways, that Daniel loved him? How could she know that in this marriage her son would be okay as he had not been before?

She rounded the final corner, and there he stood – capable and strong in a pair of jeans and a T-shirt that was just tight enough to show off his muscles beneath it.

Glancing up from the knot he had been tying in the rope he was holding, Jack met her gaze, a welcoming smile on his face as he stood quietly waiting.

She took a step towards him. "I've come to tell you my answer."

With a single nod of his head, he indicated his understanding.

"You saved Daniel's life." She wished he would help her.

"You owe me nothing for that," he stated firmly. "Besides, so did Chase."

She shifted her weight forward onto her other foot. "You do care for Daniel, don't you?"

"No, I love him and his old-before-its-time little soul. He's part of you. I consider myself to have been blessed with a package deal, and I love everything about both of you." His eyes narrowed. "And you? What do you feel?"

She took another step, drawn forward by the need for him to take her into his arms and tell her that everything that had been lacking for so long in her and Daniel's lives would be all right once placed in his care.

"I love you," she answered him simply. "Differently, but as much if not more than I love Daniel, and I recognize each time we're together that I've never before known love like the love that I feel for and receive from you."

"Then it would seem that everything's settled." He reached out his hand, and she extended hers, allowing him to draw her to him.

"Yes, I will marry you, Jack Jefferson," she said.

Whereupon he kissed her so tenderly that her heart once again filled with warmth and a welcomed sense of peace and contentment before he tightened his hold and released his own passion, for the first time revealing to her the depth of his need and igniting a flame within her stronger than any she had ever known.

"Have you told Daniel yet?" Jack asked a few minutes later, holding her close. "If not, I'd like us to tell him together this evening."

"I told him that he and I might be having a wedding."

"But not that you would be marrying me?"

"No, we'll do that together as well as discuss with him what our new living arrangements will be," she agreed.

"What was Daniel's response to your question about the wedding?"

"He asked if we could invite Max."

Jack threw back his head and laughed. "That'll be a guest for the groom's side of the aisle."

"You would seriously allow Max to come to our wedding?" his betrothed asked pleased, but surprised.

"Certainly, if it would help the little guy make the adjustment."

At which, Susan again slid her arms around his neck. "I have made the right decision for the three of us," she asserted, joy now bursting forth and filling her face, as the love of her life picked her up and twirled her around and around as if she were weightless in his strong arms.

CHAPTER XLVI

Promptly at five o'clock, Jack noted Susan's car approaching along the drive and hurried onto the front porch to greet her and her son.

"We're here, Jack!" Daniel ran to him once he had been released from his child seat.

"I see that." He picked the boy up in one arm, throwing his other one around Susan's shoulders when she joined them on the porch and dropping a kiss onto her cheek. "I've missed you," he whispered into her ear and then released her, holding the door open and gesturing for her to go first.

"Lady says that she wants one of those small bones," Daniel announced once they were inside, hurrying to fulfill the dog's wish once her owner had agreed.

Taking advantage of the opportunity, Jack drew Susan to him. "I love you." He dropped a kiss onto her lips.

"I love you, too." She grinned up at him. "I feel like I'm bursting with happiness inside." But then a crease formed between her brows. "I can't figure out how to tell Daniel," she admitted.

"Why don't I give it a try?" he asked.

"If you wouldn't mind…" A look of relief filled her face.

"Lady was really hungry," Daniel informed them as he and his furry friend rejoined them.

"Why don't we all take a seat in the study?" Jack suggested, pleased when Daniel climbed into his lap once he had settled onto the sofa next to Susan.

"There's something we would like to discuss with you," she addressed her son.

"It's about Lady, you see." Jack took his cue. "She doesn't have a boy like Casey does, and I think she's unhappy about that."

"She has me," Daniel pointed out.

"Yes, but you're not here most of the time," Jack countered. "The fact is, Tiger, that I've fallen in love with your mother, and we would like to get married."

"Like Chase and Adrianna?" Daniel asked.

"Exactly like Chase and Adrianna, who we would invite to come to our wedding along with Max if you would like for us to," Jack agreed, "only in our case, there are five of us – you, your mom, Casey, Lady and me."

"Would we live here all together?" Daniel's eyes filled with hope, much to his mother's relief. "Your house is big, and then Casey and I could be here for Lady so she wouldn't be lonely."

"Sounds like the perfect answer to me." Jack did a good job of looking surprised. "What do you think?" He turned to Susan. "Would you be willing to live in this big, happy house with Daniel, Casey, Lady and me?"

"I'd be ecstatic." She beamed at both of them.

"Would I have a room and everything?" Daniel asked in his serious way.

"How big a room would you need?" Jack looked as if the matter hadn't occurred to him. "There's the closet under the stairs. You'd be welcome to use it. We could put a window in the door to let some light in, although I'm not sure there would be room for both Casey and Lady to be in there with you at the same time."

"Don't you have any bedrooms upstairs?" Daniel's eyes widened.

"Actually, I have quite a few," Jack admitted. "Would you want to go up and check them out? Maybe one of them would suit you."

"Can Lady come, too?" Daniel slid from his host's knee, taking his hand.

"Sure, she has the run of the house, just like you will when you live here after this wedding we're all having." Jack led the way upstairs. "Why don't we men get your mom settled first?" he suggested once they had reached the upper landing. "I'm sleeping in the master bedroom right now, and I think there would be room for us to share, if she agrees."

"I don't know," Susan teased. "I have high expectations."

"So what do you think?" Jack picked Daniel up and wedged him between his left arm and hip as they entered the large suite that ran along the back of the house.

"It's wonderful!" Susan exclaimed hurrying forward to one of two sets of French doors opening onto a balcony that formed the roof of her porch. "Look at my view! And there are rockers up here, too!"

"I thought you'd be pleased." Jack's face relaxed into a grin, his dimples clearly in evidence as she returned to his side and he hugged her to him. "I had the rockers shipped in from Georgia, including a smaller one for Daniel that you'll find on the downstairs porch. Do you think you'll be happy in this room as it is?"

Susan didn't answer for a minute, her eyes taking in the comfortable seating area that filled the rounded nook, a lady's writing desk set against a shorter section of wall, the mahogany four-poster bed and its matching dresser and chest-on-chest, a comfortable chaise lounge, a chandelier and what appeared to be a working gas fireplace with a carved mantel.

"Yes, oh, yes!" She turned her face to his, her eyes filled with excitement. "I didn't expect anything like this. Oh, Jack, it's all so wonderful!"

"I already hoped you would be joining me here when I began work on this floor, so I tried to keep a good mix of masculine and feminine in the décor, but if there's anything you want to change or add, let me know," he told her. "I haven't hung many paintings or added knick knacks throughout most of the house, thinking we would do that together so it would feel more like your home."

"It's perfect," she assured him. "Absolutely perfect."

"What's in there?" Daniel asked, pointing towards double doors to their left.

"Why don't you and your mom check it out?" Jack set him down and watched while her son pulled his mother along.

"A dressing room," she announced, pleased when the opened doors revealed a fair-sized room lined with cupboards tall enough to accommodate dresses as well as built-in drawers, a cheval mirror gracing one corner. "May I?" She put her hand on the crystal knob of one of the cupboards, wishing to see its depth.

"Of course." Jack gestured for her to go ahead.

"But it's empty." She looked back at him, surprised.

"That's because this room is yours as is the bath," he explained. "That is, if you approve." He put his hand on the small of her back as they approached the door to the bathroom. "Everything works and it's all been replumbed, but if you would prefer something more modern…"

"Daniel, look!" Susan interrupted him in her excitement as her gaze settled on the room. "There's a huge claw foot tub and a marble-topped vanity!" Her eyes were filled with joy as she glanced over at Jack. "Don't you dare change a thing!"

"The shower is a more recent addition, but Pete Marlborough was able to locate the sink and period tiles that were hand-painted with pink roses, so it looks as old as the house and allows you to have a four piece," Jack shared, pleased with her response to the suite.

"Where's your bathroom?" Daniel asked.

"It's this way." Jack led them to a door that had been cut through the inside wall just before the rounded nook and opened to reveal a masculine dressing room.

Daniel immediately swung open several of the cabinet doors that proved to be filled with high end apparel and shoes, unlike the more casual clothes Susan was used to seeing her fiancé in. The attached bathroom sported a period black marble counter atop a dark cherry vanity and one corner of the room held a modern steam shower.

"We'll have to go through to the main hall to access the rest," he explained, once again taking Daniel's hand as they moved on with their tour. "This floor had eight bedrooms. I turned one into the second dressing room and bath. This one houses the gym." He indicated an open doorway through which Susan caught a glimpse of a full range of exercise equipment. "This small one, I've turned into a linen and storage room with a laundry chute that leads to the laundry on the first floor. The rest of the rooms are all bedrooms, except for the guest bath that's the second door on the right."

"Were you thinking of one in particular for Daniel?" Susan asked.

"You're welcome to any of them," Jack addressed the boy beside him, "but I thought you might like the one I always used when I came to visit my uncle. It has its own bathroom and a window seat that allows you to see the ocean beyond the trees, and it's big enough for you to share it with Casey and Lady. Would you like to see it first?"

"Yes." Daniel suddenly looked more like a child, and Jack was surprised when the small hand in his gripped him tighter.

"It's this big room on the end, because you're going to need more space for your things as you grow older." He led the way along the rest of the hall, pausing just before they reached the door and turning Daniel around. "See? You'll have a straight shot to your mother's and my room if you need to check on us during the night, and there's a lamp on that table there that we'll leave on while we're all sleeping."

"And this was your room?" Daniel confirmed.

"Whenever I visited," his host replied. "The only problem I experienced was one spring when a family of birds moved into a nest perched on the drain pipe that runs down the outside of the window seat. Of course, I got to watch the baby birds hatch from their eggs in exchange for having to put up with their chirping. I wish you could have watched them grow with me." He let go of the boy's hand as they entered the room.

A queen-sized bed with a curved oak headboard was centered on the wall straight across, topped by a bright quilt. An oak bachelor's chest stood on either side, each holding a bedside lamp. A large dresser held pride of place on the opposite wall, and a comfortable armchair and footstool filled one corner accompanied by a good reading lamp. Two tall built-in bookcases with under cabinets flanked either side of the window seat.

"I've spent a lot of happy hours in that chair over the years," Jack shared as he sent Daniel a smile. "Why don't you check it out? I was hoping you might let me help you meet your goal of reading bigger books. We could work on it together some evenings before you go to bed. That's why there's a copy of

Tom Sawyer on the table. We would both fit in the chair if you sat on my lap. What do you think?"

Daniel climbed into the chair, where he reached over the arm and patted the German Shepherd's head. "It's just the right height for Lady and me, so it should fit Casey, too." He seemed pleased.

"The cabinets and bookcases will look better once you've filled them with your books and toys, and we can put in more shelves if you need them. Your bathroom is right through that door, and the teddy bear was mine when I was a boy. I thought maybe you and the dogs would let him stay in here with you," Jack added as he sat on the broad, upholstered footstool at the boy's feet, Susan being content to watch from where she had seated herself on the edge of the bed. "Would you mind adding him to your entourage?"

"What's his name?" Daniel asked.

"I'm afraid I never got past Teddy." Jack looked ashamed. "Perhaps, you could come up with a better one."

"I could call him John like your real name," Daniel suggested. "Then he would be both of ours."

"What a great idea!" The bear's original owner approved. "Do you want to check out the other rooms before deciding?"

"If this is my room, will we be a real family?" Daniel asked as his face once again filled with hope. "My mama and I need a big house and a real family."

"Not anymore you don't." Jack pulled him onto his lap, teddy bear and all, and held him close. "This will be both your and your mom's home with me as a family for as long as you both want it, once we all have our wedding. I'm hoping you'll both agree we can have our wedding really soon, because I love both your mama and you and having you both living here with me will make me the happiest man in the whole world."

"Can we look at the book we'll be reading now?" Daniel pointed towards the copy of *Tom Sawyer*.

"Sure." Jack reached over and retrieved it.

And as she looked on, Susan felt much of the worry leave her, replaced with relief, recognizing that a huge chunk of her son's needs had already been met by her acceptance of this man she loved so much, who would take such good care of them both going forward.

CHAPTER XLVII

Jack had been required to go to New York to take care of some personal business, so it wasn't until Friday evening that the three of them were able to get back together.

"I'll pick the two of you up on the way home from the airport," he had called Susan around three. "We can order pizza and cheesecake in from Armando's."

Forcing himself to maintain a sedate pace as he headed up The Cove's drive, he wasn't surprised when Daniel burst through the front doorway and greeted him once he alighted from the Mercedes.

"Jack!" The boy hurtled himself at his mother's fiancé's knees. "We missed you so much! Mama says she isn't going to let you ever go away without her again, and I plan to come along."

"Glad to hear it!" Jack threw an arm around Susan's shoulders where she now stood beside him, dropping a kiss on her lips. "I missed you." He held her gaze for a moment before releasing her and lifting her son off the ground, preparatory to putting him into the new child seat that now graced the second row of seating in the SUV.

"Mama, look!" Daniel drew her attention to the new acquisition. "I've already moved into Jack's car!"

"No one can say he isn't excited about his new living arrangements now, can they?" Jack asked his bride-to-be as he opened her door for her, catching her to him once again before she slipped into the passenger seat – this time kissing her more thoroughly. "I really did miss you," he whispered into her ear before standing back.

"I have a couple of surprises for the two of you," he announced to his passengers once they were headed along the main road. "You'll see the first one once we get to the house if you haven't stopped by while I was gone."

"I didn't want to go when you weren't in residence," Susan shared. "I no longer have the old need, and it would've served as a reminder that you were out of town."

"Jeff Stuart has been taking care of Lady for me the last couple of days," Jack informed the boy in the back seat, "but I imagine she would be glad to play Frisbee with you until the pizza gets here, if you're game."

"She'll want another of her little bones, too," Daniel replied in his firm way, "and Mama has two of my books."

"I hope you don't mind, but he insisted I bring two of his picture books in my purse," Susan filled her fiancé in. "I've explained to him that it's a little early for us to move in."

"Well you'll just have to unexplain then," Jack replied. "As far as I'm concerned the sooner the better. Think of me as a kid who can't wait for Christmas. What would you say to our getting married two weeks from tomorrow?"

"You meant it when you said you wanted to marry us soon, didn't you?" She glanced his way.

"Yes, I did," he confirmed, his tone more sober as he reached over and took her hand, squeezing it gently. "I'll hardly be able to stand dropping you two off at The Cove this evening."

"I'll hardly be able to stand being dropped," she admitted. "And as for that one there…" She nodded towards the back seat. "He'd spend the night tonight if you asked him."

"So what do you think?" Her groom-to-be asked as he brought the SUV to a halt at the head of the drive and then dropped into a Texas drawl. "I thought I'd spruce the ol' place up a bit, ma'am, now that there's going to be a lady and child in residence."

"Oh, Jack!" Susan surveyed all that he had arranged to have done in his absence.

Immediately to the right of her door, a low bronze sign with gold lettering indicated that this was the entrance to Blue Wolf Manor, calling on two clans of their ancestors. The old gravel drive had been replaced by a wider one of thick black pavers edged with new boxwood plantings that here and there sported solar lights between them. The house itself had been freshly painted, although where once it had been plain white the trim had now been returned to its more original painted lady glory – the shutters shiny black, while the rest had been enhanced in shades of blue with touches of gold.

"We can change out any of the colors you don't like, but I wanted it freshened before our wedding," Jack offered.

"It's beautiful just as it is," she assured him, the excitement reflected in her eyes when she met his gaze confirming her words. "Frankly, I'm relieved that you've taken it upon yourself to do all of these things to the house. You're so creative, and you have fabulous taste, not to mention that you keep Daniel and me in mind at all times. Besides, you make things happen so much quicker than I would. I would've fretted about those color choices for weeks, while you knew they would look good and proceeded."

"We make a great team, don't we?" Jack leaned over and kissed her cheek.

"Aren't we going to let Lady out?" A small voice from the back seat reminded the two adults that they weren't alone.

"Absolutely!" Jack headed the SUV along the drive, and then taking care of what he was sure would be the youngster's next priority asked, "What do you want on your pizza when I order it?"

"I take cheese, and my mama wants pepperoni," Daniel placed his order as once again, his soon-to-be stepfather noted, he saw to his mother's needs.

Three hours later, Daniel fell asleep on the couch in the parlor while listening to show tunes being played for his mother on the piano, and Jack took Susan's hand and led her onto the porch – this time asking her to join him in the double rocker.

"Daniel was thrilled with the train set you brought back for him," she said as she rested her head on his shoulder. "That was really thoughtful of you."

"Not as thoughtful as you think," Jack chuckled. "Most men still harbor their boyhood love of trains. I'll probably get as much pleasure as he will from it as we enjoy it together."

"Still…," she started to say, but he cut her off with a kiss.

"I brought a little something back for you, too," he reminded her, pulling a signature Tiffany's box from his pocket.

He opened the lid, revealing a wedding set of his and hers platinum bands along with a ring comprised of a large pink diamond surrounded by smaller white ones, and then removed the engagement ring, slipping it onto her finger. "I love you, Susie Chesterton."

"Oh, Jack! It's beautiful and so unique!" She held out her hand, allowing the stones to flash in the light coming through the French door to her left.

"I wanted to make sure all the other guys would know that you're already taken," he teased her. "Besides, it had to be the most beautiful ring they could produce. Otherwise, you would've outshined it."

"I love you, Jack Jefferson." She slid her arms around his neck, drawing his face down to hers for a kiss.

"That's all I'll ever need, Susie," he assured her. "You'll never know how much your and Daniel's love means to me."

"I feel like I'm living in a dream," she said, hoping as she did so that their love would be enough to release him from his pain once and for all.

"So do I," he beamed down at her.

"There's something else we need to discuss." Susan turned her face towards the ocean spread before them.

"Anything." Jack pulled her closer, still basking in the glow of having his ring now on her finger.

"Our wedding…"

"Yes?" He fought not to hold his breath, hoping that she didn't want to postpone it.

"I had the wedding of all weddings when I married Bill, and look what it got me." Susan straightened, slipping out of his arm as she faced him. "The thought of going through a similar ceremony makes me physically ill. But then, I remember that this is the first time for you, and I feel so selfish that I can't stand it."

"Why don't I describe to you the most beautiful wedding ceremony I ever attended," Jack suggested. "Perhaps, we could come up with something similar. It would satisfy me, and it would certainly relieve your concerns. Then I want to tell you about some things I accomplished when I met with Chase at your office before heading out of town, and there's a little something else you should know before we go any further in our relationship."

"Whose wedding was it?" she asked, more intrigued by the first part of his statement than the latter.

"It was the wedding of a Greek peasant girl on an island surrounded by the deepest blue water I've ever seen," he began his tale, and as he shared his memory with her in his calm way, Susan once again snuggled close to him, safe and secure within his encircling arm.

Buried somewhere in this strong, quiet man's many diverse memories, she now realized, was the solution to every problem that would arise during the course of their lives together, and once again, he had indeed drawn forth their answer. It would be no trouble at all to have the ceremony of his dreams in only two weeks.

CHAPTER XLVIII

Jack's proposal for their early wedding date agreed upon, Susan was relieved when he took charge of their move to Blue Wolf Manor, stating that even with the short timeframe he felt they should make it as easy on themselves as possible. Since then, he had helped her to bring over a few boxes and some hanging clothes each evening, setting up Daniel's room with him while she had begun making the dressing and bath rooms of her dreams into her own.

"I feel like I'm playing house," she laughed as she felt his arms come around her from behind. "All the drawers and cabinets are now lined, and what I still have to bring over won't even begin to fill them."

"Feel free to play in here as often as you want." He bent and kissed her neck where it joined her shoulder, pleased when she responded by arching it for more. "As for the other, you'll simply have to do some serious shopping and fill this all up after we're married. Perhaps, we can get you started on our honeymoon."

"Lady says it's time for my dinner," a small voice piped up from behind them, reminding them they weren't alone.

"That it is!" Jack hoisted the youngster into his arms. "How about you and I throwing some steaks on the grill?"

"Can I turn mine?" Daniel asked. "You can hold me."

"As long as I'm with you, I don't see why not, but you'll have to wear one of the big gloves," Jack agreed.

"What can I do, while you men are busy outside?" Susan asked.

"I've already started baked potatoes, but it would help if you would toss a salad," Jack stepped back, indicating for her to go first.

Dinner consumed and the clean-up finished, Jack and Susan adjourned to the parlor to continue work on a jigsaw puzzle, while Daniel headed upstairs to play in his future room with his furry companion, occasional shouts from upstairs peppering the adult's conversation.

"I've found it!" Susan pressed a piece of blue sky into place, just as Daniel and Lady tore into the room.

"Hurry, Lady, we have to get them!" he called out before running back along the hall and up the stairs.

"I'm afraid all of this has left him overexcited," Susan apologized as she met Jack's gaze.

"I want him to feel comfortable here," he stated, a thoughtful look on his face.

A minute later, the sound of footsteps pounding down the stairs could once again be heard. "I think they went this way," Daniel shouted as the panting dog followed him into the room.

Susan opened her mouth to reprimand her son, but never got the words out.

"Daniel…" Jack said, his voice calm and quiet. "Is it absolutely necessary to maintain that level of noise?"

Surprised, his fiancée felt a flash of anger. Who did this man think he was disciplining her son? But before she could speak, Jack continued.

"I thought we had discussed appropriate behavior in a house when we were visiting Chase and Adrianna the other day," he addressed her son in the same calm voice. "Do you remember, or am I mistaken?"

"You said it would be best if I would keep things with Max down to a gentle roar," Daniel admitted, his face reflecting his embarrassment as he met the man's steady gaze.

"Good, you were paying attention." Jack smiled at him. "Because we men need to stick together, and I'm counting on you to hold up the side."

Amazed, Susan watched as her small son's shoulders straightened.

"I'm hoping I can count on you to watch my back when I'm not around, too," her fiancé continued.

"You can count on me," Daniel promised, his face intent. "We men always have to remember the ladies' sensa…sensa…"

"Sensibilities," Jack finished for him.

"That's right." The four-year-old nodded his head in agreement. "They have sensibilities, and we men have to keep them in our minds." He turned his back on the two adults and addressed the dog, who was seated on the floor behind him, waiting for his attention. "Lady, you have to keep them in your mind, too. Otherwise, I might forget."

Finding it hard to repress a giggle, Susan worked to keep a straight face as her young son started to leave the room, but then he paused and turned.

"Will you be watching my back, too?" Daniel asked, his face filled with so much hope that Susan held her breath, willing the man beside her not to hurt her child.

"Come here, Partner," Jack called him forward, sliding his chair away from the table and taking the boy onto his lap. "That's a serious adult question, and it deserves a serious adult answer." He met Daniel's worried gaze. "Know that you can always count on me to watch your back, to be there for you day or night, rain or cold, thick or thin. If you need me, I'll be there quick as a wink."

For a moment, the room fell silent except for the ticking of the clock on the mantle as Daniel considered the words he had just heard.

"Cross your heart and hope to die?" Hope again returned to the boy's face as his fingers marked his narrow chest.

"Cross my heart and hope to die." Jack took the smaller hand in his and marked his own broad chest.

"Word of honor?" Daniel asked, his expression so serious that his mother caught a quick glimpse of the teenager he would become.

"Word of honor as a gentleman." Jack's face reflected the same serious expression.

For a moment, Susan heard the voices of men she had truly admired and trusted – her father, her uncle Augustus, Andy, Larry and Chase – each of them having at one time or another used similar words in the same serious manner.

And as she watched the man she loved more than life itself hug her son to him, drop a kiss on the boy's disheveled blond waves and then smooth them gently with the fingers of his strong hand, Daniel snuggling against this man's chest, she wondered how she could've ever doubted, even for a moment, her Jack's ability to be the father that her child so needed.

CHAPTER XLIX

In the master suite of Sheffield Place Inn, Kate Sinclair took a long curly lock of her naturally blonde hair between her thumb and forefinger and lifted it out one-quarter inch further from her head, before giving her reflection a brief nod of appreciation.

It had been a long time since she had taken so much trouble over her appearance for any man and even longer since she had laid eyes on this particular gentleman - too long. After all, this was the one man in the world she had ever loved, her only hero, despite all the strong forces that had joined together to keep them apart.

Slipping a tube of lip gloss into her purse, she spritzed a bit of perfumed mist on her left wrist and then rubbed it against the other, remembering the birthday when she had opened the box containing the first bottle of perfume he had given her. Every really meaningful gift she had ever received had come from him, along with the postcards and letters sent from all over the world, and yet, she had neglected him shamefully as life had drawn her forward in its hard, relentless way.

Well, no more…

Picking up the security card from where it lay on the writing desk, she paused for a moment and took in the lovely view, wondering if his home had a similar one. Then she took a deep breath before crossing the room, determined.

Jack Jefferson, she thought, was about to receive the surprise of his life.

Anderson heard Susan C's deep, sexy voice even before he saw the curves of her body outlined against the glass of his office door. The 'bad guys' as her son had called them were all put away. Now settlement of her account and cementing their relationship in some way were the only two things left on his agenda.

"May I come in?" She asked, opening the door herself, and he gestured to her that it was okay even as he sent her a broad grin.

But instead of taking the seat that stood ready on the other side of his desk, she gracefully made her way around to his side, pausing until he swiveled his chair around to face her and then surprising him by taking a seat in his lap, her light scent filling the air around him.

"I've come to say thank you and goodbye." She bent and brushed her lips across his. "You've been amazing, and there's really no way that I can thank you enough."

Yes, there was, he thought to himself, unable to get any words past the lump that had formed in his throat.

"Now, though, I'm taking my son to my mom's place in L.A., so that both of us can breathe a bit easier and heal from all of this," she continued perfectly aware, he was sure, of what her nearness was doing to him. "I'm going to miss you, and I hope you're going to miss me. In the meantime, maybe this will help keep the flame that's been ignited between us burning."

And then, she took his face in her hands and kissed him as he'd never been kissed before as he brought his arms around her and held her close.

"Soon, Big Guy, I'll be back real soon." She drew away, undid his grip on her and stood - her beautiful blue eyes awash with tears, pausing to remove a check from her purse and leave it face down on his desk, before walking out of his life through the glaze that now filled his own eyes.

Jack glanced up from his computer, the motion of Susan's car approaching along the drive outside having caught his attention. Clicking on Save, he hurried to meet her.

"I've brought some more boxes," she announced. "Daniel keeps insisting that I bring more of his books and toys, and I tossed in the last of my suits and dresses."

"Let's get them inside then," he replied as he drew her to him, kissing her with the passion she had come to delight in – a promise of things to come.

"No one can say that I haven't done my stair stepper routine for the day." She laughed a few minutes later as they deposited the remaining boxes from her car's trunk onto the floor in front of the window seat in what was soon to be Daniel's room. "I love the way the light fills this space."

"I want him to feel he's in a happy place," Jack said, throwing an arm around her shoulders. "I was a little concerned it might be too adult for him, but he seems to have taken to it like a duck to water."

"He's thrilled with it in part because it was yours," Susan shared with him. "I keep telling you he has a bad case of hero worship."

"You two and your heroes." Jack rolled his eyes and then held her gaze. "All I need is for both of you to love me." He drew her to him and planted a firm kiss on her lips.

"I'm afraid I'll always think of you as my knight in shining armor," she teased once his grip loosened.

"I suppose there are…," he started to reply, but the sound of the old-fashioned doorbell announcing a visitor downstairs interrupted whatever he had been going to say. "I wonder who that is." He released her. "Back in a jif," he said over his shoulder as he once again headed for the stairs.

"I've come," Kate Sinclair announced when he swung open the door a few moments later, barely getting the simple words out before her shoulders shook with the sobs she had held in for so long.

"Yes, you have." He stepped onto the porch and clutched her to him, blinking back tears of his own. "Welcome to my home."

And so it was that Susan came downstairs a moment later to find her groom-to-be holding a gorgeous younger woman with a figure to die for tightly to him.

CHAPTER L

Lady choosing that moment to nuzzle the back of her owner's knee, Jack glanced up to find Susan watching them, a confused look on her face, and held out his hand to her. "Susie, I'd like you to meet my sister Kate who has come for our wedding," he introduced them.

"I'm so glad!" Susan stepped forward immediately, a welcoming smile on her face. "Have you driven far?"

"Only from the Sheffield Place Inn this morning," Kate replied as she sent her brother's fiancée a watery smile in return. "I'm afraid I'm making a fool of myself, but seeing Jack, well…"

Susan laughed as she put her arm around the other woman's waist and drew her towards the front door. "I'm glad it's you that's crying all over him this time and not me – long story that I'll explain after we've all settled down for a nice chat. I don't know what it is about your brother, but he seems to attract teary-eyed females."

Never having imagined that he would see the two women he loved most in the world together in the same place so soon, Jack worked to pull himself back together as he followed them to the kitchen.

"I haven't seen him for so long you see." His sister's words floated back to him. "Not since I was married to the man of my mother's dreams four years ago, but that is all over now as are a lot of things."

"Which would you prefer, coffee or tea?" Susan asked their guest.

"A cup of coffee would be nice," Kate stated, her eyes taking in the warm atmosphere of the large kitchen.

"Jack, would you mind calling John Thornburg and my mother?" Susan asked over her shoulder as she filled the large kettle from the stove with water. "Tell her that I'll be home before five."

"Sure," he agreed, understanding the need both to arrange for another plate at the rehearsal dinner that would be held that evening at Montgomery's and to ask his future mother-in-law if she could add the care and feeding of Daniel to her day.

"Where would you like to sit?" Susan asked his sister as he reentered the kitchen and accepted a mug from his fiancée filled with cream-laced coffee fixed exactly like he preferred. "The porch has a lovely view, and we could give you a tour of the downstairs on the way."

"I wondered if you would have a view like the one from my room at the inn." Kate turned to him. "You always have loved the water."

"The porch it is then." He opened the door to the butler's pantry. "Let's go through here." He responded to Susan's raised eyebrow with an affirmative nod as his sister passed through the doorway, pleased by what a great team his Susie and he made in the face of an unforeseen circumstance. "Thank you," he mouthed the words as she slipped past him.

Once the home's downstairs had been admired and they were all settled in rockers on the wide porch, Kate turned to her brother. "I imagine you're wondering how I found out about your wedding."

"No, it's simply an answer to prayer," he said, his dimples in evidence on either side of his smile, "but why don't you tell us just the same?"

"I found this in the trash at Mom and Dad's." She placed the printed invitation he had sent, now creased and stained, on the pine table.

"The last letter I mailed to you a few weeks ago had come back, and an internet search hadn't yielded any results," he explained. "I hoped this might find its way to you one way or another. Do they know that you're here?"

"Yes, which won't make for an easy homecoming when I return on Sunday, but I don't really care," she replied, the crease between her brow belying her words.

"Did I overhear you saying that your marriage is over?" her brother asked.

"Yes, four weeks ago I finally reached the point where I couldn't stand one more minute of it," Kate shared. "I arranged for a moving company to show up three days later, while Samuel Meriweather Sinclair V was gone on an overnight business trip, and they removed my clothes and the few things I had brought to my farce of a marriage. Most of the clothes are now crammed into my room at Mom and Dad's, while the rest is in storage until I definitely decide where to go." She turned to her soon-to-be sister-in-law. "What you must think of me!"

"I think you've gone through a rough time, the same as I did," Susan said, not surprised when Jack reached over and took her hand in his. "My own divorce was final after six empty years this past April, and I moved back from D.C. to Captain's Point, just in time to meet your brother when he first arrived. Basically, he's spent the past months helping me put myself back together enough that I could consider his wonderful proposal, which wasn't easy for him because I had a fairly closed mind when it came to allowing another man in my life."

"Additionally, Susan had carried the concern of how her divorce was affecting her four-year-old son," Jack filled in the blanks for his sister's benefit. "You'll meet Daniel tonight at our rehearsal dinner, which we're having uncharacteristically early since there is no need for an actual rehearsal and we don't want Daniel staying up too late beyond his normal bedtime so he'll be rested tomorrow. He's a charmer, and I hope you'll learn to love him as much as I do."

"I'm sure I will," Kate said, suppressing all the questions she would've liked to ask for some another time.

"Why don't you arrange for your sister to ride over with Edmund and Marissa?" Susan addressed Jack.

"Good idea." He lifted his phone and settled the matter. "I stayed at the inn myself while I was completing the renovations here," he explained to his sister after disconnecting the call, "so Edmund and Marissa were the first friends I made in Captain's Point. They, Adrianna and Chase Sheffield who own the inn and live next door, Susan's family and a small number of common friends make up our guest list, so you shouldn't feel too lost in the shuffle. We'll all be sitting around one large table."

"We're having a very simple wedding as well," Susan continued. "I couldn't face another big one, and your brother drew forth a lovely solution from one of his experiences."

"He has a wonderful way of doing that." Kate's eyes filled with affection.

"So what are you planning on doing now that you've left what's his name?" Jack asked.

"I'm not really sure," Kate replied. "Thanks to the pre-nuptial Dad arranged, I don't have to work, so I can take my time deciding. I know more what I don't want than what I do. I know I don't want to continue life as I've known it. I had been thinking about a possible move to somewhere in Europe to place me closer to you."

"Good thing you caught up with me then." Jack chuckled. "I can offer you the farm in Virginia or the condo in New York, if either of them would suit you on a temporary basis until you decide where you want to go permanently."

"You always have been the kindest of all brothers," Kate said, blinking back tears, "but I've been giving somewhere else some serious consideration since I found this." She tapped the invitation with a well-manicured fingertip. "Once you two are back from your honeymoon, I would like to return for a visit, during which I would seriously consider moving here to Captain's Point."

"Of course, you must come!" Susan stated immediately. "You'll always be welcome in our home." Then thinking that she might have spoken out of turn, she turned quickly to her fiancé for confirmation, relieved to find only gratitude in his eyes as they met hers.

"I couldn't have said it any better." He smiled back at her.

CHAPTER LI

"Jack!" Daniel ran forward and greeted his mother's fiancé with his normal exuberance, when the groom entered the large private room at Montgomery's that evening. "I was afraid you were going to be late for our dinner."

"Now you should've known that I wouldn't let the side down like that." Jack lifted the child into his arm and straightened the little guy's clip-on bow tie. "I must say you look rather elegant in your suit."

"I wore this one when I helped Adrianna marry Chase, and Grandpa says it's a miracle that I'm getting so much use out of it," Daniel filled him in. "I have a new one for our wedding tomorrow in case I spill something on my shirt tonight, but I'm going to be careful."

"So am I," Jack commiserated with him. "This is a brand new tie." He casually freed the length of expensive silk from where it lay crumpled beneath the child's knee.

"Mama said it's the cream of crab soup that I have to watch out for," Daniel stated. "It's delicious, but it stains."

"Thanks for warning me." Jack's eyes searched the room, pleased when he found both of his women standing with a group in the far corner that included Adrianna and Bev.

"Glad you could make it." Larry joined them from behind.

"Jack wouldn't be late for our dinner," Daniel stated in his firm way. "He watches my back."

"And I thought I was doing that." Larry put on a hurt look.

"Two people are always better than one," Daniel quoted another adultism.

"I'd like to meet with you professionally once Susan and I return from our honeymoon," Jack addressed Larry. "Chase and I set some things in motion for the little guy here when I met with him last week, and the next step for me will be transferring some securities. You would be the logical person after Susan to have access to those."

"Sure, give me a call whenever you're ready," Larry said. "We aim to please. By the way, who's that gorgeous blonde with my cousin?"

"Which gorgeous blonde?" Jim Laidlaw had joined them just in time to hear the critical words. "Oh, the one standing by Susan. You're right, she's a looker."

"Who is our newcomer?" Paul Lynch, who would be officiating at the wedding, asked as he approached. "The one with the lovely blonde hair?"

"I see Susan and Adrianna have your sister well in hand," Chase entered the conversation fresh from the kitchen where he had been chatting with John Thornburg.

"Your sister?" Larry and Jim asked in unison, as each tried to remember what their initial comment about her had been.

"My one and only," Jack confirmed, adding a stern look to his face, "and you know how big brothers are about their little sisters. Perhaps, I should mention that I have a black belt hanging on a hook in my closet."

"My belt is brown," Daniel spoke up, fingering the strip of leather that was holding up his suit pants. "I'll wear my black one tomorrow."

Having glanced over her shoulder, Susan picked this moment to lead her fiancé's sister forward to meet them. "Kate, this is my cousin Larry, Chase who is Adrianna's husband and the inn's owner, Jim, our local veterinarian, and Paul Lynch, our minister," she handled the introductions. "You can only believe the things Chase and Paul say."

"Unfair!" Larry held up his hands as if warding off a blow. "And after all the times I've been there for you over the years."

"I've never told but one lie in my life," Jim objected, "and that was when I said I didn't know who had cut an inch off your pigtail."

"Who did?" Daniel's eyes widened.

"Your Aunt Courtney," Jim told him. "She was playing hair stylist and got carried away, but I wasn't going to be the one to tell on her."

Kate laughed. "I believe I'll have to give all of you the benefit of the doubt."

"I'd like one of those," Daniel whispered in Jack's ear as he pointed towards the trays of hors d'oeurvres that the restaurant's staff was passing around.

Jack signaled one of the servers and she hurried over, handing him a cocktail napkin as Daniel helped himself to a miniature crab cake.

"Did everything go all right?" Arthur drew the groom to where Edwina waited for them, as Daniel grabbed another crab cake in passing.

"Yes, she's going to love it," Jack replied, referring to a painting of his Susan's view that he had commissioned from Arthur to hang over the bombe chest in the foyer of what would soon be their joint home. "That particular bit of scenery holds a lot of meaning for her, and you did a marvelous job. Not everyone can capture the essence of a seascape. She won't see it before tomorrow, so mum's the word."

"You can count on us," Edwina stated, "and you're right. I keep telling Arthur that his seascapes are really quite special."

"I wondered if you would be willing to paint a portrait of my bride from the photograph that will be taken tomorrow afternoon," Jack said. "Could I get in touch with you when we return from our honeymoon?"

"I'd be honored," Arthur agreed, obviously pleased at having been asked. "I feel as if I'm standing at the beginning of an entirely new life."

"That makes two of us." Jack sent him a grin as he threw his free arm around his intended, who had managed to pull herself away from the larger group and had just that second joined them.

"We're going to be a family," Daniel announced. "Jack, Mama, Casey, Lady and me. We have a big, happy house."

"Yes, you do." Edwina smiled at him. "You're a very lucky little boy."

Wondering what had become of his sister, Jack glanced to where an even larger group had now gathered around her – the only other woman in the assemblage being Adrianna, who stood at the back of the crowd with her husband's arms wrapped around her from behind.

Five hours later, the highly successful dinner party having been enjoyed by all present, Kate stood at the window of her room in the Sheffield Place Inn, looking over the moonlit water of the ocean that lay beyond the expanse of lawn below her. Tomorrow afternoon, her confirmed bachelor brother would say a few words and be married, and she could honestly say, having gotten to know Susan, that she was glad for him and pleased she would be welcome in their home.

Jack had been right about Daniel, too. He was a charmer. She already loved his sweet smile and open nature, and it was obvious that the child hero-worshipped her brother.

How she had dreaded this evening, and yet how welcome she had been made to feel! Who would've known that, in the space of only twelve hours, she would reunite with her brother, be received with open arms by his bride-to-be, have her cheek kissed by her new nephew, and meet the love of her life? There was now no doubt in her mind whatsoever. She would be moving to Captain's Point – the sooner the better.

CHAPTER LII

"Mama! Mama! Wake up!" Daniel ran into Susan's room the next morning. "We have to get ready for our wedding!"

A glance at her alarm having told her that it was only eight o'clock, Susan groaned. "The ceremony doesn't start until four." She threw back her covers. "Why don't you snuggle here with me for a few minutes, so I can wake up a little more slowly?"

"Okay, but you can't fall asleep." Daniel climbed up.

"May I ask you a question?"

"Sure," he snuggled close.

"What do you feel when you think about Jack?" she asked.

"Jack feels strong like Cousin Larry and Uncle Chase and Grandpa," he answered, once again not saying what his mother had hoped to hear. "Do you want me to tell you who will be coming?"

"If you would like." Susan wrapped the covers around them both.

"Jack is coming," Daniel began, holding up one of his fingers, "and Grandma is coming and Grandpa is coming and..."

Knowing he would continue through the entire guest list, even though the first name was the only one who would really matter in the long run, Susan allowed her mind to wander. What a lovely wedding they were having, and how much nicer it all was than the circus she had gone through before, primarily at the insistence of Bill and his mother – neither of whom had lifted a finger to help.

On the other hand, except for picking out her dress and bouquet, Jack had taken on the responsibility for this wedding's preparations himself, only asking her to choose between two possible invitations and two menus each for the previous evening's rehearsal dinner and the sit-down reception afterwards at what would soon be their new home.

"And Casey is coming and Lady is coming and Max is coming and Terror is coming," Daniel continued his litany by her side as she half dreamed of her husband-to-be's strong arms around her.

Simultaneously, the gentleman in question straightened a corner of the candlewick spread under which she would sleep between lavender-scented sheets in the four-poster bed that evening and then paused to glance around the room before checking on the progress being made on the lawn outside. There had been times when he had thought this day might never come, moments when he had doubted his ability to draw his Susie to him. And yet, in the end, she had agreed to share the rest of her life with him, not yet aware of the full extent of what that would mean for her and her child, content with nothing more than him.

Having straightened the vase of fresh flowers that awaited his bride on the dresser, he hurried downstairs where he signaled for Lady to heel as she accompanied him through the French doors and down the porch steps to the spot on the lawn overlooking the ocean view where a white wrought iron arbor had been placed.

"We'll only be a few more minutes," the florist greeted him with a smile as she tucked another flower into the vine-covered structure. "Cheryl has almost finished with the rest." She indicated oversized pots of white carnations between which Susan and he would stand while they spoke their vows to each other and six smaller pots of yellow carnations arranged in two rows of three each to form a short aisle. "You've been lucky. These unseasonably warm, sunny days are supposed to last through next Monday."

"I've been lucky ever since Susan agreed to marry me," Jack filled her in. "I'm counting on being lucky for a long time to come."

He thanked the woman and her staff for a wonderful job and returned to the house via the front door that now sported two large pots of white carnations on either side of it. Pausing in the foyer, he admired the ribbon and bow the florist had attached to Arthur's painting where it hung over the bombe chest – the first thing Susan would notice when she arrived to dress for their wedding - and then headed to the kitchen.

An hour later, having deposited bowls of nuts and candy on various pieces of furniture in the main downstairs rooms, he left extra containers of each on the counter in the butler's pantry, so that the serving staff sent by Montgomery's could refill them. Jeff Stuart had helped him add the three leaves to the dining room table earlier that day, and he now spread it with a white linen cloth and then added the candles and low floral arrangements that the florist had left for him in the pantry. A little while later, twenty-four place settings of the china, crystal and silver Susan and he had chosen together laid out in style, he pronounced the house ready and then glanced at his watch, knowing that he was supposed to leave no later than noon.

At five minutes past noon, Chase opened the door of Montgomery House. "Just on time," he welcomed Jack. "We thought the blue room would be best," he said as he led the way up the main stairs and turned left. "My bathroom is across the hall, and you're welcome to it. Penny left a clean towel and washcloth on the bed." He opened the room's closet door. "Hang your suit in here, and then let's grab a bite of lunch with Adrianna and your sister. I think they're taking a look at the rose garden."

"I appreciate your letting me make free use of your home," Jack thanked him, "and also for covering for Susan at the firm these past two days and while we're on our honeymoon."

"Not at all," Chase assured him as they made their way downstairs. "I owe Susan, and we're thrilled for both of you. Your bride is the closest thing to a sister that I'll ever have, and Adrianna has been betting on you ever since you came here for your interview. Neither of us has any doubt that you two will be as happy together in your own way as we are in ours."

"We wondered when you men would remember us," Adrianna greeted them when they entered the kitchen. "What would you like to drink, Jack? We have sodas, iced tea and lemonade."

"Iced tea will be fine." He gave his sister a hug. "How're you doing, Twinkle Toes?"

"You see how he treats me," Kate said, rolling her eyes, "and still I've come to his wedding."

"For which I am grateful," her brother replied, his tone now serious. "I, of all people, know what it has cost you."

"Everyone, grab your glass, and then we're ready," Adrianna stated as Chase led the group into the morning room that was comfortably bathed in the slanted rays of the October sun.

At half past two, Larry opened the door of his SUV for his cousin. "Nervous?" he asked once he got behind the wheel.

"Not a bit," she replied, smiling back at him. "Jack has made everything so easy. I feel like I'm living in a warm, soft dream, and I don't want to wake up."

"I don't think you will this time, Cuz." Larry brought their vehicle to a halt at the end of the drive and glanced her way. "Jack's top of the line."

"Yes, he is," she agreed, "and he'll be good for Daniel, too."

"Thanks for picking me up." Courtney slid into the backseat a few minutes later. "It's a zoo in there." She indicated her farmhouse. "Andy and Trey are riding Lizzie around on their backs. I don't think their jeans will have any knees in them by the time I next see them, and the older ones are playing loud card games."

"At least, they're having a fun time, the same as we all used to," Larry pointed out as they headed for Blue Wolf Manor.

"Just the same, I'm glad that I drew the short straw and get to help the bride here," Courtney said as she reached up and patted her sister's shoulder. "I must say that you've found a winner in Jack. Any man who arranges his own wedding is a keeper in my book, and those dimples..." She placed her hand over her heart.

Adrianna and Kate arrived at three, in plenty of time to open the door to Montgomery's catering staff and the photographer, before acting as hostesses as the other guests arrived. Chase and Jack were the last to make an appearance at a quarter to four. Jack took a few moments to welcome everyone and then ushered most onto the lawn, where Paul Lynch took up his position in front of the arbor, his back to the bride's favorite view.

The groom stood waiting in his spot by one of the oversized pots filled with white flowers, looking splendid in a black suit, white shirt and a black-shot-with-gold silk tie, the cuff links in his French cuffs flashing real ruby red in the afternoon light.

Chase held onto Max's green leash, the dog adding a bit of sartorial elegance to the occasion - the only guest outfitted in a tux. Andy's son and daughter performed the same duty for Casey and Terror, while Marissa stood quietly with Lady by her side.

At precisely four o'clock, Edmund played the first bars of Mozart that signified the bride was about to make her appearance. Kate escorted by Larry was the first to appear in the doorway, followed by Anders and Elizabeth, all four crossing the lawn and then taking up their positions on either side of the back of the floral aisle.

Finally, the bride stepped onto the wide porch, wearing a simple scooped-neck, cream dress with a gathered bodice and short sleeves, its skirt flowing softly around her ankles - the three yellow and one white roses of her bouquet signifying joy, gladness, happy love, and the promise of a new beginning. Her small son accompanied her across the lawn and then walked her along the aisle, the air filled with the mingled scent of the pine woods that lay behind them and the salt air blowing softly off the sea spread before them.

"We're here, Jack," the youngster announced their arrival as the groom took his mother's hand.

"Thank you, Daniel," his soon-to-be stepfather replied, giving his small hand a shake.

"I'll be watching your back during our wedding," the boy stage whispered and then surprised everyone, including his mother, by calmly walking back to where his grandmother awaited him.

"Who gives this woman in marriage?" Paul asked.

"Her mother and I do," Anders strong voice carried forward.

"And me," Daniel added.

The sides of his mouth twitching, Paul moved the service forward until the bride and groom had exchanged rings and been declared husband and wife, at which point he stated, "You may now kiss the bride."

Jack smiled down at Susan and drew her to him, just as a small voice piped up from behind them.

"My mama's lovely isn't she, Grandma?" Daniel asked.

In the process of lowering his lips to his bride's, Jack paused and looked over his shoulder at the miscreant – a twinkle in his dark eyes, his dimples clearly showing. "That she is, Partner," he agreed with his new son and then, finishing what he had started, kissed his bride with such tenderness that two women in the wedding party felt their knees weaken.

Not quite finished, Daniel took a step forward into the aisle and placed his hands on his hips as if defying anyone in the assembled group to challenge his next words. "I like Jack," he stated in a firm voice. "He loves my mama and me, and we love him back."

Whereupon Susan let out a small sigh as she met her new husband's twinkling, love-filled eyes, giving herself up to him completely, for the first time in a long time looking forward to her and her son's lives ahead without a care in the world.

EPILOGUE

"It's a good thing Jack and Susan took us up on our offer of the beach house in Key West for use during their honeymoon, since they didn't want to leave Daniel behind for too long." Chase glanced up at Adrianna, who sat next to him at the breakfast room table. "Listen to what I just found," he said and then read aloud an excerpt from his morning paper.

"'This reporter has just uncovered startling news that will send women all over the world into deep mourning. Award-winning author John Jeffers – known for the Anderson Detective Series and literary novels *Leaving It All Behind*, *Drifter*, *Adventures*, *Red Plains*, *White Water*, *Tall Peaks*, *Jungle Places*, *Desert Skies, Destined, Delivered*, and most recently *Heading Home* – long considered to be one of the world's Ten Most Eligible Bachelors, was married yesterday in a private ceremony on his secluded property in Captain's Point, Maryland.

"'Those of us here wish him and his new bride, Susan, the best!'"

"I'm almost done with this one." Adrianna picked up a paperback copy of *Leaving It All Behind* from beside her plate. "You're sure you can put your hands on all the rest of them, aren't you? I can't wait to read them."

"Absolutely, I know right where they are," Chase assured her, "but you really need to read them straight through before you get to this one." He pointed to his own paperback of *Heading Home*.

Smiling, he remembered placing his copy of *Delivered* on the bench seat between the two of them after Jack's interview - the opening quote 'The world was my oyster, and I preferred to travel life's road to the beat of a different drummer.' that appeared in the front of each book having blown the author's cover when he had repeated it to one of his most loyal and sympathetic fans.

Love's Journey

The next novel in the Captain's Point Stories series is coming soon!

A Special Treat for You!

From

Charlotte Kent

A Clue for Adrianna

Chase and Adrianna's Courtship

Chapter One

Viewing the tarmac beneath her, Adrianna Montgomery could see Chicago's Midway Airport's ground crew loading last minute luggage and truly relaxed for the first time since her arrival home to her condo in Seattle the previous evening.

"Is this seat taken?" a shy, cultured voice asked from the aisle to her right.

Turning, she found herself looking into a pair of worried blue eyes. Reflexively, she straightened the seat belt and lowered the arm that would separate them as she replied, "No, it's free. Help yourself."

"Thank you." The elderly woman joined her. "I don't often fly, and I've been dreading hours spent aloft beside a crying child." With the toe of a tiny shoe, the newcomer pushed a large patent leather handbag beneath the forward seat before fastening her seatbelt.

A light fragrance of honeysuckle wafted its way towards Adrianna, reminiscent of early childhood summers spent playing in the gazebo behind her great-aunt's seaside mansion, breezes blowing off the Atlantic lifting her dark curls. Despite her parents having left her behind as they had traveled the world in search of archeological treasure, those had been happy times.

But then, she had grown old enough to accompany them, and the summer visits had ended. As promised, she had written to her great-aunt of her travels, her childish script filling pages with stories of her adventures – a camel ride in Egypt, a mosaic at a dig in Turkey, a Minoan vase her mother had uncovered on a Greek isle – the list had gone on and on.

"My name's Edwina Foster." Her traveling companion broke through her thoughts. "I'm flying to visit my grandson and his wife."

"This trip is strictly business for me," Adrianna replied.

"Actually, it's more than a visit." The blue eyes now twinkled. "They're in their mid-thirties, and Ginny is expecting their first child. Jason has to attend a long conference in New York and didn't want to leave his wife alone this close to her due date. They've just moved to Captain's Point, Maryland, and haven't had time to make friends."

"Captain's Point?"

"Do you know it? I hear it's lovely."

"I haven't been there for any length of time since I was seven – almost twenty years ago, but I liked it back then. The town was full of little shops, but my favorite memory is of looking for shells on the beach."

With a start, Adrianna realized she had just lied. Her favorite memory had nothing to do with the beach, but rather with the wind-tossed woods behind the giant house.

One day during the early part of her last summer visit, she had found an old butterfly net stuffed between the croquet sticks and badminton racquets that were stored in a deep closet beneath the staircase. Not wanting to disturb her great-aunt's pre-dinner nap, she had gone outside to play with it, neglecting to tell the housekeeper where she was going. Happily chasing a bevy of yellow and white butterflies, she had left the manicured lawn and entered the cool quiet of the woods.

Other paths covered in pine needles had crossed, joined and then separated from the one that she had followed, and as the sun had set, she had realized that she was lost. A twig had snapped sharply somewhere behind her, and she had started to run, her way partially revealed through the leaves of the trees by a full moon rising overhead. Inevitably, she had tripped on a root and fallen to her knees, her right one striking the corner of a sharp pebble as she had let out a cry.

"Who is it?" A voice had called out up ahead.

"Adrianna," she had responded, forgetting her great-aunt's careful instructions about speaking with strangers.

"Stay where you are," the voice had commanded. "I'm coming."

A light rounded the bend ahead and came towards her, at first blocking her view of the boy who was carrying it. "What are you doing out here?" He had dropped a backpack onto the ground. "Miss Martha will be fit to be tied."

"You know my great-aunt?"

"Everyone knows Martha Montgomery." He had shrugged, calmly pulling a first aid kit from his pack and cleaning the cut on her knee with water from a Boy Scout canteen. "These woods aren't safe at night for a little girl."

"You're here," she had pointed out.

"But I'm older, and besides, I'm collecting specimens for my merit badge."

At the time, she hadn't known what a merit badge was, but it had sounded important. Silently, she had watched as he had applied an adhesive bandage to the cut by the light of his flashlight.

"I'll walk you back." He had held out his hand, and she had taken it gladly.

As the aircraft's engines roared to life, Edwina's voice broke through Adrianna's long ago memories. "I'm sure I wasn't the first person my grandson called on, but still, it's nice to be needed," Edwina admitted.

"I know they'll appreciate your help," she assured her traveling companion.

Turning towards the window, Adrianna watched as the runway flashed by, wondering if she had ever been needed by anyone – certainly not by her bright, shining parents, who had left her at a Swiss finishing school just two weeks before they had plunged to their deaths from one of the infamous curves along the Amalfi coast. And yet, here she was, flying from one end of the country to the other in response to two letters – one that had been more a command than a request and one that had broken her heart.

Another Special Treat for You!

From

Annie Acorn

Murder with My Darling

Chapter One

"Hi! Have a seat. I've been waiting for you forever. Where have you been?"

So began my conversation with my Chunk of Hunk, Dave Crockett, the courageous and bold sheriff of Missing County, Tennessee, on that fateful morning about which I have decided to tell you.

Yeah, I know, his name's kind of weird, but with a face like his, he can get by on it. Thick black wavy hair, deep blue eyes, and a dimple in each chin – all coming at you from atop a drop dead gorgeous body, and you've just about got him.

Me?

Why, Sugar, thanks for asking. I'm a blonde, but the shade depends on which month we're in. This month it's Golden Tiger. Yrraaah!

What? Did I scare you? Now, I didn't mean to do that. Please, forgive me. Now, where were we?

Oh, yeah, Dave had just managed to amble his way into the Coffee Mug down on Main Street, where I had been waiting for at least twenty minutes. Well, okay, maybe it was ten, but then, I had known he was going to be late - everyone in town did.

Having just fished Johnny Brown's body from the big fishing pool down on Possum Creek, Dave was sure to be having a rather long conversation with the coroner.

Since Nick Jones, Missing County's Coroner, also owns the local sporting goods store and deer hunting season was just two days away, well, you get my drift. Those two guys were sure to talk hunting of more than one kind – deer hunting as well as Dave's hunt for a murderer.

Yes, I said murderer, because that is what my drop dead Chunk of Hunk was going to have to go after first. The bullet hole right smack dab in the middle of Johnny Brown's skull had made that much pretty clear.

"You know where I've been, Bonnie Lou." Dave sent me one of his signature grins – the one that turns my knees into something akin to raspberry jelly.

"I know where you should've been, but that isn't quite the same, is it?" I met his deep blues head on without flinching – a little sass goes a long way with a he-man like him.

"I've been with Nick, and no, we weren't talking about deer hunting. Well, okay, maybe we did touch on it just a little. Johnny Brown always was a bother, though, and you know it. Why'd the old skunk have to go and get himself killed right before deer season starts?" He waved for Denise to wander over when she had a chance and take our order.

Since Denise was making girly eyes with her overly lined, crow feet enhanced browns at some trucker who wore his forehead low and his jeans lower, I figured my two over easies with a side of bacon might be a while. My stomach, of course, just kept growling.

"It was bad." Dave dropped onto the turquoise vinyl banquette across from me. "Real bad, but don't you go telling folks."

"Cross my heart." I leaned forward.

"This wasn't some kind of accident," Dave paused and looked around, before lowering his voice even further. "Whoever it was had tied Johnny's hands behind his back real tight-like. There were rope burns."

"And?" I positioned the girls on the tabletop in just such a way as to interest him.

"Nick says it looks like he was beaten first, too. There are bruises all over his body."

"Sounds nasty." I sat back a bit, figuring that I had given him enough of a show.

"I said it was bad." He relaxed in his normal lounge position against the banquette.

I smelled Denise's Eau de Paris before I could see her and hoped that the trucker she was after didn't have allergies.

"What can I get you two lovebirds this morning?" She leered at my man, having plastered on one of her the-better-to-eat-you-with smiles, but then, I couldn't blame her.

Missing County's Greatest Sheriff looked mighty fine sitting there in his uniform, especially when you compared my guy with her trucker and his big hairy hands. Why, her dubious catch looked like he was wearing parts of a gorilla suit beneath his old oil-stained jean jacket. I mean, really. Who would want hands like those touching them?

Well, obviously, someone like Denise would.

"I'll have one of my usuals." I sent her a smile as I reached out with my perfectly manicured index finger, my color looking so much better than her out of date Spicy Orange, and stroked my guy's hand just to, you know, kind of stake out my territory. "What about you, Davey?"

What was that? Oh, I did my nails just this morning. It's called Sizzling Pink. Glad that you like it. Come to the shop after this is all over, and I'll do yours myself.

"Fix me a plate with a couple of eggs, an order of grits, and a side of chipped beef gravy over a biscuit." Dave replaced the menu he hadn't needed into the rack with its brothers.

"Coffee?" Denise ignored my empty mug.

"Black." Dave had the good sense to turn his gaze back towards me.

I made a show of pulling out a couple of napkins from the dispenser and laying them out for the two of us. It's a nesting thing, but the old girl got the message.

"So who do you think did it?" I asked as soon as Denise had brought a twin of my mug for Dave and left us one of those insulated pitchers of coffee that she almost spilled because she wasn't watching what she was doing. Women her age... Well, we won't go there.

"There's no telling." Dave picked up his spoon and twirled it back and forth through his fingers, just like I had taught him when we were both in the fourth grade and I still had to practice my baton twirling. "Johnny didn't have any friends."

"He didn't have any enemies either," I pointed out. "He was one of those guys that are just in the way – always coming in the door just when you were going out, know what I mean?"

"Yeah." Dave exchanged his knife for his spoon, and it quickly became no more than a silver blur in the shape of a circle. "He was always in front of you in line at the Post Office, just when you were in a hurry, but people don't kill for that. Well, maybe in New York City or Chicago, but not here in Missing County."

For a moment, we both sat and sipped on our coffee, thinking of poor, bothersome Johnny Brown lying on a cold slab in the morgue. No one, not even someone who's such a bother, deserves that.

Then I let out a giggle, and Dave shot me a look.

"It sure will be quicker to mail off our Christmas gifts to your sister this year." I felt laughter bubble up from inside of me.

"And the line at the movie theater will be shorter on dollar night." Dave let out a chuckle.

"Two over easies with a side of bacon, and just what you ordered." Denise finished off her statement by plopping my Chunk of Hunk's plate down before him. "You all need anything else? Ketchup? Some orange juice? Nothing?"

The poor floozie seemed genuinely disappointed when we didn't ask her to stick around for a bit. After all, murders don't happen all that frequently around here. At least, not ones that anyone cares about.

Anyway, it seemed kind of mean not to let her in on our conversation, but my eggs and Dave were awaiting and not exactly in that order. So I sent her one of my steel magnolia smiles, and she got the message. Thank goodness!

Dave was wolfing down food like there might be no tomorrow, so I crunched on my bacon and gave him a moment. After all, Rule # 6 in *A Southern Gal's Guide to Keeping Your Man* is – Be agreeable, and you can believe me, there's nothing a man wants more for his woman to be.

Finally, he slowed down and began to chew a bit, so I waved what was left of my second slice of well-buttered toast smeared with grape jelly and asked him the $64,000 question, "So what are you going to do about it?"

"Honestly?" Dave glanced up from his plate, and the look on his face was just pitiful. "I don't know."

"Weren't there any clues? Footprints in the mud? Something?"

"Yeah, there were tons of them. Everyone in Missing County goes there to fish, and you know it."

And therein lay the problem. A man no one really cared about one way or the other had been beaten and shot and then dumped in everyone's favorite fishing hole with no useful physical evidence to show for it.

What's more, deer season was starting in only two days.

A Special Treat for You!

From

Juliette Hill

Pink Lemonade Diary

Chapter One

Thirteen year old Victoria Gray, Vicki to her friends, fumbled through the pockets of her school uniform jacket for the key to her family's Manhattan apartment.

"Finally!" she exclaimed, as the key turned in the temperamental lock. Brushing her long, blond hair from her eyes, she opened the door. "Summer vacation! Freedom! No more homework!"

Her Siamese cat, Spice, and Pom-chi, Cinnamon, welcomed her with enthusiasm. Spice meowed loudly for attention, while Cinnamon ran circles around her in his little dog way.

The apartment felt comfortably cool after the walk from school in the June heat and humidity.

"Hey, guys, wait a second. Let me put my backpack down!" Dropping her pack where she stood, Vicki kicked off her shoes and removed her jacket from her long, slender frame, before she headed along the hall to her bedroom to change into more comfortable clothes.

Jess, her BFF since first grade, was waiting on a call about getting together later, both girls anxious to celebrate. Her friend, though, would just have to wait.

"Mom...Dad?" Vicki called out as she looked through her closet for something to change into. "Anyone home?"

Suddenly, despite her excitement about summer vacation, a sense of impending doom that had hovered all day overwhelmed her.

Last night, her parents' muffled voices from the living room had mentioned her name several times as she drifted off to sleep, and this usually meant something unpleasant - a dentist appointment, perhaps, or a stint at a summer camp.

"All I want to do this summer is hang out with my friends," Vicki muttered to the dog, who looked back with a slight tilt of his head. "They never tell me anything until the last minute!" She pulled on a pink tank top and matching shorts.

Picking up the cat, she rubbed her cheek against his soft fur. "Let's get a snack." Vicki strode to the kitchen, where she discovered some of her favorite homemade chocolate cupcakes. The fridge, though, revealed nothing but pink lemonade, and she turned back to the dog. "Mom knows I hate pink lemonade as much as I hate eating brussel sprouts!"

Cinnamon barked in agreement as he followed her around, begging for a treat.

Taking a seat at the marble-topped island, Vicki heard the rattle of the front door.

"Sorry I'm late," her mother called out. "I had some last minute shopping to do."

"I'm in here, having a snack. Why the pink lemonade?" she shot back. "I can't stand the stuff, so what's up?"

Having set down her shopping bags, Vicki's mother joined her in the kitchen. "I guess I felt nostalgic for the 'good ole' days."

"Huh…the what?"

"Last night, your father and I were discussing summer break, and I was reminiscing about a vacation I spent with my Auntie M on that barrier island off the Georgia coast, when I was about your age. "I'll never forget that special summer."

"You're so sentimental sometimes." Vicki's feeling of dread returned. "I thought I heard my name mentioned when I was falling asleep," she added.

"Why don't the three of us go out for Italian, and we'll talk."

"Oh, no, what have I done now?" Vicki's mind raced as she swallowed hard. "Jess and I want to get together later and celebrate. It's Friday, so you know how crowded the restaurant will be."

"Your father will be home any minute. I'll make a reservation, and you go text Jess."

"Whatever," Vicki said in a bored tone, and headed into the family room where she turned on the TV.

Left alone, Sophia Cassandra Gray, Cassy to her friends, tapped a manicured fingertip on the marble countertop, as her mind drifted back to conversation of the evening before.

"I'll never forget those carefree days." She had handed her husband his customary brandy. "We spent hours lying under the magnolia tree sipping Auntie M's ice-cold pink lemonade."

"Urban living is harsh, unforgiving and competitive." Max had met her gaze. "I want Vicki to have a variety of experiences like you did - a quieter, gentler alternative to the glitz and glamour of fast-paced city life."

Now, again, her memory returned to Auntie M's barrier island. Once, there had even been a boy that she had liked in a way she had never felt before, but they had only shared a few glorious weeks and then he was gone. Years later, when she had met Max, something in him had reminded her of that long-ago love. How lucky she had been!

Bringing herself back to the present, Cassy peered into the family room. As usual, her daughter had the television blaring, cell phone in hand. Some things never change," she thought, or could they?"

Now, all they had to do was break the news to Vicki.

OTHER TITLES AVAILABLE FROM ANNIE ACORN PUBLISHING LLC

By Annie Acorn

Chocolate Can Kill

Murder With My Darling

A Stranger Comes to Town

The Young Executive

When to Remain Silent

On the Road

The Magic Sand Dollar

One More Christmas Past

One Last Gift To Go

A Haunting Christmas

Too Busy for Christmas

An Afghan of Many Colors

A Tired Older Woman: Loses Weight and Keeps It Off!

How to Survive Your New Home Purchase

How to Survive Your 203K Mortgage

<u>Annie Acorn writing as Charlotte Kent</u>

A Clue for Adrianna

A Man for Susan

A Christmas Kiss

<u>By Beverly J. Crawford</u>

A B-17 Christmas

The Christmas Child

The Best Homemade Christmas

While Shepherds Watched

Towards the Sun

<u>By Peggy Teel writing as denise hays</u>

Niki Knows the Dirt – A Niki Edgar Mystery

Monkey Business – A Niki Edgar Mystery

Merry Christmas Minus One

Walking for Weight Loss

By Peggy Teel

God and Grandma

Christmas in Tartan Glen

The Best Worst Christmas

A Merry Mary Christmas

Twelve Bells for Christmas

By Juliette Hill

Pink Lemonade Diary

Two Beaux for Christmas

Country Cabin Christmas

Christmas Shoppe Magic

The Christmas Spirit of Starlight Cove

By Angel Nichols

Christmas in the Mojave

Christmas Love Exchange

By Sheila Lawrence

The More the Merrier

A Silent Night

Ho Ho Ho and a Bottle of Rum

By Billie Thomas

Murder on the First Day of Christmas

Annie Acorn

Annie Acorn is the pseudonym of a prolific, internationally published author, whose readership recognizes her mainly for her women's fiction, cozy mysteries and richly woven stories with a warm southern flair. She writes her romantic women's fiction/family saga Captain's Point series as Charlotte Kent. She is a founding member of From Women's Pens – A Cooperative of Women Writers.

Annie is the mother of two sons, one of whom is married to the best daughter-in-law in the world. She lives in the Washington, D.C. area, where she has done extensive technical writing as a contractor.

She owned a tri-state medical outsourcing business for a number of years and was the Director of a behavioral healthcare firm. She once flipped a comic book and collectible retail company comprised of five stores, and she has managed cemeteries and funeral homes. She is the owner of Annie Acorn Publishing LLC.

Ms. Acorn has published in *The Inspirational Writer*, and she edited an in-house publication for the State of Mississippi. She is a contributor of ezine articles.

In her spare time, Ms. Acorn enjoys reading, writing mysteries, listening to classical music, playing cards, and spending time with her family and friends – often at a restaurant serving delicious food.

Annie is the author of the blog at annieacorn.com. You can friend her on Facebook and tweet her at Annie_Acorn. She will respond to your email sent to annieacorn11@gmail.com.

Juliette Hill

Juliette Hill is the pseudonym for a creative writer who is passionate about all things vintage, traveling with her husband and exploring family history. She enjoys treasure hunting at local antique markets and estate sales, searching for her next great 'find' that will spark her imagination. Her desire to discover the story behind each treasure motivates the writer within.

Juliette's other interests include planning family gatherings, scrapbooking, cooking, shopping and dining out, to name a few.

Her works, including *Pink Lemonade Diary, Christmas Shoppe Magic, Country Cabin Christmas, The Christmas Spirit of Starlight Cove,* and *Two Beaux for Christmas* involve multi-dimensional characters and generational plots which bridge the gap between the past and present. She is a founding member of From Women's Pens and is currently working on several projects for Annie Acorn Publishing.